Resounding praise for EDNA BUCHANAN and
PULSE

"THE QUEEN OF CRIME"
Los Angeles Daily News

"BUCHANAN TELLS GREAT STORIES—
hot, horrible, homicidal stories."
The New York Times Book Review

"ONE OF THIS SPRING'S BEST NEW CRIME
NOVELS...Buchanan has no trouble sustaining the
drama or inventing enough credible plot twists."
Chicago Tribune

"A GREASED-LIGHTNING THRILLER FROM
THE PULITZER-WINNING CRIME REPORTER...
Buchanan rides her irresistible
premise hell-for-leather."
Kirkus Reviews

"FRAUGHT WITH SUSPENSE AND DANGER...
Buchanan hooks you with the first line."
Jacksonville Florida Times-Union

Other Avon Books by
Edna Buchanan

CONTENTS UNDER PRESSURE
MIAMI, IT'S MURDER

EDNA
BUCHANAN

PULSE

AVON BOOKS NEW YORK

AVON BOOKS, INC.
1350 Avenue of the Americas
New York, New York 10019

Copyright © 1998 by Edna Buchanan
Inside cover author photo by Jim Virga
Library of Congress Catalog Card Number: 97-32292
ISBN: 0-380-72833-8
www.avonbooks.com

First Avon Books Paperback Printing: April 1999
First Avon Books Hardcover Printing: May 1998

AVON TRADEMARK REG. U.S. PAT. OFF. AND IN OTHER COUNTRIES, MARCA REGISTRADA, HECHO EN U.S.A.

Printed in the U.S.A.

WCD 10 9 8 7 6 5 4 3 2 1

For Ann Hughes,
true friend, free spirit,
and brave heart.

PULSE

CHAPTER
ONE

Sudden death saved his life.

His first conscious thoughts were not of that stranger whose death had saved him. Soon he would think of nothing else, but now, beyond the distant hums and hisses of the machines to which he was tethered, came only a single jubilant thought, I am alive!

He struck out for the surface, like a lethargic underwater swimmer, broke through and glimpsed his wife, Kathleen, and her sister, Ann, tearful at his bedside. Drifting, he sank back into sleep's warm embrace and dreamed again of running, fast, strong and light on his feet. This time he was not alone. He saw his companion's shadow and heard the familiar sounds of footfalls and measured breathing as they matched one another stride for stride.

*   *   *

What Frank Douglas wanted for the next twenty-four hours was the respirator tube out of his throat. No one seemed upset when he managed to remove it himself the following day.

He forced himself from bed on the third day, obsessed about washing his hair. Two nurses helped him to the sink. There was a mirror. He needed a shave, his hair was wild and he felt light-headed, but his elation grew as he stared at his reflection. The difference was striking. His color had returned, his skin glowed, his lips were rosy. His new heart was working.

The incision was sore. No surprise there, his rib cage had been cracked open and his beating heart removed, for God's sake. He wondered, but did not ask, what they had done with that battered and swollen organ. Despite its failure, it had brought him a long way. But heart transplant patients recover far faster, he knew, than recipients of other organs. The heart is a pump, the transplant team had told him. That's all it is. Replace a failing pump with a new one and the system sings.

Tentative and uncertain at first, Frank trudged a hospital treadmill and was pedaling a stationary bike inside of a week.

While dying, he had slept like the dead, but now that he had been restored to the living, vivid and chaotic dreams invaded his sleep, disturbing visions he could not quite recall upon waking, leaving him with a driving need, a yearning rooted, he was certain, in his fervent desire to go home.

The heart biopsy came first. Blood tests will detect rejection of a liver or a kidney, they told him, but the only way to learn if a heart is being rejected is from the heart itself. Surgeons opened the big vein in his groin, threaded into the right side of the heart lining and cut away a snippet of tissue for microscopic scrutiny. The news, after twenty-four hours, was excellent.

Determining the precise level for his immune suppressants required exquisite fine-tuning. Started on doses of powerful drugs, he was weaned away, monitored carefully as the combination was adjusted up, then down in a delicate balancing act.

His new heart filled with fear and relief when Kathleen came to take him home. He studied her carefully, as though she were a stranger. She wore a simple white shirtwaist and sandals, her chestnut hair pulled back and tied with a ribbon. He already wore an eighteen-karat gold bracelet stamped with a crimson heart that would instantly identify him to any medic as a transplant patient, a life member of The Mended Hearts, Inc. Tucked under his arm, a small black leather bag containing the medications vital to his survival, an impressive array of pharmaceuticals.

The fat gel capsules of cyclosporine, an immunosuppressant, were the big guns, backed up by another antirejection drug called Imuran and powerful steroids that would continue to be reduced gradually after weekly heart biopsies. Tiny blood pressure tabs called captopril would counter their side effects. Antibiotics would guard his immune-suppressed system against infection, while big chalky purple pills protected his stomach lining. Strong vitamins and calcium would counteract the bone-weakening steroids, with more multivitamins, iron and folic acid to boost his bone marrow.

He was to swallow them with a glass of milk twice a day, every day, precisely at ten o'clock, A.M. and P.M., for as long as he lived. It was crucial to maintain the same levels of medication in his body at all times. He was to never leave home again without that leather bag. Patients had been lost after missing only several doses, he was warned. By the time they showed symptoms, they were dying.

The immunosuppressants were to be stored and dispensed at temperatures no higher than eighty-six degrees. He and Kathleen were told the cautionary tale about another successful transplant patient more than once. An avid sportsman, the man loved to hunt. He did, leaving his medication locked safely in the car, parked in the sun. He died.

Frank was also issued a wallet-sized card for emergency use at any pharmacy should he ever find himself without his medication. The irony was not lost on him. Until his illness, he was a man who took pride in never swallowing anything stronger than aspirin. Now his prescriptions were instantly accessible from a computerized national registry to be filled immediately. Anytime, anywhere.

Leaving the safety of the hospital excited and frightened him. So many times he had been sure he would never leave alive. He had arrived dying. He was running when it all began, pounding to the crest of the Rivo Alto drawbridge under Miami's teal blue sky, the water a turquoise shimmer, the brilliant day falling hot and humid around him. He had blamed summer heat and too much wine at dinner the night before for his unusual breathlessness. The bridge tender activated the caution lights and a forty-five-foot schooner hove to as warning bells sounded. The barrier gates slowly descended as he jogged in place, heart hammering as the bridge trembled and the span rumbled open. He checked his pulse rate on his runner's watch, a twentieth-anniversary present from Kathleen—and did a quick double take.

What the hell? He shook his head, droplets flying, as he squinted at the timepiece. Nearly new, the damn piece of junk had gone totally haywire.

The schooner's mast glided by. Its captain signaled the all

clear with two taps of his horn, the bridge shuddered and began its creaky descent. Gears ground, bells clanged, the span inched down, then locked into place. Stiff wooden arms rose and clogged traffic streamed by. Low-hanging clouds swirled as he trotted out onto the metal span, a red-hot sun ballooned, blistering the sky, and the cargo-loading gantries at the port loomed on stiltlike metal legs, ungainly monsters out of science fiction. Was the bridge opening again beneath him? Or did that trembling come from his own legs? His skull, as heavy as a bowling ball, dropped back on his shoulders. The roadway rose resoundingly to meet him. A startled motorist leaned on his horn.

The bridgetender called 911.

Kathleen arrived at the emergency room pale and frightened, wearing tennis whites and out of breath. He wanted to go home, but they insisted on tests, which led to other tests and eventually to bad news.

The word the cardiologist used was *cardiomyopathy*. No easy way to tell a man he is dying.

Kathleen cried and clung to him, closer than they had ever been. Calm and analytical, as always, he consulted experts, calculated the odds and scrutinized projections.

The finest cardiologist in South Florida said he would die without a heart transplant. He nearly did. Now, after a year of waiting, weakening, liquidating his business, arranging his affairs and his own funeral during a roller-coaster ride of near misses, disappointments and false alarms, he was leaving the hospital not only alive, but with a future, in a wheelchair he tried to refuse. Hospital policy prevailed and he was rolled out as required. He would return for heart biopsies once a week for six weeks. Eventually there would be one a year. At the last moment the hospital suddenly seemed safer and more secure, but that moment passed. Nothing could compare to the familiar warmth of the sun on his skin, and the moist kiss of exhaust-scented city air. He was different now, but they were the same. He didn't recognize the car Kathleen drove up onto the ramp. He had never seen it before.

"Nice." He settled in beside her on a comfortable leather-covered seat. A Mercedes-Benz. Sleek and silver, it gleamed like a polished piece of fine jewelry. "Whose is it?"

"Surprise." She smiled. "It's our new car."

"Ours?"

"Yours, actually." She pulled away from the curb and merged skillfully into moving traffic. "I still have the Catera."

"You bought it yourself?" Kathleen had never car-shopped. He had always shielded her from the sharks. "Did you get a good trade-in on my Benz? It was in great condition. Why . . . ?"

"Only what the insurance company allowed."

"Insurance company?"

"Shandi wrecked it."

"She had an accident? Anybody hurt?"

"The good news is, air bags work. Nobody had a scratch, but the car was totaled."

Their eldest daughter, Shandi, was nineteen. The accident, Kathleen explained, took place two days before his transplant. Her own car was being serviced, so Shandi had borrowed his to help friends move into an apartment near the university. They had cruised South Beach afterwards, but not for long. The other driver was drunk and had been arrested.

"Why didn't you tell me?"

"You were busy, sweetheart, surviving." She patted his knee reassuringly.

"Anything else you're not telling me?"

She rolled her eyes and chuckled. "Where shall I begin?"

"Is that why they're not with you? Are they both in Dade County Jail?"

"Not yet, but it probably won't be long."

Frank laughed, and suddenly felt carefree. No problem exists, he thought, that we can't face together. How many men win a second chance? He was going home to start life anew and keep the promises made when he thought he was dying.

He had loved his dark blue Mercedes sedan, but what the hell, it was only a car. What had somebody in the hospital said?

"Don't love anything that can't love you back." That was it. Jack had said it, he remembered, poor dead Jack.

A muscular man with unruly red hair and eyes the shade of the sea, Jack was ten years younger, age thirty-four, a firefighter, with a pretty, plumpish wife named Danielle, four small children and pericarditis. A simple virus, nothing more serious than a strep throat, had destroyed the lining of his heart.

Frank liked the man, his family, and his wisecracking, smoke-eating buddies who blatantly ignored the families-only rule, when they dropped by to tell war stories.

Before their hearts failed, the two shared little in common, but he and Jack had shared a room, and talked endlessly about the futures they hoped for. They assiduously avoided one subject. Both were athletically built, roughly the same size, and they shared the same blood type. Heart transplants do not require extensive tissue typing, all that counts is size and blood type. Both were status one, in imminent danger of dying. They knew they could be competing for the same heart.

The night Jack was prepped for surgery, Frank was thrilled, but envious. Why him and not me? he wondered.

"I think I'm about to have a change of heart," Jack drawled, as he was wheeled out on a gurney, his wife at his side.

"Now I know the real way to a man's heart," Danielle said, mirroring her husband's bravado and black humor. "It's through his rib cage."

He's got his chance, Frank thought. Will I ever get mine?

"You're next, man." Jack flashed a thumbs-up, as though reading his mind. "Hang in there, buddy."

Frank was propped up in bed, reading a novel, when Dr. O'Hara, chief of the transplant team, appeared three hours later, still in scrubs.

"I wanted you to hear the news from me, Frank. I know you were friends." O'Hara's eyes were weary. "Jack crashed, died on the table. It was not the heart," he emphasized, "the heart was good. But underlying medical complications unique to Jack's own condition—"

"You say it wasn't the heart," Frank interrupted, "that it was good. Give *me* that heart." He grasped the doctor's arm. "You can do it!"

"Impossible." Lost time, surgical procedures and the drugs injected had rendered the heart useless. The donor, a thirty-year-old motorcyclist, had been left brain-dead after a crash. His heart might have been saved, but was wasted. Frank was ashamed that he had grieved as much for that as he did for Jack.

"This one has side air bags as well," Kathleen was saying.

"Hope to God we never need 'em," Frank muttered. They glided up the entrance ramp onto the Dolphin Expressway and headed east, a rush of metal and humanity roaring around them. He studied the faces of other motorists, strangers intent on their own dreams and destinations. He was back in the mainstream.

The car swooped down off the highway onto Biscayne Boulevard, past the scruffy window washers and their squeeze bottles, and approached the Venetian Causeway. Frank and Kathleen had decided years ago that one of the green islands in Biscayne Bay would be the ideal place to raise their daughters. Inspired by Venice, 1920's developers dredged, filled and built Rivo Alto, DiLido, San Marino and San Marco Islands, linked by twelve bridges that stretched between Miami and Miami Beach. High-rises stab the sky at each end, but the verdant, man-made islands between were quiet and residential.

The familiar landscape brought a massive lump to his throat. Had he been gone a hundred years, or only a moment? The lush greens were greener, the royal palms taller and more stately, the pentas madly blooming along the swale blushed a brighter pink than he ever remembered. He felt like a stranger seeing it all for the first time. The graceful columns, the arched entrance, the mullioned windows.

The wrought-iron security gate stood open. "I've missed you," Kathleen said softly.

"Me too. I know it's been tough on you, but things will be different now, I promise."

They rolled triumphantly up the driveway's gentle incline as people spilled out of the house. Shandi, and their youngest daughter, Casey, his sister-in-law Ann and her children, his secretary, Sue Ann, their next-door neighbors, the Bishops, their housekeeper, Lourdes, even Daisy, the dalmatian.

Balloons festooned the shrubbery and a huge handmade sign stretched between the live oaks flanking the driveway. Decorated with red hearts, it said: *Welcome Home, Dad.*

Kathleen kissed him, her mouth warm and sweet, fingers laced gently behind his neck. "Welcome home, Frank."

Eyes wet, they entered, hand in hand, enveloped in applause, love and laughter. Fresh flowers, silver and crystal glistened in the dining room, his favorite foods piled high on the good china. The bay danced and sparkled in the splashy midday light beyond the windows. His eyes rested lovingly on his oldest girl. Shandi looked like nineteen going on thirty-five. Her once long dark and silky mane was now short and sleek, a mottled tricolor he had never before seen on a human scalp, and her ears bristled with gold wire earrings. Lots of them. Smiling, he fought the urge to count how many times needles had pierced those tender pubescent lobes. She kept pushing her shorn hair back behind her ears, making it hard to resist. But to mention it now would be bad timing. She came into his arms for a gentle hug. Was her nail polish black?

He sat at the head of the table. The food looked mouth-watering but tasted oddly flat. "Do we have any hot sauce, Tabasco?" he asked, as everybody dug in. "And I'd love a cold beer."

Kathleen, filling his ice tea glass, looked startled. "Who is this man? Don't let Lourdes hear you," she murmured accusingly. "She's been in the kitchen since dawn. You've never liked hot sauce, and since when are you a beer drinker? What went on in that hospital when I wasn't there? Did they give you new taste buds, too?"

She leaned down and he tasted her lips as they brushed his.

"All I know," he said, peering down the neckline of her dress at her breasts, "is that you should always give your heart what it craves."

"Is that so? We'll see."

"Would you check the bar," he persisted, "for the beer,

and the Tabasco? Didn't we keep some there for Bloody Marys?"

The beer quenched a craving he had felt since soon after his surgery, and the Tabasco was exactly what his food needed.

Hours later, company gone, they strolled out to watch the setting sun change the bay from sea green to shimmering gold, then bloodred to black. Tree frogs, crickets and night birds began their chorus as the night city across the bay awoke in a cacophony of color. Mirrored skyscrapers, multi-colored neon and the glow of sodium-vapor anticrime lamps, underlined by the moving lights of traffic.

He felt slightly hurt that both girls went out with friends his first night home, but was thrilled to be alone with his wife. He swallowed his pills promptly at ten o'clock, then arm in arm, they slowly climbed the balustraded stairs.

"It's so good to be home," he sighed, as she came to bed. Her nightdress was white and silky, her lustrous hair brushed and loose around her shoulders. She tapped in a sequence of numbers on a bedside panel to arm the security system and turn out the lights.

He reached for her in the dark, his lips finding her throat.

"Do you think that we . . . ?"

"Yes, oh yes," he whispered.

"Are you sure you can . . . ?"

"They say the captopril affects some men. So far, no problem." He guided her hand to his penis. "I've been this way all afternoon."

"Isn't it too soon after surgery? How—"

"If you help me, love. You know they said it's okay, I just can't do any strenuous pushing or pulling for a few weeks." He sensed her hesitation.

"So," she said lightly, "you expect me to do everything."

"I could live with that."

Her silky gown brushed across his face as she pulled it over her head and tossed it aside. Her fingers gently traced the still angry scar.

"Let's turn on the light," he whispered.

"The light?" she murmured.

"I want to see you."

"Aren't we full of surprises." She reached across him, her bare breast resting against his cheek as she switched on the bedside lamp, then sat on her heels, back arched, eyes focused almost shyly on his face. The sight of her naked startled him for an instant, it was as though he had expected another body, more compact and muscular. Had it been so long that he did not even recognize his own wife?

"What's wrong?" she asked, as he stared.

"Nothing," he whispered. "You're beautiful." More softly rounded after twenty years and two children, she was still the same blue-eyed girl he had married.

"You were right." She gently straddled him. "You definitely do not suffer the dread side effects from your medication."

"Lucky us," he breathed.

Gingerly she caressed and fondled him, never fully relaxed. "Are you sure this is all right?" she kept asking.

"Yes, yes, yes."

"Frank, I really think we should talk to the doctor to be certain . . ." He wilted against her thigh as she pulled away at the wrong moment.

Not the greatest sex they had ever enjoyed together, he thought; she was nervous and uncertain and he felt . . . different. But it was no total fizzle either. God bless modern medicine and pharmaceuticals. He was home, alive, still a man.

He felt the delayed reaction of his transplanted heart, now

pounding passionately, and smiled ruefully. The doctors had explained that his new heart would not immediately respond to a sudden scare or the sight of a naked woman. Like pumps, transplanted hearts are hooked up to all the vital plumbing but not to the sympathetic nerves that deliver instant messages from the brain, speeding the pulse. Enzymes in his blood stream would do the job instead, accelerating his heartbeat, but they take longer, requiring more time to warm up and to cool down after exertion.

Getting used to his new heart would take time. His thoughts were scattered and restless. Sex was not the problem, he knew that would get better. He was lucky to be alive, lucky to have Kathleen's soft presence beside him in the dark. When working his way through college, he had had two jobs, ambition and no time for love. Then he had seen her. He had earned extra money chauffeuring a retired professor who no longer drove but still babied the ancient Cadillac in his garage. Frank drove him to the supermarket, to medical appointments, on errands, and studied while waiting. He had had a four-o'clock class that afternoon and was rushing the old professor through the library, when there she was, reading *Peter Pan* to a group of rapt preschoolers.

He perched on a pint-sized chair, as enthralled as the other bright-eyed listeners until the professor finally came looking for him. Frank had returned to the library several times, lurking like a pervert in the children's section, but she was not there. Then, by chance, he spotted her on campus and followed like a puppy.

She was from Connecticut, a drama major who volunteered to read to children bussed in from disadvantaged neighborhoods. Soon they were on their first date in the professor's borrowed Caddy and Frank was the disadvantaged child basking in her nurturing radiance. Who would have thought, he wondered, that he still would be, nearly twenty-two years later?

He should have been totally content at this moment.

"What are you thinking?" Her words were dreamy in the dark.

He paused. "Being home today with you and the kids was insanely awesome, as Casey would say, but something's bothering me and I just realized what it is." He propped himself up on one elbow. "I keep thinking about the donor."

"But he's gone," Kathleen said softly, taking his hand.

"I know." He sat up. "I'm surrounded by the people I love. What about his family?"

"Your job now is to take good care of yourself."

"But what about his wife? His kids? There must be something I can do for them."

"You don't even know if the donor was a man or a woman." She sighed. "It could be a teenager."

"It was a man," he said, without hesitation.

"How do you know?" She sat up, too, and began to massage his shoulders and the back of his neck. "I thought they didn't tell you."

"They didn't. But I know. It was a guy."

"How can you be so sure?"

He thought for a moment. "I don't know how, but I know. Maybe I overheard something at the hospital when I was groggy."

"Get some rest, sweetheart." She kissed his shoulder and sank back down on her pillow. "Coming home was a big hurdle. You're exhausted."

"There must be something I can do to thank them, to show my gratitude."

"Bad idea," she said sleepily. "They're grieving, trying to

put a loss behind them. Intruding into their lives would only remind them of their tragedy."

She rolled over and curled into her usual sleep position. He stared at the ceiling, mind racing. His gut said it was the right thing to do. *When our peril is past, shall our gratitude sleep?* Who said that? Was it his father? What was it from? he wondered. Why did he recall it? The phrase repeated, an endless loop through his mind, until restless, he slipped out of bed, careful not to disturb Kathleen. He tapped in the by-pass code on the alarm keypad, then walked to the French doors, opened them quietly and stepped barefoot onto the balcony. The night was hushed, the stars pinpricks of white fire in the cool majesty of a vaulted heaven. The water shimmered like rumpled silk below the bridge, a skeletal rigging to the south. There was no traffic at this hour, only an occasional car overriding the yellow beacon of its own headlights.

As he inhaled a deep breath of night air, a sudden movement caught his eye. From shadows below, as though emerging from a sudden crack in the darkness, a solitary figure appeared on the span. Frank blinked. The lone pedestrian was still there, on the bridge between DiLido and Rivo Alto. The figure was tall with a hint of urgency in his long-legged stride. Perhaps his car had broken down, Frank thought, as he watched, mesmerized. Though his features were obscured by distance and the night, the man looked oddly familiar. He paused at the crest of the bridge, his silhouette silvered by moonlight. Then, as though aware he was being watched, the figure turned to stare directly up to the balcony where Frank stood. Fear and foreboding rushing over him like water in an icy stream, Frank shrank back, retreated inside and closed the doors. When he peered through the glass a moment later, the bridge was empty in the silent night.

Frank fought the urge to rush downstairs to check the

doors and the locks. He feared for his family. His daughters were out there somewhere sharing the same night with that spectral figure. Casey was sleeping over at her best friend's on Bay Point. But Shandi . . . His stomach pitched. He forced himself to think rationally, crawled back into bed and lay there listening until she came in. He heard her visit the kitchen. The slam of the refrigerator door, minutes later the sound of her footsteps on the stairs to her room. He arose again once all was quiet, padded down the hall and saw the reassuring glow of light under her door as he went downstairs to be sure that she had turned the dead bolt behind her and reset the alarm. Without switching on lights, he moved easily through each room. He knew this house so well, but tonight it seemed different, almost strange—and frightening.

He returned to bed and a fitful doze, but someone called his name and he awoke disoriented. The room was unfamiliar. Who was he? Where was he? The answers came to him slowly as he lay there pondering how odd it was that the hospital had installed a ceiling fan in his room exactly like the one above his bed at home.

CHAPTER TWO

He got star treatment. Other members of the transplant team looked in during his exam, exclaiming and beaming at his progress like proud parents. His tests had continued to go so well that after three months he was being released with only six-month checkups for the next year. After that, if all went right, only an annual exam.

He did not ask the question that nagged at him until he was fully dressed, seated with Kathleen in front of a cluttered desk and a small bank of computer equipment in his surgeon's small office.

O'Hara frowned. "This sleeping problem you mentioned . . . I could prescribe—"

"No, thanks." Frank grinned. "I take enough medication now. Everything seems to be working fine, no point in tinker-

17

ing with the formula. It's annoying as hell, but I can handle it. I think I'm still adjusting to the new heart, to being home, and being healthy again. I'm catching catnaps during the day. You can hold the prescription for now, Doctor, but there is something I do want." He took out his Mont Blanc pen and his small leather pocket briefcase, poised to jot down the information.

The doctor listened to his request, his lean body relaxed in his leather chair, his long slim fingers pyramided in front of him. "No," he said simply, then leaned forward and began to move around some papers on the desk in front of him. "The policy of the transplant program is to maintain confidentiality and I'm in total support of that."

"In no way do I intend to intrude upon the family," Frank said confidently, "but I do want to help. I'm in a position to do so, and I owe them so much."

Dr. O'Hara shook his head. "Not necessary," he said briskly, his voice pleasant. "Donor families know that their consent is a gift. Accept it in that context."

"Please understand." Frank was firm, but polite. "I merely want to know if the family has a mortgage, or a child in need of an education. I was left fatherless myself at an early age. I know what that's like. If I can spare some kid—"

"And you turned out all right." O'Hara studied him shrewdly, eyes narrowed. "Didn't you?"

"I only want to make their lives a little easier." Refusals were foreign to Frank. He did not digest them easily.

"Focus on your own life, Frank."

The two men, each accustomed to having his own way, studied each other for a long moment, tension building. Kathleen stirred uncomfortably beside him, placing her hand over his in a cautionary gesture. Indignant, he wanted to shake it off.

"Look," the doctor said, "in the early days of transplants, recipients and donor families were able to meet. Many did. In some cases it didn't work out. There were some real problems, in fact. That's why a policy of confidentiality was adopted, and believe me, Frank, it's better this way."

"I agree." Kathleen sighed in relief. "Thank you, Doctor. Frank, are you sure you don't want the doctor to prescribe something that will help you sleep through the night?"

He shook his head, he didn't trust his voice.

O'Hara got to his feet, smiling. "Go home, enjoy your life," he ordered good-naturedly.

The man's refusal was too glib, too quick, Frank thought on the elevator. Perhaps he knew the question was coming. He studied Kathleen out of the corner of his eye. Had she spoken to the doctor? Gone behind his back?

They celebrated his sterling checkup over lunch at the newest "in" restaurant on South Beach. He fought his frustration, relying on his usual allies, logic and reason. They never let him down. No need to go to war with the doctor, or with Kathleen. He smiled across the table at her as they dined on smoked pheasant served by a muscular waiter who wore a T-shirt announcing that *Only my teeth are straight*. His wife's attitude and the doctor's stubborn resolve confounded him, but there were other ways to learn the information he needed. And he did need it. He was right. He was never more sure of anything. The decision to track down the family of his heart was exciting and slightly subversive, an irresistible challenge.

He could hardly wait to finish lunch.

Selling F.D. Douglas, Inc., had been wrenching. Frank had built his business from nothing, lived it, breathed it, ate it. It was his life's work. But selling was the wisest course of action when he was a dying man, a name on a list of forty-eight thousand patients awaiting organ transplants. His company brought even more than he had expected, a goddamn fortune he was too sick to enjoy. What good was the money? Money could not buy him a new heart. But he had known all along that if he beat the odds and survived, he could and would start over. He had kept a small but comfortable office in Miami Beach, on Lincoln Road Mall, and one employee, his longtime trusted secretary. Sue Ann was like family, devoted to him and the job. Divorced, fifty-five and efficient, she lived within walking distance, in a condo with her cat. Her husband had remarried and was raising a new family with the much younger woman he had abandoned her for. But Sue Ann was not alone in the world. Her son was a career Marine with a wife and children, and she had a daughter, a struggling would-be actress in New York. Frank had kept Sue Ann on the payroll even after he was far too ill to conduct business. He had arranged, in the event of his death, for her to remain on full salary and benefits for as long as necessary, one year minimum, to help wrap up his affairs, close the office and assist Kathleen with the inevitable details. His alternate plan, now in motion, was to ease back into business on a smaller scale, look into some investments and dabble in real estate.

He called the office after lunch, from the privacy of his study, and instructed Sue Ann to arrange an appointment ASAP with Nicolas Lucca.

He could probably handle this little job himself, Frank thought, but he might tread on some toes. Lucca was a pro, discreet and efficient, and Frank trusted him.

From a Chicago family of cops, Lucca had resisted the badge until moving to South Florida for the health of a chronically ill child. He joined the Metro-Dade police department at age thirty-nine, largely for the benefits and the medical plan, he said later. Transferred to homicide, he quickly established a reputation. The new man on the squad was always saddled with the missions impossible: unidentifiable victims left in fields or murky Everglades canals. More than whodunits, they were whoisits, nameless victims who could be drug dealers, illegal aliens or felons on the run from anywhere. Luck, they said, when Lucca solved the first one. He solved the next one, and the one after that. Then his superiors dusted off an old, cold case nobody could crack. He solved it. He closed eleven in a row. He had a talent.

The local newspaper, *The Miami Herald*, featured his accomplishments in its Sunday magazine. The detective scowled off the cover, wearing a rumpled trench coat and a menacing sneer. The story made him a local hero. Though they had never met, Frank dictated a brief note of congratulations after the article appeared, thanking the detective for his efforts on behalf of all crime victims.

Murder always intrigued Frank. Homicide investigations had fascinated him since childhood, when a detective was kind to him and his mother during the worst moments of their lives. He had planned at one time to apply to the FBI Academy, but by the time he graduated from the University of Miami with a degree in accounting he was mad with love for Kathleen and driven by the same entrepreneurial zeal that had consumed his father, that tragic figure, the man he scarcely knew.

The article spelled the end to Lucca's police career. The publicity was priceless, the name recognition too valuable to waste. His streak unbroken at twelve, he turned in his badge, got rid of the rumpled raincoat, which had been borrowed for the photo shoot, bought some expensive suits and set up shop in North Dade where he practiced PI work for lawyers in Miami and Fort Lauderdale.

Frank had forgotten his note until a reply arrived months later, Lucca's new business card. From then on, Frank had hired him when he needed to sort out legitimate competitors, investors and would-be business associates from the con men, scam artists and fast-buck operators South Florida is famous for. Tough and plainspoken, Lucca was a straight shooter, a class act who took no window-peeping or divorce cases. He relished being his own boss and probably banked more in a good week than his squad-room buddies took home in a month. Frank looked forward to seeing him again.

Kathleen strolled with him to the car. She had made it a habit since he resumed driving, urging him to be careful, kissing his cheek. She still fussed and worried, despite the fact that her once-dying husband now exuded more energy than he ever had. He often wondered if his recycled heart had belonged to an athlete, or someone much younger than himself. Kathleen had been right about one thing, he thought, the Mercedes. Smooth and responsive, it handled like a dream.

Lucca was punctual, as always. He was a big man; his legs looked too long for his rugged torso. His black hair bristled, thick and shiny, with a brushy mustache to match and a deep, distinctive voice that evoked the shadowy hills of Sicily. In his well-cut dark blue suit and immaculate white shirt he resembled a suave soap opera villain or a Mafia kingpin more than a former cop.

They exchanged a firm handshake as Lucca appraised Frank and the new, downsized office. "You still have a secretary?"

"Yeah, she's out."

"What you need here, boss, is security cameras to monitor the reception area so when you're alone, you can see who arrives before they see you."

"Good idea. Handle it for me."

"Sure. Heard you had ticker problems and got rid of the business. How ya doing?"

Frank took his seat behind the desk as Lucca folded his big frame onto the soft leather sofa. "Had some surgery," he said evenly. "Kept my secretary and this small office and I'm about ready to get back into business."

"Need some new associate checked out?"

"It's personal this time."

Something in Lucca's eyes changed. "I don't do marital problems."

"Good." Frank smiled. "I'm a lucky man. I don't have any. This is something else. You knew I was sick."

The detective nodded.

"You probably didn't know how sick. Sudden death saved my life." He paused. "Somebody else's death, not mine."

The detective's expression never changed as Frank laid it out, explaining what he wanted. "He died on Saturday, July twelfth. That's the day I was reborn. I don't know how long he was on life support before they gave me his heart. What do you think?"

"No problemo." Lucca looked pleased. "First one of these I've had."

A man accustomed to daily death and disorder must find a fresh challenge a welcome diversion, Frank thought.

Lucca scratched his neck and took out a small spiral notebook. "From what I understand, the body-to-body window for a heart is only a matter of hours."

"Four to six hours, with four preferable," Frank said. "It's called ischemic time, that's how long the organ can survive outside a body."

Lucca jotted down the date and time of the surgery. "As I recall," he said, "a national computer network matches patients to compatible organs as they become available."

"Right." Frank was impressed. "The United Network for Organ Sharing. Didn't know you knew that much about it."

"Come on, boss. I used to deal with the organ procurement team all the time when I worked in homicide." He raised a shaggy eyebrow. "I hate to say this, boss, but you may not like what I find out."

"Meaning?"

"You know, they want you to think that your donor was a brilliant, clean-cut, young premed student killed in some tragic traffic accident. Actually"—he casually crossed one long leg over the other—"with helmet laws, car restraints and tougher drunk-driving laws, thanks in large part to MADD, traffic deaths are down by at least forty percent. Most organ donors these days are gunshot victims. There'd be even more, except that the lifestyle that got 'em shot usually means that locating the immediate family is a problem and the hospital can't keep 'em going long enough for us to find 'em and get permission in time. In homicide we tried to work with 'em as much as we could, but the investigation has to take priority. Our manpower hadda be spent looking for the shooter, not the victim's next of kin. Just so you know, your donor was probably no Eagle Scout." He shrugged.

"I'm not harboring any fantasies." Frank pushed away from his desk and stepped to the window overlooking the bustling mall below.

"For the most part," Lucca said, "people die like they live. We're probably gonna come up with a shanky character, or some gang member who got himself popped."

"I don't think so." Frank shook his head. "But no matter. You don't know what it's like." He turned to face the detective. "I feel like I'm sixteen years old again. Starting over. Got a whole new lease from a stranger. In my book you don't accept gifts without a thank-you, especially when that gift is the miracle of life. It may sound corny, but this is payback time. If the family doesn't need anything, the least I can do is thank them."

"Can't argue with that, boss."

"But I can't shake a gut feeling that something is waiting out there that I need to do for them. I can't sleep, thinking about it."

"I always say, never argue with your gut. But don't say I didn't warn you. How far you want me to go?"

"Just the name of the donor and the address of the family member who gave permission. I'll take it from there." He moved back to his desk. "You'll want to start in Florida. Here's how it works. When a donor becomes available, the computer searches statewide for a match. If none is found, they check the entire region. That includes Louisiana, Georgia, Alabama and Tennessee. If no suitable recipient is found, they go nationwide. He could be from anywhere. That's a lot of turf to cover."

Lucca's dark eyes took on an amused glint. "I wouldn't lose any more sleep over it, boss."

The detective got slowly to his feet. They shook hands and he headed for the door.

"How long you think it will take?" Frank called after him.

"How's tomorrow sound?" Lucca said over his shoulder. He turned and faced Frank. "Tell you the truth, you could be the poster boy for heart transplants. I never would have guessed." He paused for a moment, then nodded at the black leather bag on Frank's desk. "Your medication, right?"

Frank nodded.

"You shouldn't leave that thing lying around."

"Who would want it?" He felt puzzled. "Nobody could use it to get high."

Lucca's weary look said he should know better.

"That stuff's expensive, right?"

"More valuable to me than money, but you're right, there's one pill alone that's a hundred and fifty dollars every time it's filled."

"Exactly. That's why it's easy for a thief to sell it back to the pharmacist."

Frank winced. The thought had not even occurred to him.

Once the detective left, Frank found himself unable to focus on the prospectus he was reading. His mind raced. Lucca would most likely tap into death records, cross-check with the Division of Motor Vehicles. Their licenses designate whether Florida drivers agree to be organ donors. He would list the names of those who died during that time period, then rule out the diseased, drugged or otherwise ineligible, come up with a short list, then narrow it down to the right one by process of elimination. The magic of computer technology. Dead or alive, he thought, nobody has privacy now.

Frank locked the office and strolled Lincoln Road Mall. Renovations, rebuilding and remodeling were under way everywhere. While he was growing up, the once swanky shopping mile was fading into shabby disrepair. Saks Fifth Avenue and Lillie Rubin moved out, replaced by the sleazy shops of gypsies and grifters who preyed on unsuspecting tourists and lonely senior citizens. Once the South Beach renaissance began to flower, artists and performers discovered the neighborhood and its low rents, transforming the pedestrian mall into a Bohemian venue much like the Greenwich Village of the 1950's. Now in full bloom, the area had become the American Riviera, wildly popular with the rich and famous.

Property values and rents soared, the artists were being forced out and a glamorous new rebirth had begun.

Frank ordered an iced cappuccino at an outdoor café. Oddly enough, though he had never smoked, he wanted a cigarette. Really wanted one. It would be insane to start now, he decided. A notion intrigued him. What if he had inherited the tastes, the desires, maybe even the characteristics, of the stranger whose heart beat in his chest? During support sessions at the hospital, other recipients had discussed the possibility of spiritual links and emotional connections to the original owners of the organs that now kept them alive. Nonsense, of course. Like the counselor, he had scoffed at the idea. But what if his donor was a chain smoker? If so, Frank was grateful the habit hadn't damaged the man's heart. What if his transplanted heart had arrived with likes and dislikes, a personality and memory of its own? Perhaps his odd sleeping habits, his early rising, his troubled dreams, were not his at all, but someone else's.

The sight of a stunningly statuesque woman, probably a model, interrupted his thoughts. On Rollerblades, she wore skintight short shorts and a tank top and pushed a bright yellow baby stroller. She smiled at him as she skated gracefully by and he sneaked a peek in the stroller. The passenger, a pampered white poodle, wore a flashy rhinestone studded collar and yellow hair bows. Frank laughed aloud. Life was good. Lucca was on the job. Soon he would know all about the donor whose death saved his life. Like a schoolboy at Christmas, he eagerly anticipated what lay ahead.

A low-flying jet, inbound for Miami International Airport, blocked the sun for a moment and a shadow fell across the sunny mall. A fleeting millisecond of doubt followed the chill he felt, remembering the oft-heard warning. *Be careful. You might get what you wish for.*

*   *   *

He announced at dinner that night that in a week or so, after he had cleared up a few minor matters, they would all go to Disney World for a few days. He expected squeals of delight.

"Daddyyy," they chorused in protest. Casey rolled her eyes. Shandi wrinkled her nose.

"You loved it. You both begged to go back last time." His voice was plaintive.

"Daddddy, I was six and Shandi was thirteen," Casey whined. "I can't go now, our first coed dance is coming up." She lisped slightly through a mouth full of metal. Her braces would not come off for months.

"I've got school," Shandi declared flatly. "I have to study."

He regarded her thoughtfully, her tricolor hair, dark blue nail polish and studded earlobes. "I'm so glad you've finally seen the light and made school your number one priority."

He glanced back at Casey, busy attacking her dessert. "I just thought it would be nice for us to spend some time together as a family."

"Why start now?" Shandi asked flippantly.

He didn't like her attitude or the way she simply seemed to push the food around on her plate without eating.

"That's no way to talk to your father," Kathleen said calmly.

"What is it with that nail polish?" He could not resist the question.

She studied her manicure. "Everybody wears it. It's vamp."

"It makes you look like you should be thawed out."

Casey giggled.

Shandi shot her a contemptuous look, then smiled unexpectedly at her father. "It's really popular. All the models wear it. Dad, do you think I could borrow the new car this weekend?"

"What's wrong with yours?"

"That piece of junk?" She made a face. "It's embarrassing to be seen in."

"It's a pretty decent set of wheels for a college kid without a job. When I was in college—"

Shandi groaned. "I know, I know. You worked, you paid your own way. You didn't have a car. But," she added boldly, "you didn't have a father. I do."

He put his fork down. "Your car is only four years old. If it is a piece of junk, that means you're not taking responsible care of it. Maintenance is important, and given what happened last time you used my car—"

"Not my fault," she said quickly.

"That's right," Kathleen said quietly, "the officer said she was clearly not at fault."

He didn't like being double-teamed. "Well," he said, "if you hadn't let her drive it—"

"She didn't!" Casey burst out, her freckled face flushed. "Mom said she couldn't, but Shandi took it anyway."

The painful silence that followed told him it was true.

Lourdes, on her way in to pour coffee, heard the exchange, turned around and disappeared back into the kitchen. He pushed his plate away. "Is that true?"

Shandi stared sullenly at her nails.

Casey watched, eyes expectant.

"It doesn't matter," Kathleen explained haltingly. "At least no one was hurt."

He ignored her. This was the time to wrest back control. "You're grounded for a month, except for school."

"A month!" Shandi looked astonished. "You can't do that!"

"Oh, yes, I can."

"Mom said it wasn't my fault. You heard her."

"But it was my car you wrecked after taking it without permission. I'm not your mom, I'm your father and I'm still in charge."

Shandi looked to her mother for support and saw none. Kathleen avoided both their eyes.

"I'm a grown woman, in case you hadn't noticed. You can't just, just put me under house arrest!"

"My house, my rules."

She started to respond but didn't. "When does this start?" she finally muttered.

"As of now."

"No way!" she yelped indignantly. "I have a date tonight."

"Call and tell him it's postponed."

"I can't do that!" She checked her watch. "He's already on the way. Mom, do something!" she demanded.

"Perhaps there could be a compromise," Kathleen suggested, slowly folding her napkin. "Since this date was pre-planned, perhaps Shandi could start . . . house arrest after this evening."

What the hell was going on? He felt bewildered and a bit betrayed. They had always backed each other up on discipline. On the other hand, perhaps canceling this date would be unfair to the boy.

"That's doable, I guess. Who is this boy?" he asked.

Casey giggled.

"Someone new," Kathleen said casually, and began to clear dishes from the table as Shandi dashed upstairs to get ready.

After a short time, the bell rang at the front gate and Shandi scampered downstairs. "That's him," she sang out. "See you later." She headed for the door.

"Hold on," Frank said. He pushed the buzzer that opened the gate. "I'd like to meet him."

"Daddy!" Her tone was exasperated.

"Sit."

She sat nervously on the arm of a chair.

"Remember," he said. "I always meet your dates."

"Not for more than a year."

"From now on, we're back in the habit."

She sighed audibly.

He answered the door. The visitor was not who he expected. Frank stared. They had met before. Shandi's high school drama teacher, Jay Bowden.

Bowden stepped confidently inside. Kathleen rushed forward, took his arm and turned to Frank with a bright smile. "You remember Jay, don't you?"

"Bowden, isn't it? Jay, what brings you by?"

"I'm just here to pick up Shandi," Bowden said. "Good to see you again, Frank."

Shandi whisked him away as Kathleen told them to have a good time. "Drive carefully," she called after them, then closed the door.

"That's her date?"

Kathleen nodded, expression resigned, expecting his reaction.

"Jesus Christ! The man is nearly as old as I am! He's thirty-nine if he's a day. His goddamn hairline is receding and he's got a ponytail. Was that an earring he was wearing?"

"I knew it wasn't a boy," Casey trilled, from a front-row seat on the wide staircase. "He's an old guy."

"Baby, I want you upstairs. Now." He watched as she

obeyed, a pout on her face. He wanted to hug her. Was she the only one in this household who wasn't hiding something from him?

"We need to talk," Kathleen said softly.

"Damn straight. You knew she was seeing this guy? You went along with it? She's been out almost every night lately. Is it with him? How long has this been going on?"

They sat in the Florida room, knee to knee in wicker chairs.

"Sweetheart, I'm sure you know it wasn't easy trying to keep everything under control all that time you were sick." She sounded hurt, eyelashes lowered. "They're both spirited girls, Frank. I had to make you my top priority."

"But you had to know that dead or alive, I would not approve of that guy," he said, less vehemently. "Something is obviously wrong with a man that age who is interested in nineteen-year-old girls."

"But that's exactly the point, Frank, she is of age. She's nineteen. If we try to ground her or forbid her to date a particular individual, she is perfectly capable of moving out, or even marrying inappropriately, because she is so headstrong. Many of her friends already have their own apartments. She could find a roommate and be gone tomorrow."

"Who would pay the rent on this apartment? It might do that girl some good to get a job and learn how to live like a responsible adult."

"If she moved out, we'd have no control whatever."

"Looks like we have none now."

"She's safer living at home. What do you think I would have done at that age had I been told I couldn't date you?"

"I see your point, Kath, but that was different. I was a fellow student, not some predatory professor. Does the school know about this? If it's not illegal, it's certainly unethical for him to date teenage students."

"He quit teaching. He's the artistic director at the new Golden Glades Playhouse. Frank, I trust her to have enough good sense not to—"

"Like you trusted her not to take the car when you said no?"

"You're impossible! I don't know what's wrong with you lately!" She sprang to her feet, flushed and angry. Left alone, he tried to figure out where he had gone wrong. As he saw it, his only crime was suggesting a wholesome family vacation they could spend together. Now everybody was pissed off at him. He thought of the promises he had made in the hospital, how he would make it up to them if he lived, be a better father, a better husband. He remembered Kathleen holding his hand all the way to the operating room, praying aloud. ". . . though I walk through the valley of the shadow of death . . ." She had urged him to pray with her.

"You pray. I've got other things to think about," he had said, focusing every fiber on survival, on his will to live, determined to do his part. He had made it, and now he had to focus on keeping his promises. Though he knew the thought was ludicrous, he wondered if they wished he had never come home from the hospital.

He poured a drink. Scotch and soda. The first sip was good. He carried it up to his study. The red light on his message machine was flashing. He punched the play button.

"Hey, boss," Lucca said. "Got what you wanted. You were right. This guy wasn't some street punk. See you tomorrow."

CHAPTER
THREE

Frank was the quarterback. Fans stomped and roared, rocking the stands. He had the ball. A voice he should recognize, but didn't, urged him on, entreating, demanding. But what was the play? Where were the goalposts?

Frank had worked since age eleven, he had never played football, yet that predawn dream left him as frustrated, breathless and bathed in perspiration as a man accustomed to a helmet and shoulder pads. Some suppressed desire, a latent childhood fantasy? He went to the office early, and studied the morning paper. The usual madness in the streets had spread to the halls of justice where a robber had filed suit against the city for his injuries, suffered in a crash while trying to flee police. He alleged that their roadblock endangered his life, violating his rights.

Frank was pacing when he heard the outer door. Lucca saw the open newspaper, the drained coffee cup. "You got here early, boss."

He slid an eight-by-ten manila envelope across Frank's desk. "Tell you the truth, boss, this was a breath of fresh air. Something contemporary, something sophisticated. A helluva lot better, I gotta admit, than standing for hours in some nasty ghetto apartment watching a parking lot where another dead dope dealer got shot off his milk crate."

Frank stared down at the envelope.

"It's all there," Lucca assured him. "You were right. This guy obviously had a few problems, but he was no street punk."

"What was his name?" Frank sounded hoarse.

"Mister Daniel Alexander," Lucca said succinctly. "White male, age thirty-eight. His widow, Rory, age thirty-two, signed the consent form."

"Children?"

"Thought you might ask." Lucca fished out his spiral notebook. "One, a son William, age eight."

Frank winced. "How did Alexander die?"

"Gunshot wound, self-inflicted."

Frank blinked in surprise. "Suicide?" That seemed wrong, not what he had expected. How ironic, he thought; he had fought so hard to live and did, only because another man chose to die.

"It's all in there. Even his obit."

"What do I owe you?" Frank reached for the desk drawer and his checkbook.

"I'll send you a bill. Need anything else? I could run a little credit check on Alexander if you're interested."

"I'll call if I need something more." Oddly agitated, he was impatient to peruse the contents of this envelope in private.

Lucca shrugged. "Pleasure doing business with you, boss. As usual."

When he was alone, Frank closed the door to his inner office, poured more coffee, and stared at the envelope. He had asked only for the names, but Lucca had obviously done his usual thorough job. His hands shook slightly as he slit open the flap with the small knife on his key chain and removed the contents.

Daniel Paul Alexander, a 38-year-old, five-foot-eleven, 175-pound white male, was born in Darien, Connecticut, on June 29, 1959. Place of death, Miami.

That had to be why the transplant team did not divulge even the usual basic facts about the nameless donor, such as age or manner of death. Too close to home. The thought stunned Frank. He and Alexander might have passed on the street, idled alongside each other in traffic, shared the same dentist or dry cleaner.

The printout reported Alexander's driver's license number. Expiration date: June 29, 2000. The driver had expired long before his license, Frank thought ruefully. He scanned the page. The dead man's telephone number, a list of his last three addresses, all local. Alexander had no arrest record, no known aliases, no traffic accidents in Florida and no workmen's comp claims. He did have a concealed weapons permit. Frank wondered if the man had bought a gun to protect his family and then used it on himself. There was even a profile of his home, the purchase date, selling price, and current tax assessment. His vehicle registration was for a Lexus LS 400. The printout included the car's VIN number, original cost, current value and insurance carrier. Alexander had some sort of business licenses as well. Frank skimmed those details until he found what he wanted.

Married June 11, 1988, to Aurora Lee St. Jean, white female born March 14, 1966, in Mount Olive, North Carolina. First marriage for both. One child, William Douglas Alexander, born February 4, 1990.

The printout listed the grid of streets surrounding the Alexander home, along with the neighbors' names, addresses and telephone numbers.

The last sheet was a copy of a brief newspaper obituary printed in agate type. *Alexander, Daniel P., 38, of Miami, died Saturday. Visitation 5 to 9 P.M. Monday. Van Orsdel Funeral Chapel. Services 11 A.M. Tuesday.*

A *Miami Herald* clipping was attached, short and concise, dated the same day as the obit.

RESTAURANT OWNER SHOT IN APPARENT SUICIDE
The shooting death of a popular restaurant owner was an apparent suicide, Miami police said Sunday.

Daniel Alexander, 38, was discovered wounded by a single gunshot to the head at his South Coconut Grove home on Saturday. He was later pronounced dead at Jackson Memorial Hospital. Police said Alexander was alone in the house at the time of the shooting. His wife, Rory, 32, found the victim when she returned home and called police.

Homicide Detective Joseph Thomas said the victim was apparently despondent and had left a suicide note. Alexander and a partner operate the popular Tree Tavern Restaurants in Miami Beach, Coral Gables and Kendall.

That was it. A man's life and death reduced to crisp black and white words and numbers, minus the passion, the joy, the sweat and tears.

How incredibly lucky, Frank thought, that Daniel Alexander did not fire the bullet into his heart. He would have killed us both. Frank had been so weak, so close to death, that within days, if no donor had been found, it would have been too late. He read the news story twice, feeling inexplicably let down. The information brought no enlightening revelation. What had he anticipated? He had no clue. Impulsively he reached for the telephone and dialed Alexander's number. It rang three times.

"Hello." A young woman answered, her voice soft and deep-throated. He realized he had no idea what to say. Words froze in his throat. "Hello," she said again. "Who is it?"

He hung up, hating himself. What could he say? What should he? Why did he dial without thinking? What was he doing? How totally unlike him to be so rash, to act without thinking things through first.

Was Kathleen right? Would his intrusion only inflict pain? Good God, he thought, closing his eyes. The woman's gift saved my life and I just repaid her with a harassing phone call. He knew how frightening those could be to a woman alone and grief-stricken. His eyes watered, remembering his widowed mother's tears.

He read through Lucca's material again, more carefully this time.

Alexander lived in a good neighborhood, he had driven an expensive car and owned a business. Most likely he was well insured, his wife and son well provided for. What value could he bring to their lives? His fantasies about stepping in to ameliorate their situation were just that, fantasies. Was he motivated by gratitude or merely morbid curiosity? Kathleen had been right.

Sue Ann arrived, carrying the mail, as he left. "Hey,

there," she chirped, upbeat as always. "You're an early bird. Need anything?"

He shook his head. "I'm going home. I may be back later. The coffee's fresh."

He retrieved the car from the municipal parking lot behind the building and started home. He must at least, he thought, say thank you. He could do that in an anonymous letter of gratitude delivered through the transplant program. That was the soundest course of action. A face-to-face meeting was out of the question. Why didn't he feel relieved? Without thinking, he turned east, toward the ocean, then north on Collins. Troubled and restless, he parked the Mercedes at a meter, then climbed the wooden plank stairs to the boardwalk, inhaling the salt air and broad horizon. Few sunbathers on the sand this early on a weekday during the off season. He descended onto the beach at Thirty-sixth Street. The ocean slapped its big salty body against the sand as usual, now and forever, evoking a nostalgic sense of longing. He loved the sea and the endless sky and always thought better when walking the beach. A force as strong as the tide was tugging him toward Daniel Alexander's widow. Common sense told him it was a bad idea, but his heart—his heart, that was funny, he realized, smiling to himself—his heart wanted him to go to Rory Alexander, the person who gave it to him.

Who knew what can of worms that could open? Better not to know. The woman could be a total bitch who hounded the poor bastard to death. Perhaps she had cheated on Alexander, or intended to divorce him, prompting his last desperate act. If she bore a burden of guilt, Frank would be a reminder of what she had done. Go with the intelligent decision, he told himself, not illogical emotions. Taking the high road had always worked for him.

It was time to go, the sky was changing as a thunderstorm boiled up offshore and roiled swiftly toward the beach. He should have joined the few bathers who scooped up their beach towels and fled. But something kept him. He sat on an unattended wooden lounge and watched slanted rain streak the horizon, churning the sea from brilliant blue green to gunmetal gray under low-flying, fast-moving clouds. The air freshened as a skirling and relentless wind whipped his hair. He had never felt more alive, stimulated by the energy of the electrical storm racing across open water. Bam! An earsplitting thunderclap following a lightning bolt that skittered crazily across the sky. Cool, scattered raindrops began to fall. He was alone on the beach now, except for a lifeguard closeted in his pastel art deco station.

More lightning. Frank never flinched. The storm's awesome power thrilled him. The odds against being struck by lightning were huge, at least six hundred thousand to one, he knew. He was more likely to win the lottery or be mauled by a shark. The odds would be no consolation, of course, should a bolt seek him out. Even if he saw it coming at sixty thousand miles a second, he could never outdistance it. He could run, but he couldn't hide. But he felt confident, almost cocky. God had granted him a new heart, a medical miracle, a new life. He certainly would not take it away now in a bolt from the blue.

Frank turned to leave, then saw it. A small boat tossed viciously, out beyond the breakers, helplessly buffeted by the storm. A man stood precariously in the bow, waving both arms, signaling frantically.

Jesus Christ, he thought. The guy's in trouble. His cell phone was in the car blocks away. Rain pelted faster now. Frank jogged toward the lifeguard station, shouting, "Call the Coast Guard!"

He nearly staggered up the wooden steps and pounded on the door. The window slid to one side with a gritty rasp.

"What's your problem, buddy?" The guard, snug and dry, eyed him suspiciously.

Frank gasped for breath. His doctors should see him now, he thought. "Did you call the Coast Guard? That guy's in trouble out there!"

The guard's blue eyes remained flat and uncomprehending. "What guy?"

"The boat, goddammit! The boat!" He couldn't help but see it. Frank turned in to the pounding rain to point back to where he had seen the floundering craft. All he saw was raging surf.

"My God, he capsized." He squinted, searching for a survivor in the water.

The guard looked unperturbed, hunched in his Beach Patrol windbreaker. "I didn't see anybody out there, and if I were you, buddy, I'd get off the beach in an electrical storm. It's not safe."

"Are you crazy? Call the Coast Guard! He was right there."

The guard lifted his binoculars, focused, scanned, then shook his head and put them down.

"I'm telling you, he was right out there. A small boat, about a sixteen-footer." The needlelike downpour, hard and cold, soaked his shirt, slacks and shoes. This was not the soft, warm, splashy rain of summer. Lightning lit up the sky, thunder crashed.

The guard picked up his walkie-talkie. "Randy, you see anything out there? Got a guy who claims he just saw a boat in trouble right here off forty-one." He paused. "Yeah. Me too. Right."

He hit another button, apparently accessing a central frequency. "This is forty-one, anybody see a small boat in trouble offshore?"

The replies were all negative.

Wet to the skin, hair plastered flat, water cascading down his face, Frank knew how he must look to this stranger.

"Listen," the lifeguard shouted, over the sounds of the storm, "sometimes the waves are like clouds. You think you see things. Now, get off the beach, buddy, before you drown. You're soaked." He slammed the window shut.

Gusts of wind-blasted rain nearly shoved Frank off balance as he went down the stairs. He stared at where he had last seen the doomed boater. Nothing but stormy sea. The stretch of beach that curved north toward the Fontainebleau was empty except for the raging surf.

"You'd better make a report on this," he shouted furiously, knowing his words would be drowned out by the wind and the rain, " 'cuz when that guy and his boat wash up onshore, 'buddy,' I'm turning you in!" His eyes stung and his shoes made squishing sounds as he slogged across the wet sand, climbed the steps to the boardwalk and trudged back to his car through the rain.

He sat shivering in the Mercedes, his water-soaked clothes oozing onto the sculpted leather seats. His Italian-made shoes were ruined. Some poor son of a bitch just drowned out there, he thought. So why am I thinking about that damn woman? Rain pounded the windshield, drummed on the roof, echoing an inner voice demanding that he find Rory Alexander.

He stopped at the fast-food window of an art deco Burger King, ordered a carton of milk, swallowed his pills, then drove home, teeth chattering.

Kathleen was horrified when she saw him.

"My God, Frank. What happened? Did you take your medication? You'll catch pneumonia!"

She dispatched Lourdes for towels and hot soup, and insisted on helping him peel off his wet clothes. "There had to be a place to take shelter," she fussed. "You look like you nearly drowned. Look at those shoes!"

She filled the Jacuzzi in the master bath, ordered him into the steaming water and returned with a big stoneware mug. The soup was hot, aromatic. Chicken. Homemade. Jewish penicillin. She sat on the marble ledge around the oversized tub and spoon-fed it to him. Then she lathered his hair with her fragrant shampoo, massaging his scalp. Had he been a cat, he would have purred.

He knew what she was doing, of course. This was in part a diversion, a warm, delectable and delicious diversion from their squabble the night before. He had heard Shandi come in from her date at about 2 A.M. He had never suspected Kathleen's motives before, but right now he was in heaven, the moment too good to spoil. Who knows, he thought, perhaps the situation with Shandi would resolve itself. Some do.

He felt completely relaxed. "Something happened at the beach, Kath."

"What was it?" She rubbed conditioner into his hair.

"I saw a boat in trouble, floundering in the storm."

She paused. "Anybody aboard?"

"One man, he saw me and was signaling for help."

"Did they save him?"

"By the time I got the lifeguard's attention, he was gone. Nobody else saw him."

"What about all those cliff dwellers in the high-rise condos and hotels along the beach?" She sounded cheerful and matter-of-fact. "Lots of them have nothing better to do than scan the horizon with their telescopes and binoculars. You know how eager they all are to be the first to spot dead bodies, beached whales and Haitian boat people. Surely they saw him and called for help.''

''I hope so,'' he said doubtfully.

She handed him the cup and he drained the last satisfying dregs. He smiled up into her eyes, the water easing the tightness in his muscles. ''You saved me again,'' he said, his head clear. ''Home is really the place where they have to take you in.''

''I was so worried when I woke up and you were gone. Where did you go off to at the crack of dawn?''

''To the office, had an early meeting.''

''Don't ever do that again without telling me first.'' Her voice was tender, though she shook her head in mock exasperation. ''I worry about you.'' She brought him towels from the warmer, thick and fluffy. ''What you need now is a nap.''

She was right. He meant to thank her, to tell her she had been right about everything, all along, but he felt drowsy. He wore his bathrobe into the bedroom, sank into bed and pulled the down comforter over him.

He awoke refreshed, the room in soft shadow, the setting sun spilling its golden glow between narrow cracks in the blinds, the sheers billowing in the breeze off the water. Disoriented for a moment, he was not sure whether it was dawn or dusk.

He was sure he was not alone. Someone had just spoken his name. Someone was sitting in the comfortable overstuffed chair between the bed and the fireplace, where Kathleen often sat reading to him when he was ill.

''You don't have to watch me sleep anymore,'' he mumbled. ''I'm okay now, Kath.'' He rolled over to reassure her, comfortably drowsy in the fading light. "I'm sure you have . . ."

The stranger smiled faintly, his eyes bright.

Frank jerked to a sitting position. The shock sent cold fear coursing through his body. The man looked familiar, though his face was in shadow. The high-backed chair blocked the waning light from the window behind him.

His rumpled clothes seemed stained and spattered in the uncertain light. The intruder remained still, exhibiting no threat, no sense of menace.

"Who the hell are you? What are doing in here?" Frank fumbled for the bedside keypad, then mashed the panic button.

The shrill siren howled an earsplitting warning, automatically alerting the monitoring station. Police would be notified. But the man seemed to take no notice. Still seated, he extended his right hand in a gesture of supplication.

Frank scrambled out the far side of the bed, the down comforter sliding to the floor. He pulled his robe tight around him, eyes on the intruder, and edged toward the door.

"Kathleen!" he bellowed. "Lourdes!" The alarm continued to wail.

He heard voices, somebody pounding up the stairs.

"Call the police!" he shouted. "Call the police!"

The door burst open. The siren's shrill sound spilled even louder into the room. He took his eyes off the man and saw the frightened faces of Kathleen, Casey and the housekeeper. His daughter was wide-eyed, hands over her ears.

"Frank, what is it?"

"Don't come in!" he warned, wheeling. "Somebody's in here!"

Kathleen hit the light switch. The room was empty. On

the chair, only a pillow and an open magazine. The intruder had escaped that quickly.

"Casey," he instructed, "go downstairs, go outside, stay there and wait for the police."

No one moved. They all stared at him.

"Go! Go!" he shouted.

"Do it," Kathleen said, touching Casey's shoulder, never taking her eyes off him.

"Did you call the police?" he demanded, as Casey trotted out of the room, turning to stare at him over her shoulder.

"The alarm company will send them, unless we cancel," Kathleen said calmly.

"He must have gone through the bathroom." His words sounded tense, choked. "He could be anywhere." If the siren would only stop, he could think.

The leather bag with his medication still lay on the nightstand. Frank snatched it up. The closet where Kathleen kept her jewelry seemed intact, the wall safe undisturbed.

"Come on." Hurriedly he shepherded them out into the hallway, then downstairs and into the foyer.

Lourdes squinted, gritting her teeth against the shrieking of the alarm. "I'm going to turn it off," Kathleen said.

"No! The son of a bitch is still in the house!"

"Who?"

"I don't know."

"You were asleep, Frank. You must have been dreaming."

"No!" he said fiercely, as the first hint of doubt gnawed at the pit of his stomach. Why did the intruder's face look so familiar, so beneficent, as though he belonged there?

A patrol car pulled into the driveway. Frank used the remote to stop the siren. In the sudden, blessed silence, Frank saw their next-door neighbors at the side gate. Gardiner Bishop's paunch hung over the top of his walking shorts. He held a revolver in his hand.

"Is everybody all right?" he called.

Frank nodded as he stepped out to greet the first patrolman, ears ringing, the alarm still sounding in his head.

Two police officers and a K-9 dog searched the house from top to bottom. Daisy the dalmatian barked her brains out at the men in uniform and their canine partner, a harnessed German shepherd who ignored her. The searchers found nothing amiss. Doors, screens and windows all intact.

Frank and Kathleen talked to the officers in the living room. A lanky, weary-looking cop who appeared to be in his forties and his partner, a burly, slightly oafish man at least ten years younger.

No one else saw the intruder. Daisy never barked until the police arrived. Now she refused to stop. Yes, Frank had been sleeping during the day. Well, yes, he was on medication but nothing hallucinogenic.

Shandi came running into the house, past the police cars blocking the drive.

"What's going on! What happened?" she panted, eyes frightened. "Is everything all right?"

"Daddy said he saw somebody, upstairs, in their room," Casey blurted.

"He's still recuperating," Kathleen was telling the officers, "from major surgery. He was in the hospital for months."

"I'm fine now," Frank protested. He realized how it sounded, and looked. He had been barefoot, in a bathrobe, when they arrived. "I simply took a nap because I was up very early this morning and got drenched in the storm this afternoon." He read Kathleen's face as he spoke and realized she didn't believe him either.

No one was seen leaving the island on foot, no strange cars had been spotted. The man might have escaped along the water. But if so, the others downstairs and Lourdes in the kitchen should have seen him.

"So you wake up and he's just sitting there?" the younger cop said again. "You didn't see a weapon?"

"No, it was shadowy, but I didn't see anything in his hands."

"He wasn't exposing himself?"

"No," Frank said impatiently. "Not that I saw. I think he was trying to tell me something. His lips were moving."

"Maybe he was reading that magazine," the cop suggested. Kathleen's copy of *Southern Living* had been left open on the chair. He turned to Kathleen. "That was there when Mister Douglas went in for his nap?"

She nodded.

"Didn't look like anybody sat on it. Maybe he took the magazine off the chair, then put it back before fleeing." He shrugged and glanced at his partner.

"What did he say?" the older cop asked.

"I couldn't hear, didn't wait around to find out," Frank admitted.

"You just got out of the hospital," the cop said quietly, "where people are in and outta your room all the time. Maybe you woke up and thought you were still there. You know how you can wake up confused for a moment."

Frank knew, all too well.

"The light can play tricks on you, especially if you've been dreaming."

"No," he said stubbornly. "I saw someone. He was there."

He saw the way they looked at him. The eyes of the lifeguard that afternoon had reflected the same expression.

"We've had a few driveway robberies on these islands," the older cop conceded, getting to his feet. "But no home invasions."

The officers remained respectful and left promising to patrol the island more often, but Frank knew they didn't believe him.

Dinner was nearly ready, but he wasn't hungry. He needed a drink. He poured one and sat sipping it, staring at the gathering darkness. The household was subdued. Little was said, but he knew what they were thinking. The Bishops called to make sure all was well. He remembered Gardiner at the gate, a gun in his hand.

A gun, Frank thought. He had always feared and hated firearms because of his father. But now he realized the world, his life, had changed. He had to protect his family. That was it. He needed a gun.

CHAPTER
FOUR

In bed that night, he spoke to Kathleen about upgrading security, not only in the house but the entire neighborhood.

"I'm going to the next Homeowners Association meeting," he said, "to propose a plan for manned security gates on each island." As past president, he had the clout. They would listen to him.

"Who would pay for it?" she asked, her voice doubtful in the dark. "Wouldn't it be expensive?"

"Each homeowner would be assessed their fair share based on their property value."

"But taxes are so high now," she protested. "People who've lived here forever, especially the older ones on fixed incomes, are having a tough time financially. I'm sure there will be opposition."

"But we have to protect ourselves. You saw what happened today."

She took his hand. "Sweetheart, you may have been mistaken. After all you've been through . . . Perhaps we should talk to Dr. O'Hara," she said softly. "He could reevaluate your medication."

"I'm fine," he snapped. "I'm calling Guard-Tec in the morning. I want security cameras here at the house."

Her silence was eloquent. She soon slept, but he did not. His heart prevented it. No pain, no discomfort, no precise symptom he could positively identify. He was simply aware of every heartbeat. He heard each one. Did Daniel Alexander's widow sleep well, he wondered, or did she lie awake somewhere listening to her own heartbeat? He knew now that he had to see her, just once.

His heartbeats faded into the gentle creaking of the house, Kathleen's restless sighs and the faint, faraway music from a midnight party boat passing in the bay.

Frank pored over the morning paper and tuned in to the radio news. No reports of a drowning victim or a missing boater. He called Lucca, instructing him to expedite installation of surveillance cameras at the office, and hired him to consult with his home security company on design of a similar system for the house. "I also need your recommendation on the right weapon to buy, a gun."

"You got a problem, boss?" the detective growled. "Anything I should know about?"

"Nothing serious. But we had a prowler yesterday."

"That's always a wake-up call. What did the local gendarmes have to say?"

Frank wanted to avoid the details. He valued Lucca's respect too much.

"You *did* call them, didn't you, boss?"

"Yeah. They were out here. They didn't find him."

"No surprise," he scoffed contemptuously. "Those guys over on the beach couldn't pick up a wounded elephant's trail in a foot of fresh snow. How serious are you about this gun thing?"

"Dead serious."

Lucca was silent for a moment, apparently mulling over Frank's choice of words. "You're talking about a weapon to keep in the car, your office, at the house for protection?"

"Exactly. What do you suggest?"

"A good, old-fashioned, .38-caliber six-shot revolver with a three-inch barrel. That's the easiest to handle, less chance of an accident. Doesn't tend to jam like an automatic. Fires nice medium-velocity lead bullets. Anything by Smith and Wesson or Colt. Not for stopping cars or tanks, strictly for punching holes in people. That's all, you don't need no alley sweeper or elephant gun, no eighteen-shot automatic.

"Might I suggest that before you bring it home, take it to the range first. So you get the feel of it, as opposed to the Miami style, which is throwing open a back door or a window and firing a few shots in the air. Be a good idea to take your wife and the kids out to the range, show 'em how to use it, teach 'em to fire it, explain the safety rules. This accomplishes two things. One, if they're ever alone in the house and threatened, they know how to protect themselves, and two, familiarity does away with the forbidden-fruit factor. Worst thing people with kids can do is to hide a weapon and warn 'em never to go near it. That's asking for trouble. And for God's sake, boss, don't do like some people who are so scared of their own weapon that they unload it and lock the ammo in a different part of the house. An empty gun don't do you any good in a real emergency."

"Thanks for the advice."

"You follow up on that other matter yet?"

"I'm about to, now."

"Let me know if you need anything in that department."

"You've got it."

Frank had trouble selecting what to wear. He wanted to look . . . what? Reputable? Responsible? Appreciative? Like a man worthy of the gift he had received.

Kathleen was in and out of the room while he dressed. He tried on a red printed silk jacquard tie, but rejected it. Too bright, too frivolous for the occasion. He felt impatient, pressured to hurry. Why? he thought. The woman doesn't even know I'm coming. That may not have been her who answered the phone. She may not even be there. Hell, she could be in Paris, Rome or cruising the Aegean Sea by now, spending her dead husband's insurance money.

He took off the white-on-white herringbone stripe. The French cuffs and spread collar made him look like a stuffed shirt. What had even made him buy these clothes?

Wearing only a bra and lacy half slip, Kathleen fastened a pearl earring and paused to watch him try on an Italian-made blue-gray textured cotton shirt with a point collar.

"If I didn't know better . . ."

"What?" He stood in front of the mirror, holding a navy and royal blue silk woven tie up under his chin.

"You remind me of Shandi dressing for a date," she said, smiling, hands on her hips.

"Speaking of Shandi," he said, to change the subject, "we need to talk about her seeing Bowden. Is that still going on? Was she really at the library last night? She is grounded, right?"

"Of course. We can discuss all that later." She kissed his cheek and padded barefoot into the bathroom.

He looked in the mirror and decided to lose the tie. The Miami look, the casual look, was better. That was him.

First he drove to the gun shop Lucca had recommended. He chose the revolver the detective had suggested, paid for it and filled out the paperwork. His background would be checked during the three-day waiting period. Then he drove south.

The house sat at the end of the street on a cul-de-sac. Twin phoenix palms towered over the front yard, flower beds nestled at their feet. The lawn and the beds looked slightly straggly, as though neglected lately. A child's bicycle lay on the lawn, near the front porch. A white Mercury Sable station wagon, a few years old, stood in the driveway. The dead man's Lexus must be in the garage, he thought.

A gray striped cat napped contentedly in the sun on the front doormat.

Frank drove by twice. He stared at the house, uncertain. It would have been so much easier if she were gone. But someone did appear to be at home. He pictured what she would be like. Petite, dark-haired, athletic, the woman on the fringe of his fantasies, the elusive figure haunting his restless dreams. Why not? he thought. His heart had loved her. Doctors call it a pump, poets call it the place where love lives— or dies, the center of all emotions. The truth, he thought, must lie somewhere between.

He did not pull into the driveway, but parked the Mercedes at the curb and proceeded up the walk, stepping over a garden hose. A row of empty plastic flowerpots, a trowel, and a ten-pound sack of potting soil sat next to the house as though the task of repotting had been interrupted. They looked as though they had been there for some time, the pots askew, tipped one way and the other.

The cat stared, wary at his approach, then skittered into the bushes. The front screen door was strictly South Florida, flamingos and palm trees forged in art deco ironwork. The inner door stood open, to welcome the breeze. Beyond it, he saw a Cuban tile floor, rattan furniture and dappled light filtered through palm fronds outside the back windows. This house had a name as well as a number. TWIN PALMS was painted on a decorative ceramic tile over the doorbell.

He took a deep breath and rang the bell. The drive had taken nearly half an hour, mostly because he was unfamiliar with the neighborhood and busy rehearsing what to say. He had decided to keep it simple:

On behalf of my family and myself, I want to personally express our sympathy and our gratitude. You saved my life and we will never forget it. As you can see, I'm doing very well. Thank you.

Short and sweet. That would end it. This compulsion behind him, he would go on to live out his new life and sleep peacefully through the nights to come.

All was quiet inside. He pushed the doorbell again and listened to the melodic chime. A long shadow fell across the tile floor, someone emerging from another room. He held his breath as a woman came swiftly to the door.

"Mrs. Alexander?"

"Yes."

She was tall, at least five ten, lean and angular with high rounded cheekbones and a sharp little chin with a deep dimple etched in the center. She was nothing like the small dark-haired woman in his mind's eye. This woman's hair, a curly mass of red, auburn, spilled carelessly over her shoulders, cascading down her back.

"You got here so fast." She unlocked the screen door and

pushed it open. "You don't know how much I 'preciate this."
She spoke southern in a throaty drawl.

He stood there, bewildered. "Come on in," she urged,
beckoning impatiently. "I hope we kin git this all figured
out." She sighed poignantly. "It's got me totally bumfuzzled."

Hesitantly he stepped inside. He had been so certain she
would look familiar, that he would know her at once. So
much for his cockeyed fantasies. Her husband's heart might
beat in his chest, but it neither fluttered nor pounded in recognition. She was a total stranger. This was the woman who
had saved him. Slim, almost too thin, she wore a simple, subdued ankle-length print dress, short-sleeved with tiny buttons
down the front. Sandals. No jewelry, just a gold wedding band.
Her gray-green eyes were big and expressive, her lips almost
too full to be natural. He wondered if they were silicone-
enhanced, a fad Kathleen's friends had embraced a few years
earlier, when they all began to appear with suddenly swollen
lips, as though stung by bees on an angry rampage.

"Please sit down." She waved toward the rattan couch.
A book on the coffee table caught his eye, *Healing After the
Suicide of a Loved One.*

She had obviously mistaken him for someone else, so he
remained standing. He did not plan to stay long enough to sit.

"Mrs. Alexander . . ."

"Call me Rory. Sorry this place is such a mess." Newspapers were stacked on a dining room chair. Toys scattered on
the floor. She picked up a plastic truck with a missing wheel.
"I've just been runnin' in circles," she said helplessly. There
was a childlike vulnerability about her.

"My name is Franklin Douglas."

"You're not from Briscoe and Taft?"

He shook his head. He recognized the name, an accounting firm with offices downtown.

"I'm sorry." She shook her head, exasperated, and pushed back her hair. Her eyes became wary and she licked her lower lip nervously, as though expecting something unpleasant. "Then you're . . ."

"Frank." He cleared his throat. "I was very sick for more than a year. I nearly died." His mouth opened, but the words he had rehearsed weren't there. His top shirt button was open. He undid the second button, fingering the top of his incision. "I . . ." he fumbled.

"Oh my God," she whispered. Her big eyes widened. The toy truck slipped from her hand unnoticed. "You're forty-four years old? From Miami? You have two children?" Tears welled in her eyes.

He nodded, his own eyes swimming.

She clasped both hands, her expression one of joy. "Oh, you look wonderful! You're all right!"

"Yes." He smiled.

"Please sit down. Please."

He sat on the sofa, she directly across from him in a cane-back chair.

"I'm so glad. I'm so glad." When she smiled, deep dimples appeared in both cheeks. "I was so scared that it wouldn't work out. If you weren't all right, then there'd be nothin'." She leaned forward. "One of Daniel's kidneys went to a man in Orlando. They said he only had hours to live without it. The other went to a teenage girl in New Orleans. His liver went to a father of four in Tampa. I think they're all right. I haven't heard, probably won't. But you, look at you."

Her long, tapered fingers covered her face, huge eyes peering over them to stare. "Daniel would be so happy." A tear skidded down her cheek as her eyes roved to the mantel.

Frank got to his feet.

"That's him? That's your husband?"

She nodded, blinking. "The three of us. Taken a few years ago."

A small boy perched on a bicycle, his mother laughing, held him and the bike, which appeared to be new. Daniel Alexander stood behind them, smiling. The silver frame was small, only five by seven. But even at a glance Frank saw that this handsome man with deep-set dark eyes was also a total stranger, no visceral connection, no link to his troubling dreams.

He smiled at the photograph, touched by the solemn gaze of the small boy who resembled both parents. The all-American family. He wondered what happened, why it ended the way it did.

"I simply wanted to thank you." He turned to her. "You saved my life."

"Oh." She looked startled. "When they asked me, I never hesitated, not for a moment." She hugged herself as though suddenly cold, her gaze returning to the photo. "The chance was a tiny anchor in a sea of grief. We had never discussed it, but I'm sure it was what Daniel would have wanted."

She offered him coffee.

"Sure, I'd love some," he heard himself say.

"Come on." He followed her out into a sunny, country-style kitchen wondering why he did not follow his plan to say thank you and leave, wondering about the dark-haired woman he had expected. The wallpaper had a green ivy print, a reflection of the real thing growing in water on the windowsill. He sat at a hand-painted wooden table while she brewed coffee. Her husband watched, his expression serious from inside a heart-shaped magnetic frame on the yellow refrigerator. This photo appeared more recent, judging from the hairline just beginning to slightly recede. He felt compassion for the widow, and gratitude, but Frank had expected something else, a physical link, a spiritual sensation of déjà vu, here in the man's house, looking at his picture, at his wife. But there was nothing. Instead, he felt oddly disturbed and unsettled. The phone rang as she took flowered coffee mugs from a glass-fronted cabinet.

"Yes," she answered. "Is he coming?" Stretching the cord, she stepped around the corner into a hallway for privacy. "But . . ." She lowered her voice. Her muffled words sounded argumentative at first, then reproachful, and finally exasperated.

She returned, her troubled frown fading when she saw him.

"A problem?" He was prying; that was unlike him.

"The man I mistook you for. He's not coming," she said, and poured the coffee. As she stirred hers, he looked about the cozy nook. This was how she must have sat opposite her husband on more than a thousand mornings, he thought. If his heart had come to him with a memory, it now suffered from amnesia. This comfortable setting was totally unfamiliar.

"I'm so glad you came," she said. "It's . . ." She groped for the words. "It's something. There hasn't been a lot, you know, since that day . . ."

Her eyes grew shiny, focused on his.

"What I mean is, you are living proof that some good can survive even the worst moments of your life. Do you have any pictures?"

He was startled for a moment.

"Your family. Your children." She held out her hand.

He fished for his wallet and found a snapshot taken at a Fourth of July celebration. Kathleen and the girls wearing red, white and blue, Casey waving a small flag.

She studied it, holding the picture in both hands. "They're all so pretty."

"Actually," he said apologetically, "that's not too recent. Shandi is nineteen now, going on thirty-five, in her second semester at U. of M. She's got short hair now and about two dozen earrings, I'm afraid. Casey is eleven, braces on her teeth at the moment. But Kathleen, she looks the same." He wondered what his wife would think if she saw him now, in Rory Alexander's kitchen.

"Is there anything that you need?" he asked. "Anything that I can do for you and your son?"

She smiled. "You've done it," she said, "by coming here."

She walked him to the door where they shook hands. "Would you mind?" she whispered.

"No," he said, before he even knew what she intended.

She undid the third button on his shirt and slid her hand inside, gently positioning her warm palm over his heart.

It reminded him of the moments when loved ones touch a pregnant woman's belly to feel the life of an unborn child. In this case the life was not a new one soon to be born, but that of a loved one gone forever. Her eyes were closed.

"I can feel it," she whispered, then withdrew her hand.

Their eyes caught for a moment as he turned to leave. She was a radiant woman, he thought. He was nearly down the front steps when a nondescript-looking light-color, late-model Chevy made a sharp turn into the driveway and pulled up close behind the station wagon. The driver, a middle-aged man, got out, glanced up at them for a moment, then reached back into the car for something.

Frank turned to Rory, still behind the screen door. "You expecting somebody?"

"No."

"You know this guy?"

"Don't think so."

Frank hesitated, then waited as the man strode up the

walk. He wore a cheap sport coat and a bold stare. He nodded at Frank, then swaggered past him, up the stairs.

"Mrs. Alexander?" The tone was authoritative.

"Yes."

"Glad to catch you at home, I need a few minutes of your time."

Frank couldn't discern her expression, filtered through the wire screen.

"What's this about?" There was an uneasy resignation in her voice. He'd heard that tone before. Had it been in his mother's voice?

"I think you'd prefer to discuss this in private." He offered his card and she edged the screen door open to take it.

She studied it, then let him in.

"Is everything all right?" Frank asked loudly.

"Fine." She smiled and closed the door.

He went on down the walk. He should go, he thought. His new life waited. Instead he sat in the car watching time pass on the digital clock in the dashboard. The man emerged twelve minutes later.

Frank got out of the Mercedes and walked briskly up to the driver's side of the stranger's car.

"Mind if I take one of those cards, buddy?"

The man stared up at him. "Sure." He dug in his pocket and came up with a business card, slightly rumpled.

Frank read it. "Mind if I ask your business with Mrs. Alexander?"

"You a relative?"

"No."

The man looked amused. "Didn't waste no time, did she?"

Frank gave him a cold stare. "Does she have a problem?"

"Only that the broad paid for her husband's funeral with bad paper. She's a paper hanger."

"I'm sure this has been a difficult time for her."

"It's always a difficult time for my client when his customers don't pay their bills. It's not like he can repossess the merchandise or anything."

He began to squirm under Frank's scrutiny.

"Management is sensitive to the situation. Not like he didn't give her every break. He put the check through two, three times. So she writes another one, bounced from here to Homestead."

"Thanks for your sensitivity. I'll be in touch."

"Yeah. Right." The collection agent rolled his eyes skeptically and shifted the Chevy into reverse.

Frank put the collection agency card in his pocket, watched the car pull away and proceeded back up the walk. This time both doors were closed and locked. He rang the bell.

She was surprised to see him.

"We have to talk," he told her.

"What's the story?" Frank asked briskly.

Cheeks reddening, she stared miserably down at the table, back in the country kitchen.

"No story."

He sighed, slightly exasperated. "My intent is not to pry or embarrass you, but the reason I came here was to attempt some sort of payback, to help if there was anything you needed during this tough time. Under the circumstances, don't you think we should be able to talk like old friends?"

She tilted her head at him and blinked.

"Obviously you have a problem," he said. "Let's see what we can do to resolve it."

The luminous gray-green eyes drowned in desperation.

"I've never had a good head for figures." The words came slowly. "Daniel handled all the finances. It's just that I've made some idiotic moves. I don't even know which account . . ." she said hopelessly, running a hand through her thick red hair. Her fingers were slim and long, the nails neat but unpainted. "I wrote checks on the usual account, which I thought was backed up by other accounts, a liquid asset and CDs in that bank. You know that, what do they call it? Overdraft protection. The money is there," she added quickly, "no doubt about it, but I'm not exactly sure where. That's why I asked the accountant to send somebody who could help me sort it out today, but they say they don't have the files . . ."

"You're in luck, Rory." He could not help but grin confidently, thrilled to be the white knight to the rescue. "You just happen to be talking to a certified public accountant. First in my class in business administration at the U. of M. That's what I did in my early life, before launching my own company." He rubbed his hands together in anticipation. "Now, where did Daniel . . ." Speaking the man's name made him uncomfortably aware of Daniel Alexander watching from the refrigerator door. Something surprisingly chilling skittered along his spine. Unusual, considering the warmth and concern he felt for the man's widow and child. "Where did your husband keep his files and ledgers, his bank records? His office or here?"

"Here," she answered, a faint trace of hope in her voice. "In his study."

"Let me at 'em." He got to his feet. "I'll have you squared away in no time. That's a promise. No reason for you to ever have to deal with characters like the man who just left."

"That's the other thing." She remained seated, talking into her coffee cup. "His study . . . that's where it . . ." Her small voice dropped to a whisper. "Where I found him. When it was all over, I cleaned it, scrubbed it and scrubbed it until my hands bled. I haven't been in there since. Can't even bring myself to open the door."

"You can't put that off forever. And I'm here to help you with it now." He leaned over, voice comforting, his palms flat on the table.

"The insurance money should be coming soon." Her brooding eyes avoided his, roaming the room until they rested on the refrigerator-door photo. "That'll take care of things for the time being."

"It'll be far easier," he urged, "for the two of us to walk in there together and sort out what has to be done. There are estate matters. You have to be prepared for taxes . . ."

"But it's all such a mess. There's a stuffed filing cabinet. And cardboard boxes full of papers he brought home . . ." She glanced up at the clock. "I have to pick Billy and the kids up at school at two-thirty, I'm the car-pool mom this week."

"Shall we make an appointment then, and begin early, first thing in the morning? You'll have a chance to sleep on it."

"You don't have to do this, you know."

"Yes, I do."

She was smiling when he left.

He was eager to tell Kathleen, but she was out when he got home, off at some meeting. Then he decided to keep it to himself until it was a fait accompli. Then he could announce that not only had he found his donor's family, but that he had been right all along, there had been a need and he had filled it, solving their problems. This was part of some divine plan, he was convinced. Syncronicity. Lucca was right. Always listen to your gut.

They could dine out together when he was finished, he

decided. Kathleen and the girls, Rory and her son. Perhaps they would all become friends. He pondered where to take them. A really nice place, he thought.

"Whose canary did you swallow?" Kathleen always read him so well. "Is that a feather on your chin?" She shrugged smartly out of her lime green Escada jacket. Single-breasted with gold buttons, over a silky blouse. The woman knew how to dress, always did. Her hair was up, wound into a French twist. She looked like a sophisticated Brickell Avenue executive home from the fray.

"I'm just happy to see you. How goes it?"

"Well, Dave Linderman never should have been appointed to the board for the new arts center." She hung her jacket in the hall closet. "Suddenly, he's an expert on everything and all the man wants to do is argue. Not a whit of common sense. He gets in the way of whatever we try to do."

"Any way to get rid of him?"

"Nothing short of a coup d'état. He's the mayor's appointee. The man's insufferable." She fumed. "The rest of us are thinking about raising funds for a paid assassin."

He hugged her and kissed her cheek. "You're cute when you're mad."

"You've been watching old movies again, and pilfering their dialogue, haven't you?"

"No, but maybe we have time before dinner to go upstairs and make our own movies." He growled and nuzzled her neck. He closed his eyes, overtaken by the erotic image of a strong and passionate dark-haired woman, a creation, he knew now, of his own imagination.

"X-rated?" Kathleen nibbled his ear, then slipped out of reach. "I've got a surprise," she said. "We need to talk."

"Uh-oh." Kathleen had held back, obviously uneasy since

they'd resumed their sex life. Having to reassure her that gasps, moans or heavy breathing during intimate moments were signs of passion, not imminent death, was not a turn-on. Was it all an excuse? Had she ever really enjoyed sex with him? Or did she really fear he would die in her arms?

"Listen," she said cheerfully, perched on the arm of his chair. "We've got to keep this under wraps for a few weeks, but it appears that I am going to be named president of the Committee for Art in Public Places."

She chuckled, clearly delighted.

"Madame President." He stroked the silk of her blouse, his sensitive fingertips seeking her nipple. "Sounds good to me. But you're already on the boards for the South Florida Historical Museum and the new arts center. Won't it all be too demanding?"

"Of course not, silly. You know how organized I am. I may have to hire a secretary, but now that you're well and going back to the office and the girls are so busy with school, it's something I would love to do. Do you realize that with the right people aboard, our committee could change the look of this entire community?"

He waxed enthusiastic and supportive, while wondering why she had not mentioned it sooner. As he lay dying, his life slipping away, he had vowed to create lifelong memories for his loved ones should he survive. This development could put a crimp in the Norman Rockwell family image he had envisioned. No point boxing shadows, he thought, she has not been appointed yet.

His dreams that night were excitement-charged, as though he had boarded a high-speed train roaring headlong toward a secret destination. He slipped out of bed in the dark and dressed before dawn in an open-necked pullover and twill slacks. He dug his old monogrammed leather briefcase out of the closet and removed the small bars of sweet-scented soap Kathleen kept inside to keep the leather fresh and Miami's mildew away. He shoved several legal pads, sharp pencils, index cards and a calculator inside and took the laptop, a small notebook computer, from his desk.

"What on earth?" Kathleen stood in the doorway, sleepy, still in her nightdress.

"It's off to work I go," he said cheerfully.

She yawned. "Want coffee?"

"I'll pick some up on the way."

She looked doubtful. "What business are you conducting this early?"

"Have to do some calculating and organizing on investments and tax matters. Early morning is best, no interruptions."

"Can't you do that here?"

Damn, I should tell her now, he thought, but there was so much to tell, and he was impatient, a man in a hurry.

"The paperwork is there." He did not say where.

She eyed him skeptically. "You always hated to get up this early. You never did if you could help it." She touched his cheek. "Did you sleep well? How do you feel?"

"Excellent. It feels great to be back in harness."

She smiled indulgently. "Well, please don't do too much. And do come home by two. That's when the Guard-Tec consultant and that detective will be here to discuss the security system."

He slapped a palm to his forehead. "I nearly forgot. I'll be back. If I'm a few minutes late, just work with Lucca and give him whatever he needs. You'll like him. He's good."

He stopped at a Burger King drive-through for black coffee and scanned the morning paper. Still nothing about a lost boat or a drowning victim. He blamed the paper. The local section had become lackluster. That's what happens in a one-newspaper town, he thought. Coverage suffers without competition. The story had gone unreported, he thought, or the boater had somehow saved himself.

He drove with the flow of traffic, windows open. Unlike the stifling hot dead air of summer, there had been cooling fall breezes almost every day. He felt eager and energetic, ahead of rush hour, which would soon stream in the opposite direction, toward downtown. Unscrambling figures, making numbers talk until they spit out the bottom line, had always been an irresistible challenge. Heady with anticipation, he made the turn onto Rory's street. A police car sat in her driveway. He stopped, overtaken by dread. There were two uniformed officers, one retrieving something from his cruiser, the other near the front door, which stood open. He snatched his briefcase, locked the Mercedes and hurried up the walk.

"What's wrong, Officer? Is there a problem?"

Rory appeared in the doorway, wearing blue denim, her hair loose, down her back. She seemed to be all right. From behind her, a small boy stared at the policemen.

"I don't have my license and registration," she told the cop. "They're in the glove compartment."

"Swell." The cop shook his head. "That's not smart."

"I know, I know." She pushed back her hair and turned to Frank. "My car was stolen last night."

"Right out of your driveway?" He turned and stared in disbelief down the shady residential street as though the culprit might still be lurking, eyeing his Mercedes.

"I woke up this morning and it was gone. And it's my week to drive the kids to school . . ."

"We haven't had many auto thefts in this immediate area," reported the taller cop, the one with the clipboard.

"You sure another family member didn't take it in for repairs without telling you?"

"There are no other family members," she said quietly, curling a protective arm around her small son's shoulders, "just us."

"Notice anything unusual, any strangers around here lately?"

Her eyes turned to Frank.

"I swear I didn't take it. Not guilty."

"Of course not," she said.

"A Mercury Sable station wagon is not exactly the hottest set of wheels in the world of professional car thieves," the shorter cop commented.

"How old you say it was, a ninety-three? Musta stole it for parts."

"Three forty-two?" The voice of the dispatcher sounded crisp and clear on the taller cop's hand-held radio.

"Three forty-two," he responded.

"Three forty-two, that's affirmative on that vehicle at your QTH, it's on the list."

"Affirmative? Thank you. QRU." The cop capped his pen, exchanged glances with his partner and gave Rory a withering look.

"Nobody stole your car, lady. It was repossessed."

"Repossessed?" She sounded shocked.

"Yeah."

"But how could that be?"

"Simple premise, lady. You don't make the payments, the repo man takes the car. Let's go, Bill."

"But wait," she protested, "my license, registration and some of my son's baseball gear, his uniform and his mitt, they're all in the car."

"You'll have to take it up with the lender, ma'am."

"Will they give it back, Mom?" The small boy plucked at her elbow. "Will they give it back?"

Frank wondered if the child meant the car or his baseball uniform.

Her eyes filled. "They just come and . . . and steal it from your driveway?"

Halfway down the front steps, the cop turned back to her. "They didn't steal it, ma'am. It belongs to them."

"But they don't even notify you?"

"It's easier that way, ma'am. They notify us."

Piqued at the waste of their time and talents, the two cops meandered on down the driveway to their car.

The little boy fought back tears. "But Dad gave me that mitt."

"We'll get it back, Billy. We'll get it back." She wiped her eyes, and sniffed loudly.

The boy turned and ran into the house sobbing. His mother sank down onto the front stoop, took a deep shuddering breath and put her head between her knees.

Frank still stood there with his briefcase. "This," he said to the top of her head, "may be a bit more complicated than I thought."

CHAPTER FIVE

"You're late to school anyway," Frank said over his shoulder. "Want to stop at McDonald's for a Happy Meal?"

"No, sir." The boy answered in a barely audible monotone and only after a nudge from his mother. Rory had wanted Billy to sit in the backseat of the Mercedes because of the air bags. Billy had refused to climb into the back unless she sat with him. So she did, her arm around him.

"So you've already eaten breakfast?"

"Yes, sir."

The kid was not easy to strike up a conversation with, Frank thought.

"Where do I turn?" They were approaching an intersection. "Remember, I'm the only one aboard who's never been to Coconut Grove Elementary. I need a good navigator."

Billy leaned forward and pointed. "It's that way." His disgusted tone made it clear that anybody with any smarts wouldn't need directions.

Frank smiled to himself. He had arrived, briefcase in hand, ready to delve into the Alexander family finances. Instead he was driving their kid to school. Did that make him the car-pool mommy?

"Mom?" piped up the small voice of the boy in the backseat. "Do we have any money?"

"Of course, sweetheart."

"Are we poor?"

"No, we're not poor. Daddy worked very hard and left us enough money to take care of everything."

"Then why did they take our car?"

"Because Mommy made a mistake. She won't do that again."

"Do I still get ten dollars if I get all A's on my report card, like Daddy promised?"

"If Daddy promised, you'll get it—if your report card is all A's."

Frank watched them in the mirror, heads together. They shared the same coloring, wide eyes and fringed lashes. The boy closed his, burying his face in his mother's shoulder.

"Voilà." Frank glided the Mercedes to a stop in a *No Parking* zone outside the sprawling Mediterranean-style elementary school. "Didn't think I'd ever find it, did you?"

Rory smoothed the boy's hair and straightened his collar. "Mommy loves you. Have a good day, sweetheart. Tara's mom will bring you home with the others. I'll be waiting for you."

"Promise?"

"I promise." She handed him his lunch, packed in a brown paper sack. A frantic search earlier had determined that his *Star Wars* lunch box was gone, left in the station wagon.

Frank smiled reassuringly as Billy turned to him.

"My Dad's on a trip," the boy said. "He'll be back." He scrambled out the door and darted through the empty school-yard into the building.

"Wait," Rory said, watching, "I want to make sure he's all the way inside."

Frank turned to her. "You can ride in the front seat now, ma'am. If you'd like to."

She tossed her head back and laughed heartily, an infectious, pleasant sound. "I'm so sorry about all of this. I swear." She settled into the front passenger seat with a sigh. "That boy has turned into a child of Satan."

"Seems fine to me."

"Shoulda seen us this morning. Billy gets absolutely hysterical about the car. So does the other mother, forced to take over the driving today. Had to cancel an appointment with her dermatologist. Then Billy flat out refuses to get in her car with the other kids and insists on waiting for the police. He totally freaks when they show up. Then, once they're gone, he insists on going to school. Says he can't miss his fourth-period art class." She sighed and shoved her hair back. "I usually refuse to let an eight-year-old run my life, but right now I'm cuttin' him some slack."

"Why do you think he insisted on being there when the police came?" Frank asked quietly.

"Thinks he's the man of the house now and didn't wanna miss a thing."

"It's probably more than that."

She paused. "I kin see it," she said, face solemn. "Last time the police came his daddy was taken away. Now the car is taken away and here come the police again. Maybe he was afraid that when he got home from school, I'd be gone too."

"Bingo."

"You're good," she said, with a sidelong glance. "As demented as I have been lately, that did not immediately occur to me. It helps to talk things out with another parent."

She appeared on the verge of tears, so he changed the subject. "Want to stop for breakfast?"

"If you don't mind, I think I would."

He pulled into a Denny's. Rory walked ahead of him to the booth. She moved with a lithe, careless grace that turned heads. When the waitress brought the menus, she removed the sunglasses she'd worn since they left the house and folded them on the table.

"I started wearing them 'cuz my eyes were always red and puffy," she explained.

"How are you doing now?"

"Much better," she assured him. "There were days when just getting up and putting on clothes was an effort. If it wasn't for Billy, I would not be making it."

"You had any help?"

"The transplant program has an aftercare coordinator. She sent me a bereavement packet. For his birthday she's gonna help us arrange another service, a celebration of Daniel's life." She brightened. "Maybe you can come."

He nodded. How could he not go? It would be a celebration of his own life as well.

"Billy and I are working on a patch for the donors' quilt. He's a pretty good artist for a third grader. He made that plaque over the doorbell."

She ordered a mushroom omelette and hot tea. "Want bacon or sausage with that?" the waitress asked.

"No, thank you. We should be kind to our animal friends,

not eat them." She spoke the words casually as though she repeated the line often. The middle-aged waitress lifted an eyebrow and poured Frank's coffee.

"I'm a vegetarian," she said, when the waitress left.

"I gathered that."

"Now, where were we? Oh yeah, gettin' help. I've been looking for a support group, gone to a couple meetings, in fact. But so far I'm finding that most widows' groups are for older women. Can't find one that relates to my specific situation. Maybe none exists. Young widow, small child, suicide, organ donor, financial confusion." She watched for a reaction. "You knew Daniel was ruled a suicide?"

He nodded. "What about relatives, friends?"

"My own mother, up in North Carolina, has never been an especially sympathetic woman. Said I could send Billy up there for a few weeks, but I didn't want to disrupt his routine any more than it has been. My best friend, Doreen, came down from Atlanta. Known her since kindergarten, we were in each other's weddings. First thing she said was, 'Rory, I know how expensive it was for Daniel to be in intensive care on those machines and all, but why didn't you come to us first, instead of just pullin' the plug?' "

He winced.

"Then there's psycho bitch, my mother-in-law. God bless her, she's here, lives in Kendall. Can't stop callin' to tell me what a happy boy she raised. 'What happened, Rory? What did you do to him? Why was my son so unhappy?' Shit, I thought her son was happy. I had no idea he wasn't, that's what makes it so hard. She's playin' grieving mother to the hilt now, but when he was still alive she sure tried her damn level best to spoil every holiday, every occasion, never missed a chance to make him miserable, always workin' herself up into some kind of soap-opera snit."

She leaned back as the waitress slid their steaming plates onto the table.

"This is my first step in the right direction," Rory said, lifting her orange juice glass. "Gettin' straightened out, if you're still up to it."

"Definitely." He dug into his eggs.

"I know I've got to snap out of it and get this show on the road for Billy, to get him over it. He's become so clingy. He's not really that way, least he never was." She chewed on a piece of whole wheat toast.

"Nobody gets over it when they lose a parent at that tender age."

She nodded, then swallowed. "You have no idea what it's like to lose someone so suddenly."

"Oh, yes I do." He fiddled with the spoon on his saucer, then raised his eyes to meet hers. "I most certainly do."

"What happened?"

"My father was murdered when I was a child."

He heard her shocked intake of breath. She set her fork down. "How old were you?"

"Ten, almost eleven, not much older than your son. Robbers killed him in his shop. My mother sent me to bring him home because he was late for supper. I found him."

"Lordy, did they solve it?" She leaned forward, an odd intensity in her eyes.

"Yeah, two punks. They went in there with a gun, to rob him. He knew them, had refused to buy stolen property from them in the past. So I'm sure they intended to kill him all along, though they denied that. They were only convicted of robbery and second-degree murder. They got life, but in those days all life meant was about seven years. They've been out for decades, if they're still alive."

"Did you go to the trial? Did you see them?" She had stopped eating and was totally focused.

"I saw them once. Dressed up for court, wearing suits and ties. Nice haircuts. Their families were there. Fancy lawyers. My mother took me on the first day. I had to testify about finding him. She cried all the way home on the bus. Out loud. Embarrassed the hell out of me. Everybody stared. We didn't go back for the rest of the trial, she was too drunk."

Rory closed her eyes and took a deep breath.

"We wouldn't have known the verdict except for a little paragraph in the newspaper. And the detective, he came by one day to tell us it was over, that they'd been sent upstate to Raiford Prison."

Frank hadn't discussed his father's murder for years. He wondered why he was talking about it now.

"At least you had resolution, some kinda justice," she said softly.

"Justice," he said. "A rare thing."

"I know." She cleared her throat. "I want to tell you something, Frank. Please don't call me crazy."

"I promise I won't."

Her voice dropped to a white-hot whisper. "I don't believe Daniel killed himself."

"What do you mean?" His gaze remained steady, but his heart thudded so loudly he wondered if she could hear it.

"He did not commit suicide. Daniel did not put that gun to his head. He was murdered. I'm sure of it."

The electricity he felt had to be generated by her intensity. "What makes you believe that?"

"Nobody will listen to me, but I swear, somebody else did it, somebody killed him."

The hair on his arms tingled and stood on end.

"He couldn't, wouldn't leave us that way. He had no reason. He loved life too much. Daniel always loved the good things, good food, good drink, good sex. That man would never put a gun to his head."

"Didn't he leave a note?"

She hesitated. "Yes. But it was on his computer screen. It was cryptic, apologetic, all it said was good-bye. Anybody could have typed it, or forced Daniel to type it."

"Who do you suspect?" He wondered if she heard the slight tremor in his voice. Was this why he was here?

"I don't know. That's just it. I thought perhaps someone he'd argued with at the restaurant. He was a tough boss. Or robbers, but I don't think anythin' is missin'."

"What did the police say?"

"They were useless," she said impatiently. "Didn't want to listen. They were nice at first, then they quit returnin' my calls."

His watch began to beep. "Do you have to call someone?" she asked.

"No, it's an alarm watch. Kathleen bought it, just the other day. Reminds me, as if I could forget, to take my medication." He asked the waitress for a glass of milk, spread out his array of pills, then swallowed them, as she watched.

"I'm no shrink," he said calmly, as they drove to the tow company's lot, "but I've heard that the families of suicides often refuse to believe it."

"It's called denial," she said flatly, "and it ain't a river. I know all about it. Survivors can't accept that they failed to see the signs, that they ignored the cry for help. Daniel had no family history of suicide, it does not run in his family. He was not mentally ill. He didn't talk about killing himself. He had no prior attempts."

"That you knew of."

"Don't you think I'd know?" Her voice rose, then fell. "I

guess that's unfair, because you didn't know us. You couldn't know his lust for life. His death was like a nightmare. I kept telling myself that when I woke up, I'd find it really didn't happen. It can't be, I kep' thinkin'. He was so young. Weren't we enough for him? I grasped at straws. Maybe he was sick and didn't tell us. But the medical examiner did an autopsy and said he found no sign of any illness. It seemed so unfair. He took all the answers with him. I didn't ignore his cry for help, I never even heard it. I was blamin' myself. If I hadn't gone out that day, if I'da come home sooner. I could have stopped him. But the more I thought about it, the more I realized, he didn't. He couldn't. He wouldn't. I knew that man, we were together for almost twelve years."

The towing company, west of the city, returned Rory's inventoried personal possessions in a cardboard box, but the man in charge wouldn't even let her see the car.

"Looks like I'm a pedestrian now," she said flatly.

"What about your husband's car?"

She sighed. "He had a Lexus. I couldn't bring myself to drive it. The damn car had his smell in it, the aftershave he always used. I couldn't even stand to see it, after he . . . was gone. I sold it. Daniel was in the restaurant business. The manager of the Miami Beach restaurant offered to take over the payments. Even now, I still expect it to pull into the driveway with Daniel behind the wheel."

"I'll call my lawyer this afternoon and see how we go about bailing out the station wagon."

She smiled. "Thanks. I'd like to have it back, but no sweat, if it's too much of a hassle, forget it. I can buy us a new one once I get the bank business straightened out, or the insurance check comes in. Should be any day now."

"No more excuses," he told her. "It's time for us to get back to your house and get to work."

She nodded. "Let's do it."

The day was bright and brilliant. Headed for Coconut Grove, he opened the sunroof and turned on the sound system. Her hair blew in the breeze, glowing red in the sun, and the music flowed around them. Daniel Alexander may not have been a certifiable mental case, he thought, but he had to be crazy to leave a woman like Rory.

He pulled right into the empty driveway. The cat didn't run this time. It purred around Rory's legs as she unlocked the front door. Inside, a trio of kittens performed rough-and-tumble aerobatics around the stairs, peering between the wooden balustrades, attacking each other with mock ferocity.

"Where's Daniel's study?"

"Upstairs."

He extended his arm. "Shall we?" She could lean on him, he would be the pillar of strength and see her through this, he thought.

She hesitated, halfway up the stairs. "The key! I forgot the key. Be right back." She turned and ran down, hair flying.

Briefcase in one hand, the other on the polished banister, he gazed up at the arched window at the top of the stairs, overwhelmed by a sudden sense of déjà vu. He had seen that glimpse of sky and treetops through that glass before. The memory was not pleasant.

She rejoined him moments later, breathless, with a single key dangling from a simple ring. "Didn't want Billy snooping around in there," she explained.

The carpeted hall beckoned to him as Rory prattled on, oblivious. "It was originally a guest room, but Daniel converted it to his home office."

He knew which door it would be before she stopped and handed him the key.

"Ready?" His stomach clenched into a knot.

She nodded and smiled. He inserted the key, the bolt snapped back and the door swung open. The blinds were closed, the drapes drawn. The smell of bleach hung on the air, masking another faint foul odor.

"The light switch is to your right," she said. Her voice echoed as though from the bottom of a well.

He hit the lights. He had intended to support Rory should she falter. Instead, details of the room flashed in relief before the light exposed them, the wall-to-wall carpeting, the massive file cabinet, the heavy desk with its bordered blotter. The effect was that of a baseball bat slammed into his midsection. An explosion echoed in his ears and his knees buckled. The drapes, the lamp, the molding at the top of the door, were all familiar parts of the recent dreams that had haunted him. For an instant he heard and saw chaos, but the image vanished before he could see it clearly, gone like a forgotten dream.

"Oh my God! Oh my God!" She was on her knees beside him. "I'll call the rescue squad!"

Slumped against the wall, he flailed out. "No! No!" His hand caught hers, his heart already beating wildly, a racehorse pounding down the stretch.

"Is it your heart?" She held his arm. "What is it? What's wrong? Do you need your medication?"

He shook his head, fighting to breathe, eyes wildly roving the room. "It's a flashback," he gasped.

"I didn't know you were in Vietnam."

The spinning slowed. "I wasn't."

CHAPTER
SIX

"**S**hall I call your wife?" Rory asked as she helped him into a sitting position.

"No, no." Frank got to his feet, embarrassed, leaning for a moment against the wall. "No reason to alarm her. I'm sorry. That room." He shuddered and shook his head. "I just felt queasy."

"It's the smell." She wiped his brow with a handkerchief. "I should have aired it out first. I'll open the windows and turn on the ceiling fan. We should do this another day."

"No, I'm fine." He had to know why this was happening to him, what had happened in this house, in that room.

Despite his resolve, his knees trembled when he stepped back into the room, his eyes drawn like magnets to the faint outline of stains, scrubbed but not entirely obliterated, on the ceiling and the wall behind Daniel Alexander's massive mahogany desk. The rug beneath the leather chair was discolored, bleached from efforts to clean it. The hair prickled on the back of his neck and he wanted to close his eyes to shut out the sight.

They decided to lug the boxes and the file folders downstairs to the dining room table.

Frank set up his notebook computer and took out his reading glasses. "Is there a copy here of your husband's will?"

He glanced up when she didn't answer. "Did Daniel have a will, or a living trust?"

"I'm not sure." She sat at the end of the table, her back rigid. "We talked about it once, right after Billy was born, about who was to raise him if somethin' happened to both of us. But I don't know. Daniel was goin' into the restaurant business at the time and I remember signin' lots of papers with him."

"Have you heard from his lawyer?"

She shook her head.

He sighed. "Well, let's see what we can find. How much life insurance did he have?"

"Quite a lot," she said with certainty. "One policy for fifty thousand dollars that he got when we were first married. Later he changed it to another one, for half a million dollars."

He frowned. "Actually, five hundred thousand is not a lot. Not with a wife, and a son to raise and educate. You've got a good ten, eleven years before he's ready for college, and with inflation . . ." He did some rapid calculations. "It's not a great deal. You'll have to invest wisely."

He looked up at her. "Is there a mortgage on this house?"

She nodded, toying with a paper flower that had fallen on the table when they set up the files. "We bought it nine years ago, when I was pregnant. Has a twenty-year mortgage."

"Good, so you've built up some equity. Mortgage insurance? The kind that pays off the principal if the primary breadwinner dies?"

"I think so," she said slowly. "He mentioned once that the house was free and clear if anythin' happened to him."

"Excellent." He began to sift through and enter into a computer file records that soon indicated that Rory was a wealthy woman, or would be someday. At the very least, she and Billy would be comfortable. Daniel's investments were, for the most part, growth-oriented and well chosen. In addition to a healthy stock portfolio stuffed with blue chips and thriving mutual funds, he had contributed the maximum, about thirty thousand dollars annually, to a deferred-compensation tax-exempt retirement pension each year for the past seven years. He'd bought a number of technological stocks, including Intel and Microsoft at precisely the right time, making a killing. Nice going, Daniel, he thought.

"I told you he was smart." Rory looked wistful when he commented on her husband's astute investments. She pulled her chair up closer and sat beside him, studying the computer screen as he listed the assets. She smelled like cookies and cream. What was that scent? he wondered. Vanilla, she smelled like vanilla.

There were bank statements for two jumbo certificates of deposit, a liquid asset account and three interest-bearing checking accounts. With all this, he wondered how did she ever manage to get herself into such a bind?

"Have you been receiving the monthly income from the restaurants?" She could have paid her bills with that, he thought, shuffling through a stack of rubber-banded receipts.

"No, that ended. Daniel sold his half of the business to

his partner, Ron Harrington, five or six months ago. He wanted to invest the money and move into somethin' else. He was tired of the restaurant business, too many hours, too many hassles," she said. "He was stayin' on temporarily, as executive manager on a weekly salary, until Ron found a replacement."

"How much did he get, and where did he put it?"

"I'm not sure. He didn't talk much about business at home."

Curiously, Frank found no recent bank statements; all were six months to a year old. "We need the current file with the latest statements," Frank said. "We must have overlooked it."

She shook her head. "I think we've got them all. I'll check upstairs, but those other boxes are all old tax records."

He frowned. "Then he must have kept another file at the office, or with your accountant."

She shrugged. "I think Ron sent me all of Daniel's things after the funeral . . ."

"Do you remember any statements coming in the mail?"

She looked guilty. "Maybe." She went to a hall closet and dug out two shopping bags stuffed with unopened mail. "There's a few more bags in there," she confessed. "It's all addressed to him. I just couldn't deal with it. I never opened his mail. I . . ." She shrugged again. "The more it piled up, the less able I felt to deal with it."

"Okay," he instructed. "Find a letter opener. You start opening, I'll sort."

She began stacking the opened envelopes next to him, assembly-line fashion. Most were bills, late notices; some, with more recent postmarks, were plastered with red stickers demanding "Remit Now" or "Third Notice."

"Good God, Rory." He glanced apprehensively at the light

fixture above them. "Florida Power and Light is about to cut off your service. The phone company, too. How could you let this happen?"

"Well . . ." She ran her fingers through an unruly mound of red hair. "What checks I did write were returned. I sure didn't want to write any more bad ones. When I tried to use my ATM card, the machine ate it."

"What have you been living on?"

"Been chargin' food and gas on my Visa card. I know, I know." She held up a hand in her defense. "I was plannin' to get squared away soon and straighten all this out." She looked at him plaintively. "But I was feeling lower than a snake's belly and it just got worse and worse, 'til I didn't know where to start."

He nodded, fingering three overdue notices from Visa. He had arrived just in the nick of time.

"Some damn bank officer should have stepped in to assist you. Even with the accounts in your husband's name, you appear on them as beneficiary. All you need to switch them to your name is a copy of his death certificate. Sam Townsend, chairman of Southern Savings, is a friend of mine," Frank said hotly. "He needs to know how callous and insensitive his people are. Next time make sure your name is on everything."

The long eyelashes dipped. "I don't think I'll be gettin' married again. Daniel was one of a kind. I thought he walked on water."

He wondered if Kathleen would say something as touching about him.

"Who is your broker?"

She wasn't sure.

"No matter, I'll find it in here somewhere. I'll call and ask that you be sent copies of your most recent statements so we can establish the current value of your portfolio. That'll give us a better idea of your net worth. We have to start putting things together for tax purposes."

Even while focused on the task before him, his eyes betrayed him, straying to the stairs and the second-floor hallway to the room beyond.

Two blasts from a car horn startled them both. Rory flew out of her chair.

"My gosh, it's that time already, Billy's home!"

She opened the door and hugged the boy, who darted inside wearing a book-stuffed backpack. A woman followed, riding the crest of children's shouts behind her. Her blonde ponytail bounced, head swiveled, eyes darting. She wore leggings and an oversized T-shirt.

"Just wanted to make sure you were all right, Rory." She peered inquisitively into the dining room. "Saw the strange car in the drive. Did they find yours?"

"Oh, Jill, this is Frank Douglas, he's . . ." Rory seemed at a sudden loss for words.

"The police are still looking for the car," he lied, pushing his chair back and getting to his feet. "I'm Mrs. Alexander's accountant."

"Oh," the woman said archly. "Billy told us it was repossessed."

"Kids." Frank shook his head, smiling fondly at Billy, who clung to his mother and stared back. "They say the darndest things."

"An accountant?" The woman inspected the living room with the thorough eye of a vice squad detective seeking signs of an orgy. "I didn't know they made house calls." She flashed a shiny white-toothed smile. "How nice. We have to go to our accountant's office. Do you have a business card?"

He patted himself down in a halfhearted motion. "No, I don't seem to have one—"

"Jill," Rory interrupted, "it looks like my car won't be back by morning. Could you . . . ?"

The woman sighed loudly, rolled her eyes and slung a hip to one side. "This is screwing up my whole schedule," she complained petulantly. "You know we agreed—"

"As soon as I have wheels, I'll drive for two of your weeks, I promise."

Cries of "Mommy, Mommy, Mommy" chorused from the driveway.

"Okay," Jill said reluctantly, "but in the future we've got to stick to the schedule. It's not fair to everybody if we don't." She cast a last curious glance over her shoulder as she left. "Good luck with the car."

"She's got a big mouth," Rory whispered, as Billy scampered into the kitchen. "A *biggg* mouth." She glanced after her son. "And, of course, so does he."

"All right." Frank folded his reading glasses and stacked the files. "Too late to tackle the banks today. I'll call Sam Townsend at home tonight and rattle his cage so he can pursue it full throttle in the morning. We can straighten them out in the A.M. When we do"—he thumped a stack of papers clipped to attached envelopes—"these are the bills that must be paid immediately, first thing tomorrow. I'll have my lawyer make some calls about the car."

"Do I try to bail it out, or buy a new one?"

"It's healthier for your credit to make things right with the lender. Then you can decide whether to keep it." He snapped shut the notebook computer.

"Now, while Billy works on his homework, you need to tackle yours. This is your assignment. Call the utility companies, now, before five, explain the circumstances, promise full payment and tell them the checks are going out tomorrow. We want to forestall any inconvenience and additional charges for restoring service. With your prior good record you may be able to talk them out of some or all of the late charges. After five o'clock you start calling the credit card companies."

"Gotcha." She gave a little salute. "How can I ever thank you?"

"You already did. Besides, there's nothing to thank me for yet. We still have a lot of work to do, but we're off to a good start. I'll call you in the morning." He leaned into the kitchen. "See ya, Billy. Take care of things around here."

" 'Bye." The boy scarcely looked up from his workbook at the table.

Frank drove home in the state of euphoria reserved for good Samaritans on a roll. He tuned in to the evening stock market report on the radio, mulling over the investments he would suggest once the Alexander finances were in order. Suddenly he slapped the steering wheel, struck by a thought. They hadn't booted up Alexander's computer! Perhaps the man had begun entering his statements into a computer file. But he would still keep hard copies, wouldn't he? They had to be there somewhere.

He found Kathleen at a Chippendale table in the front hall, arranging fresh-cut flowers in a crystal vase. She glanced up coolly as he came in and kissed her cheek. "Have a good day?"

"Got a lot done," he said enthusiastically, and headed for his study.

"Glad to hear it. My day certainly could have gone better."

He paused, suddenly wary. "What happened?"

"I was concerned. We all were. Sue Ann said you never arrived at the office. She had no clue where to reach you." She used a small tool to snip the stem end of a Chinese peony. The severed clipping flew into the air and bounced on the marble floor. She ignored it and slid the sheath into the half-filled vase.

"Who says I have to punch a time clock with her?" He spoke with the righteous indignation of an innocent man. He stooped to pluck the green snippet off the floor. It was wet and slick, as hard as bone and smelled like a dark woods. "I told you I planned to work on something today. Since when do you check up on me?"

"Since you spent months in the hospital, underwent major surgery and nearly died." The curved jaws of the sharp little tool in her hand gaped open as she turned toward him.

Perhaps, he thought, she will snip out my new heart right here. He envisioned it flying through the air and bouncing messily onto the marble floor.

"Your detective Lucca was here," she said, blue eyes frosty. "So were the alarm people, ready and able to carry out your instructions—but you weren't here to give them."

"Oh, for Pete's sake. I forgot all about it." He put down his briefcase and nuzzled her neck. "Sorry. It's just security cameras. I didn't ask them to coordinate the Manhattan project."

"But they kept asking questions." She placed the tool on the polished tabletop with a click and faced him. "Do you want split-screen monitoring? Should the cameras be fixed or scanning? Should they use one of the empty cable channels on our television sets? Should all the sets be used to monitor, or only those with the picture in a picture?"

"I'll call them in the morning."

"No need," she said lightly. "I handled it, made all the decisions myself."

"So okay, what's the uproar about?"

"You." She crossed her arms, her expression wounded. "It was as though you had vanished between here and the office. I didn't know whether you were okay or I should report you missing."

He gently pushed back her wispy bangs. "Missing? You know I'm okay."

"With everything that's been happening to you"—she gave him a meaningful look—"I wasn't sure. You've always stayed in touch with me and Sue Ann before. Disappearing is so out of character for you, Frank. I even called the hospital to see if the team had heard anything."

"You shouldn't have done that." He felt embarrassed that she'd called the transplant unit looking for him. What would they think? "You know that if anything happened to me, you'd be the first to know."

She shrugged. "I wanted to call the police," she said matter-of-factly, "if it hadn't been for that detective, Lucca. He insisted that I wait until dark. Said I should call him first if you weren't back."

Thank God for Lucca, he thought. "Look, sweetheart," he said patiently. "You will not believe the day I just had." He checked his watch. "Let me make a couple of quick calls, then I'll tell you and the girls all about it. I'll be right back."

Frank burst into his study, called his lawyer first, then reached Sam Townsend, a man in a hurry, about to leave for a fund-raising cocktail party. "I'll see you there," he said.

"Maybe not." Frank frowned. "Kathleen didn't mention it. She's the one who keeps track of our social calendar. But, Sam, you've got to listen to this." He quickly filled him in on the financial trials and tribulations of the widow Alexander. "Lousy PR for your institution," he said in conclusion.

"Jesus Christ!" Townsend replied. "Give me the customer's name again. I'll track it in the morning and find out who the hell is responsible. Just like you, you son of a bitch, to drop this on me when I'm on the way out for the evening. But thanks, we'll roll out the red carpet, make it up to her."

Frank smiled and hung up. He dialed Lucca's office expecting his machine, but the man himself answered.

"You safe and sound?" Lucca asked.

"Yeah, sorry I missed our meeting this afternoon."

"Your bride was ready to send out the bloodhounds. She wanted your picture on milk cartons. Classy woman, by the way."

"Thanks. I'm glad you kept her from calling the cops."

"Try to stay in touch, boss. People worry."

"Listen, I talked to the widow in that other thing."

"And?"

"I need you to check something out." He lowered his voice even though he was alone. "I know it's highly unlikely, but she's convinced"—he rubbed the back of his neck, pacing up and down in front of his desk—"that her husband was murdered, that he was no suicide."

"Not unusual. That's common with suicides."

"The thing is, there doesn't seem to be any reason for taking his own life. She's a gorgeous woman, with a beautiful kid. They had a nice home, no apparent money problems."

"Gorgeous, huh? The plot thickens."

"You know me better, Lucca. I just thought that for her peace of mind, we should look into it. She's sure—"

"Just like your old lady was sure you were upside down in a ditch somewhere this afternoon. She know you were meeting with gorgeous?"

"I'm gonna tell her all about it at dinner. Look, I owe the woman a favor and thought you could look into it."

The detective sighed. "It's your money, boss. How far you want me to go?"

"Check out the police investigation, determine if it was thorough. Let me know if you agree with their conclusions. Nobody else has a better instinct for these things."

"What about her? If I remember correctly, the news story said she found him. If I was to do a full-blown investigation, I'd start with her."

"She's still too fragile. Lucca, you should see her."

"I'd like to. Gorgeous, huh?"

"Yeah, in a slim, tall, graceful sort of way."

"Big girl, huh? Blonde?"

"No, red hair, long, sort of auburn."

"Oh ho, a redhead!"

"I don't believe this conversation. At the very least I owe her . . ."

"Sure, sure, sure. I'll see what I can find out without spooking Big Red."

Frank went downstairs. Casey was munching potato chips in front of a blaring TV and he quickly realized that what she was engrossed in was no action movie, but live news breaking, aerial views of the hot pursuit of a trio of bank robbers by Miami cops. The chase ended before their eyes in a hair-raising crash. There were police cars, innocent victims and the suspects, fleeing on foot, scrambling up an expressway embankment. A running robber let go his bag of loot. Green-backs fluttered in the air as people scrambled, some on hands and knees, for the cash. A chaotic traffic jam, commuters, cops and ambulances on the ground, news choppers pounding the air and crowding the sky overhead.

"What a mess," Frank said.

"Cool," Casey commented, crunching a mouthful of chips. He noticed that her lips and fingers were greasy, crumbs littered the front of her T-shirt.

"Haven't you had enough of those?"

"Nope." Her eyes never left the television screen.

"You don't want your face to break out."

"What do you know?" she said grumpily.

"Casey, that's no way to talk to me."

She glanced up, mouth full. "You're not my boss."

"Wrong." He would have switched off the set, except that testosterone-fueled cops were now grappling with commuters who had been snatching up the cash. Another camera broadcast a live shot as one of the robbers plunged into a canal. News choppers hovered, churning up waves that battered and swamped him. Lunging police dogs and shouting cops with shotguns lined the banks.

No place to run. Frank swallowed and stared, his body tensed. He shared the man's panic. No way out.

Casey, banished to her room, was permitted to rejoin them for dinner. The sea bass was light and succulent in an orange chervil sauce, and Frank asked Lourdes to open a bottle of white burgundy. His celebratory mood was only slightly dampened by Casey's truculence, Shandi's sullen attitude and Kathleen's slight pout.

"Casey, could you please ask Dad to pass the asparagus?" Shandi asked.

"You can ask me directly," he said pleasantly, and passed the serving dish. Then he cleared his throat. "As you know," he said, "we're all together at our table tonight because of the generosity of another family who will never be together again. Life can't be taken for granted. And you know that I wanted to thank the family responsible for the gift that will, hopefully, allow me to see you both grow up, to dance at your weddings and enjoy many more years with the woman I married.''

Kathleen smiled and put down her fork, listening intently.

"Well . . ." He paused for effect. "I have done exactly that.''

"Could somebody please pass the rolls?'' Casey said, ignoring the moment.

"Shhh, don't interrupt your father," Kathleen said. Neither girl stopped eating.

"My experience proves again," Frank went on, "that we have to trust our own instincts. Mine were right and I spent today engaged in a little payback.''

Kathleen's lips parted, eyes widening. "You located the donor's family?''

"His widow and son. I spent some time with them today.''

"You actually met them?''

"That's right.''

"How old is the son?'' Casey showed interest for the first time.

"The boy is eight years old, his name is William, better known as Billy.''

"Who . . . ? How did you arrange it?'' Kathleen appeared incredulous.

"Where do they live?'' Shandi interrupted.

"In Coconut Grove." Turning to Kathleen, he said, "I arranged it myself. I am not without resources. And I was right, they did need my help.''

"How on earth did you approach them? Did you just call and say I'm the man—''

"No, I rang their doorbell.''

"Totally unannounced?'' Kathleen was astonished.

"Exactly."

She laughed disapprovingly. "That's so unlike you, Frank, so spontaneous. And the woman invited you in?"

"Yes. Well, at first she mistook me for someone else, but when I told her who I was, my welcome could not have been warmer, or more touching."

"Why did you choose to do this alone?" Kathleen seemed annoyed and mystified. "I would have liked to have been there with you."

Her reaction surprised him. "Well, it didn't occur to me. You were so against it."

"I still think it's a bad idea. Remember what Doctor O'Hara said? I still think it unwise, and out of character, but if it did work out . . ."

"So whose heart did you get, Dad?" Shandi asked.

"The donor's name was Daniel Alexander."

"What did he die of?" Casey said.

He hesitated. "A gunshot wound, evidently suicide."

"Gross," Casey said.

Kathleen studied him reproachfully. "Perhaps we shouldn't discuss it at dinner."

"Well, I would like to propose a toast," he said, still perplexed by Kathleen's negative reaction. "To Rory and Daniel Alexander."

"To life," Kathleen murmured, as they touched glasses.

"That reminds me, I talked to Sam Townsend earlier, from Southern Savings. He assumed he'd see us at a benefit for the Youth Museum tonight. What happened? Are we out of the loop?"

Kathleen looked up from her lime sherbet and patted her lips with her napkin. "I declined for us."

"Why? I would have liked it. I haven't seen some of those people for a while."

"I didn't think you were really ready to go out and mingle yet."

"What do you mean? You should have run it by me. I need to get back into the mainstream."

"Not just yet," she murmured.

Something about her patronizing tone irritated him. He could not dispel the image of the fleeing bank robber, the chopper-driven waves breaking over his head, shotguns and dogs waiting.

"Shall we discuss it later?" She shifted uncomfortably before his stare. "It's just that . . . we want to keep you all to ourselves for a while longer, don't we, girls?"

He and Kathleen took their coffee out on the pool patio. A high-flying full moon lit up the night and the rippling surface of the bay.

"So what's she like?" asked Kathleen, reclining in a lounge chair.

"The widow? Young, bereaved, incredibly naive about money."

"Is she attractive?"

"Some might say so," he said warily.

"An attractive woman, her age, I'm sure she'll remarry once she recovers from the trauma."

"It's hard to say. Apparently they were quite devoted."

"I'm really sorry I haven't met her, too."

"Oh, you will."

"When?" She raised her head and looked puzzled.

"I thought we could all go out to dinner once I'm finished."

"Finished with what?"

"Kath, when I arrived there this morning, the woman's car had just been repossessed."

"And so it's up to you to handle it?" she said, clearly exasperated by this new revelation. "Did her husband leave her flat broke?"

"No," he said defensively, "quite the contrary. She's just been too shocked and numb to cope. Evidently he handled all their finances and after his death she couldn't even bring herself to look at an envelope with his name on it. She was hoarding sacks of unopened mail and bills dating back to the day it happened."

"I'm sure the poor thing was traumatized, but you don't have to inherit the problems her husband left. Dayton can handle it. Why don't you put it all in his hands?"

"No, it's something I want to do myself."

"Why?" She sat up straight and faced him. "He's a superb accountant. You've said so yourself, many times. You can pay his bill and your good deed is done." She waited for his answer.

"Because this is something I feel strongly about. I need to do it for myself as much as for them."

"Why?"

Frank had grown weary of explanations. "Look, Kath, it's the difference between making an impersonal donation and getting involved. The difference between writing a check and working on Thanksgiving Day at the soup kitchen for the homeless. Remember the year we all did that? True thanks as opposed to lip service?"

She was silent. He couldn't see her expression in the dim light.

"You could just write out a check to the museum, which you do," he pointed out, "but no, you also choose to serve on the board, attend meetings, help make the day-to-day de-cisions, pitch in and do the actual labor because it's important to you. Helping Daniel Alexander's widow and their son is as important to me."

"At this particular point in time," she said, her voice distant, "don't you think it far more important to spend time with your family?"

CHAPTER
SEVEN

Kathleen arose when he did, at dawn. Uncomplaining, she brewed coffee while he scanned the newspaper.

The robber he had seen on TV was dead. Drowned. No one tried to rescue him after he had slipped beneath the surface of that murky canal. Not until police divers in wet suits arrived twenty-five minutes later. When did the world change? Frank wondered. Where had the heroes gone? He remembered them, cops who unhesitatingly kicked off shoes, stripped off gun belts and plunged into deep water, even a cloudy canal, to save a life, even that of a fleeing felon. Heroics were in nobody's job description now.

We are alone in this world, he thought. All alone.

"You know," Kathleen chirped, "your idea about a few days up in Disney World, in Orlando, was excellent." She poured coffee and sat opposite him in the breakfast nook. "Let's all go this week. It'll be fun! I'll just throw a few things in a suitcase."

Her enthusiasm struck a false note. She was never so bright and chatty at this time of day. She usually wasn't even awake. Frowning, he folded the newspaper and reached for his coffee mug. "I thought nobody liked the idea. But swell, if you can convince the girls. Just put it off a week or so, until I finish this job."

She sighed and did not bring it up again.

Frank took Rory to reclaim her car.

She wore lustrous lipstick, and smelled again like vanilla, but there were bluish shadows beneath her eyes. "How are you today?" he asked.

"Oh, I'll be perky as a puppy once I git my wheels back." She settled into the car beside him. The utility and credit card companies had responded positively to her calls, she reported.

"Lookit that skyline," she said, as they swung up onto the expressway. The city's hard edges, metal, stone and glass, glittered in the sun, crisp and clear-cut against the vast morning sky.

"Always blows me away," she murmured.

He asked where she hailed from, though he knew the answer from Lucca's report.

"Small town. China Grove, less than eight thousand population. Smack-dab in the middle a North Carolina, four hours from the Blue Ridge Mountains and five hours from the ocean. Stores down one side of the Main Street, railroad tracks down the other. The big boss in town is the cotton mill, they make sheets and towels. Charlotte is the closest big city. That's where I went to college, at the University of North Carolina."

"Do you miss it?"

"Miss the seasons some." She casually crossed her legs, exposing the graceful curve of her ankle. "The trees, the frost on the leaves. Four absolutely, positively distinct seasons changin' right on cue." She stretched and leaned back, red hair spilling across the leather headrest. "You know it's spring because the dogwood, the azaleas and the crocus tell you so. I *don't* miss chiselin' ice off my windshield. Or tree limbs fallin' and power lines snappin' because of the ice. Don't miss chains and snow tires."

"So you got married and came to Miami?"

"I came to Miami first." She leaned forward, more animated, her words picking up speed. "After I graduated from college, with a bachelor of fine arts degree, I'm thinkin' it's time to git a car, an apartment, some money. How do I find a job? My two roommates said, 'Let's go to Miami and become flight attendants.' I was like, 'Yuck. Waitresses in the sky?' But I came along for the ride, to see Miami—and guess who was the only one to land the job? I couldn't believe it. Airlines want you there on time. I go out sightseein', get lost in Little Havana. Can't find a soul who speaks English. Outa seventy applicants I'm the only one who sneaks in late, stood out like a hooker in church. They ask me, 'Are you honest?' and I give 'em an honest answer: 'Sometimes.' And they say, 'Your physical is tomorrow.' 'Oh, whoa,' I tell 'em. 'Wait a minute.' And they say, 'But we have to send you to Honolulu right away for three weeks of trainin'.'

"All right, I think, neat. Cool. It was like a whirlwind. I thought I was a jet-setter. It was waitress-in-the-sky time."

"So how did you meet Daniel?"

"On the job." The dimples flashed. "I was workin' in first class, kind of eyin' this handsome guy, and I guess he noticed me too. During a layover in New Orleans, they put on these extra-special fancy French pastries including four fat little chocolate éclairs on ruffled trays. I was starved, so I closed the curtain to try one when I was alone in the galley. It was so good that I ate another one, then couldn't stop until I finished 'em all!

"The curtain musta been cracked open. Cuz when I went out, all polite and proper, to serve what was left to the passengers, Daniel smiles up to me and says, 'I'd like a chocolate éclair.' I opened my mouth to tell him we didn't have any, and he says, 'Wait, before you say anythin', check out a mirror.' " She paused. "I had a chocolate smear from my upper lip to my nostrils." She tossed her head back and laughed, the sound drawing him in until they were laughing together.

"I could not look him in the eye. But he refused to git off that plane without a chocolate éclair or my phone number—and there were no chocolate éclairs. That was Daniel."

The repo man had stashed her station wagon amongst sad rows of repossessed cars hobbled by locking devices on their front wheels.

"There it is! There it is!" she said, excitedly pointing out the Sable to the guarded caretaker. "My poor little car. Mommy's come to git you and take you home."

The confirmation and paperwork took half an hour. "Don't I need to write a check or somethin'?" She opened her cloth purse.

"Not yet." Frank's restraining hand closed over hers and he shook his head. "No checks until we get a green light from the bank later today. My lawyer handled this."

"So do I owe him or you?"

"Let's not worry about it now. Let's just get it out of here before they change their minds."

"I will pay you back."

He nodded, then followed her back to Twin Palms where she parked in her driveway and patted the hood.

"The car-pool mommies will be so happy that this baby's home," she crooned.

"Tell them the police recovered it," he said, as she unlocked the front door.

She laughed conspiratorially. "If I kin just keep Billy's mouth shut."

Frank braced himself before stepping back into Daniel Alexander's study, but still felt chilled and claustrophobic, as though some malevolent presence were sucking the air from his lungs. Forcing himself to focus, he hastily booted up Alexander's IBM PC, and copied the contents of the hard drive onto a backup tape. Downstairs he used the tape to reenter the contents into his laptop.

The most recent file was the suicide note left on the screen the day Daniel died.

"Do you mind?" he asked Rory.

"No," she whispered. "I want you to see it. Then you tell me if it makes any sense."

Farewell, Rory. We had good times. This is the road I must travel now. Remember, I love you and Billy. This is not your fault. It's nobody's fault but mine. Don't make any fuss. I want to be cremated, to blaze as bright and as brilliant as the sun for one final moment. That's how I want you to remember me. Do as I ask, please. Then carry on. Raise Billy to be as good and as strong a human being as you are. Don't hate me. I love you, sunshine. Daniel.

A computerized suicide note definitely lacked the personal touch, Frank thought, gazing at the screen.

"What is that?" Rory demanded, leaning over his shoulder. "Can you tell me?" She turned away and paced the dining room. "It explains nothing. He couldn't have done it."

"Had he received any threats?"

"No, not that I know of," she conceded, slumping into a seat at the table.

"Enemies?"

She shook her head.

Few murder victims, he had once read, die at the hands of strangers. "What about criminal connections? Did he know any dangerous characters?"

"You meet a lot of people in the restaurant business . . ." She shook her head again. "But none that I ever knew of."

This is Miami, he thought, where anything is possible. Police can and do make mistakes. What if she was right? Did he feel a rush of excitement because he believed her, or was it merely the thrill of playing amateur detective with a beautiful woman?

"Were either of you ever the victim of a crime before?"

She chewed her lower lip, then nodded. "The house was burglarized about eighteen months before Daniel died. We were on vacation, skiin' in Aspen, just the two of us. Billy stayed with Daniel's mom. When we got home, we found the house had been broken into. Sounds small time, but God, it was awful. The TVs were gone, the VCR, Daniel's computer, all the small appliances. The silverware, what jewelry I had, even Billy's bicycle and some of our clothes. God, what a feeling. Months later, we'd look for something and realize, 'Oh God, they got that too.' That was our big brush with crime.

"The police were nice and all, even dusted for prints, but they never caught the burglars or recovered a thing. Said there'd been a rash of cases in the neighborhood. We had insurance. But the worst part was that feelin' of violation, the idea of strangers in our house, rummagin' around through our stuff, pawin' through our things.

"After it happened, a course, when we had nothin' left to steal, Daniel took the advice of the police and we burglar-proofed the entire house. That's when he bought the gun," she said bleakly, and paused. "We trimmed the hedges way back, too, installed new locks and had the security system put in."

"I've noticed how you use it," he said reprovingly.

"I guess I should," she said softly. "He wanted to protect us."

"Did the burglars steal anything out of the ordinary? Like your husband's business records . . ."

"Not that I recall."

"Who profits from his death?"

"That'ud be me. Me and Billy, I guess. There was an itty bitty little old life insurance policy that his mother had on him. Then there's the business, the restaurants. He and Ron, his partner, had . . . What do you call 'em? You know, those life insurance policies that pay off to keep the business goin' if anythin' happened to either one of them."

"Key-man policies?"

"Right. That's it. They were with the same company as our life policy. They had 'em from the start, from when they opened the first location. Ron didn't get his insurance check yet either. I spoke to him last week."

"How much were they for?"

"A million dollars."

Now, there's a motive for murder, he thought. "Any trouble between the two of them? Hard feelings about Daniel leaving the business?"

"Not that I knew about," she said, with a dismissive gesture. "Those two knew each other forever, they had their moments, but never anythin' serious. They fought like brothers."

"Well," Frank said briskly. "I'll run through these computer files looking for your bank statements. Think you could rustle up some coffee?"

While she was in the kitchen, he made hasty notes of their conversation to fax to Lucca when he got back to the office, along with a copy of the suicide note.

Daniel Alexander's computer files yielded little. Frank spent several hours scrolling through routine correspondence. Nothing relevant in his E-mail. The man had been an inveterate letter writer. There were complaints to food distributors about late deliveries, to the Miami city manager about the homeless people who panhandled and intimidated diners outside the Coral Gables restaurant and a strongly worded objection to a city of Miami Beach proposal to double the outdoor table tax paid by restaurants.

Frank started a tax file, failed again to reach Townsend, who had been unreachable, in meetings all day, and left, promising to call Rory after speaking to the banker.

On his way back to the office, he stopped to pick up the gun. His background had apparently passed muster. The gun shop operated a pistol range in an adjacent building as cold as a refrigerator. The number of Miamians blasting away at paper targets surprised him. Suburban couples, middle-aged businessmen, even little old ladies brandishing firearms. He enlisted the help of an instructor, donned safety glasses and ear protectors and took the only free cubicle. The next slot was occupied by a young Latino with a huge handgun, a .44-caliber Magnum. Each time he fired it, Frank feared the concussion would make his nose bleed.

He thought of his father, hands shaking as the paunchy

instructor with small, pale blue eyes coached him. "Don't jerk the trigger, squeeze it gently like it was a woman."

The sound startled him as the gun recoiled in his hand like something alive. The paper target, the dark outline of a man, jumped. His bullet had punched a hole in the lower left-hand corner. The instructor said Frank had a good eye. He began to feel more comfortable with the weapon, more confident. After thirty minutes, the target was riddled and torn. Surprisingly, he liked seeing it buck when his bullets slammed through it. Then the range master announced, "Lights out," and the room went dark.

"To simulate combat conditions," his instructor explained. Frank wondered why Miamians felt the need to be combat-ready, but enjoyed seeing flames spit from the muzzle, the smell of the gunsmoke, the power and heat from the metal. Someday, when he had more time, he thought, he would practice regularly, become proficient, maybe even join a target-shooting club and compete. He learned how to clean the weapon and departed after a few final words of advice.

"Never aim your weapon at another person unless you're prepared to shoot 'im," his instructor warned. "And if you ever have to shoot somebody, make sure you kill 'im. You wind up with fewer problems that way."

Frank stepped back out into the afternoon sun, the added weight of the weapon in his briefcase, and thought of Daniel Alexander. He, too, had bought a gun for protection.

Sue Ann was cheerful, despite her sneezes and the handkerchief held over her nose. Workmen were drilling, installing the security cameras, and she was allergic to dust. Townsend had called twice, she reported. She tried him, but the banker was again unavailable. Frank printed out his notes, along with Daniel Alexander's suicide letter, then faxed them to Lucca himself, declining Sue Ann's offers of help. She was bubbling over the upcoming visit of her Marine son and his family. Her grandbabies' arrival was enough to make his secretary giddy. Frank arranged tickets to the current production at the Coconut Grove Playhouse for the adults, insisting that he and Kathleen would take the youngsters for the night.

"It'll be great to have some little ones in the house again," he said, and gave Sue Ann the rest of the afternoon off. The workmen finished, demonstrated the system and also departed. Unobtrusive cameras now focused on both offices, monitored by twin TV screens mounted high on his office wall. Intercoms with small-screen monitors on each desk enabled him and his secretary to see and speak to anyone outside. Push a button and the visitor would be taped. The last to leave at night would set the system on slow-speed, to record any intruder.

He was about to leave when Townsend called, bombastic as usual.

"Just like you, you SOB, to agitate me, and give me indigestion, just as I'm headed out for the evening. How well do you know this woman?" he demanded. "This widow?"

"What do you mean?" Frank asked irritably. He had expected a more conciliatory attitude.

"She's got no goddamn blessed accounts here. The CDs, the liquid assets, all cleaned out, closed six, seven months ago. The checking accounts have been closed since the end of June. She's complaining we don't honor her checks? Woman doesn't have a dime in this institution. She was writing bad checks on closed accounts. That's a criminal offense."

"Who closed them?"

"Daniel P. Alexander. Signatures match his card."

"Where did the money go?" He rubbed his forehead.

"Don't ask me. Took it in cash. No honest man in his

right mind walks around with that much cash. Tellers say he insisted. Put it in a briefcase and off he went."

Frank sat at his desk after Townsend rang off, a hollow ache of suspicion invading the pit of his stomach. He took out his list, the names and numbers of the broker, the banker, the retirement account custodian and the savings and loan officer, the gatekeepers to Rory and little Billy Alexander's financial future.

"Sure," the stockbroker said, "I can send Mrs. Alexander a statement if she wants one. But I can tell you now, the balance is zero, zero, zero."

Half a dozen phone calls confirmed that Alexander had liquidated all his assets in the months prior to his death. He had emptied all his mutual funds, Vanguard, Windsor, American and Washington.

He had paid the early-withdrawal penalties and cashed in his retirement fund. Two remaining savings and loan accounts were also closed.

Frank felt sick. Rory was broke. Worst of all, her husband's liquidation of equity meant major tax consequences. She would owe a fortune in capital gains, and prohibitively high taxes on the money prematurely stripped from the retirement accounts. Her only hope was that Alexander had reinvested or stashed the money away. But where?

Rory and Billy had nothing left but the house and the life insurance policy. A terrible thought struck him. Perhaps the life insurance company hadn't paid off yet because Alexander had cashed it in, along with everything else.

Was the man a gambler? Hooked on drugs? Did he lose his shirt in some shady deal? There had been nothing in his files that gave a clue as to where the money had gone, or why.

He called Rory, who sounded cheerful. He heard Billy playing in the background.

"Hey!"

"Don't write any checks yet, Rory."

"But I told 'em all I'd mail—"

"I'll see you first thing in the morning. There's a snag." Why ruin her evening? he thought. Nothing either of them could do overnight, anyway. "Don't worry," he said, "we simply have to go in tomorrow to open a new account."

"But I promised Florida Power and Light the check would be—"

"Twenty-four hours is no big deal. But whatever you do, Rory, don't write any checks. In fact, just destroy those checkbooks."

"All right," she said uncertainly, "if you say so."

The other line rang; he said good-bye and picked it up.

"Hey, boss."

"Lucca. You got my fax?"

"Wasn't in my office when it came in, but got a new toy that just transmitted it to my car. I checked out that matter you were interested in. Okay for me to swing by?"

While he waited for the detective, Frank called a Coconut Grove savings and loan, spoke to the manager and arranged a twenty-five-thousand-dollar transfer from his business account into a checking account in Rory's name. They would go to the office in the morning so he could sign the authorization. All she had to do was fill out a signature card and pick up a book of temporary checks.

The security cameras worked. He watched the tall, long-legged detective step into Sue Ann's office. He wore a dark suit; his bristly mustache looked thicker and more ferocious than ever. Lucca paused, pivoted, scrutinized the nearly invisible cameras with an appraising eye, then saluted the lens with a wicked grin.

"Nice work," he said, opening the door to Frank's office. "If I do say so myself." He studied the monitors, nodded sagely and took a chair in front of the desk. "Now all you have to do is learn to lock those doors and we'll keep you from joining the crime statistics."

"You saw the suicide note?"

He nodded, looking smug. "Before you sent it." He leaned back in his chair. "Farewell, Rory. Good-bye sunshine. Boom!"

"What do you think?"

"Suicide," he said, with finality. "No conspiracy, no bushy-hair intruder, no question. The detectives who handled the case are no Einsteins, but they did a thorough job on this one."

"You're sure?"

"You tell me. A gunshot-residue test confirmed that the man fired a weapon. The gun was his. The weapon was found near his right hand. He's right-handed. No sign of an intruder, nothing missing, no strangers seen. The suicide note is just the icing on the cake. They don't come much neater. I know you felt he had no motive. But nobody knows what's going on in another man's head, his frustration quotient, his level of despair. He could have been an undiagnosed manic-depressive, he mighta had a bad childhood, maybe he couldn't stand his wife's perfume. Could be she belittled him in bed. Nobody has a clue, except maybe her. But she won't tell because she feels guilty. Happens all the time."

"I doubt it was anything like that." Something was wrong here, Frank knew it instinctively.

Lucca shrugged and rolled his eyes cynically. "She ain't telling you everything. Women never do."

"There may be a motive," Frank said reluctantly. "I'm

helping to straighten out his estate. There should be considerable assets, instead it looks like she's broke."

"Wad I tell ya?" The detective opened his arms in a cynical gesture. "He blows the bucks. He's scared to tell her. Farewell, Rory. Ba-boom!"

"Maybe you're right," Frank said.

"You pick up your peashooter yet? The gun?"

"This afternoon, why?"

Lucca shrugged. "I am sure you are aware, your old lady ain't crazy about the idea."

"Kathleen?"

"Ain't she the only old lady you got?" He raised an eyebrow.

"When did she talk to you about it?"

"At your place the other day, when you didn't show. She's not happy about having it in the house with the kids around."

What had gotten into Kathleen? To discuss him with a stranger, behind his back? She acted like he was still helpless, a dying man, to be discussed with doctors outside his presence. "Nonsense," he told Lucca, "the girls are old enough, intelligent enough, not to mistake a gun for a toy."

Frank hit the record button after the detective left, locked the office and walked the mall. Throngs of people passed by, young, beautiful and exuberant. South Beach was alive and exciting. He loved this time of year. If only the weather would stay so breezy, so cool and invigorating, year-round. Of course, that would result in tourists, foreign visitors, their traffic glut and parking woes year-round. He passed a tea room featuring a gypsy who read palms and tarot cards. He thought of Rory. What would the gypsy see in her future? He would go to Twin Palms and talk turkey with her in the morning. Her future and that of her son depended on it. She had to have some clue about where the money went.

Hungry, he realized it was nearly dinnertime. Something nagged him to call home. He stepped into the doorway of a funky boutique and took out his tiny cell phone.

"Where are you?" Kathleen sounded annoyed.

"On the mall, near the office."

"You forgot."

"What?"

"Lourdes was off today. We were going out to dinner."

He vaguely recollected a mention of Lourdes being off, but recalled no dinner plans. "Were we meeting someone?"

"No, just the two of us."

"Sweetheart, I'm bushed." He was in no mood to compete for a table in some noisy, crowded restaurant. "How about I stop by Joe's and bring home some stone crabs?"

She sighed and paused. "All right."

"I'll get us a double order of jumbos. What about the girls?"

"They've already eaten, it'll be just us. Bring some cole-slaw and don't forget the mustard sauce and drawn butter."

"You've got it, sweetheart. I'm on the way."

South Beach traffic was already bumper to bumper. Joe's, a legendary landmark, is located at the city's southern tip. No reservations and two-hour waits for a table. A take-out department was added a few years ago, a blessing for aficionados. Sturdy brown bags emblazoned with *Joe's* now vied for snob appeal with shopping bags from Sak's.

Frank sat stalled in traffic surrounded by the beautiful people in their limos, Jags, Rolls, vintage sports cars and neon-trimmed custom hot rods. A vast midnight blue sky hung low overhead, bouncing the music, the traffic sounds, the laughter, back down around him. As they all inched along, he watched curiously for the restaurant operated by Daniel Alexander and his partner, Ron Harrington. There it was. Brightly lit, patrons crowded at outdoor tables, waiters with red cummerbunds. He wondered whether the table tax increase so ardently protested by the late Daniel Alexander had ever passed.

He had called in his order from the car. A uniformed cop directed traffic in the parking lot. Frank sighed. He had never intended to spend a single precious moment of his new life waiting in line for stone crabs. He felt that he should be somewhere else, doing something important, but had no idea what it was.

Finally awarded his brown shopping bag, he escaped, delighted to go home. Traffic thinned once he cleared the South Beach congestion and driving again became a pleasure. He listened to Verdi on the CD player, part of Kathleen's endless campaign to upgrade his cultural sensibilities. The music a soothing backdrop, he rehearsed ways to break the bad news to Rory in the morning.

He turned onto the causeway with its old-world streetlamps, crossed the Belle Isle bridge, then made a right onto Rivo Alto. So did a car behind him. He rounded the curve, beneath the sheltering branches of a giant royal poinciana, and slowed, the garden lanterns above his gateposts a welcome glow. He reached up to the visor for the remote.

A man suddenly sprang from the shadows, flinging himself in front of the wrought-iron gate. Frank cried out in surprise and hit the brake, his entrance blocked. The man had come out of nowhere, tall, eyes wide, mouth agape in a distorted grimace of fear, gesturing frantically. He waved Frank away with both arms, his entire body caught up in the frenzied motions like some deranged traffic cop.

Bewildered, blinded by the bright headlights close behind him, Frank strained to see. With a shock, he recognized the man rushing toward him, the same pale, lean intruder who had invaded his bedroom while he slept!

Frank wrenched the wheel and hit the gas. The car responded, screeching away from the house. The driver behind him followed. Frank speeded past the stop sign at the causeway, cutting off a westbound motorist who blasted his horn as the Mercedes hurtled across his right of way.

On the south side of the island, Frank stood on the brakes, trembling fingers grasping his cell phone. The car following him had paused at the stop sign. He saw it in his rearview mirror, dark blue, a Gran Prix. Who were they? He stared out the back window, straining to see the two men in the front seat as they veered off, headed west. He did not know them, and noticed what appeared to be red primer paint on their left rear fender, and a tag outlined in neon.

Was Kathleen all right? He punched the speed dial. "Oh my God, oh my God." He gasped, trying to catch his breath, as the number rang, rang, then rang again.

"Hello?"

"Kath! Are you okay?"

"Frank, where are you?" she complained. "I'm hungry."

"At the far end of the island, the south side. Make sure the doors are locked. Don't open them. There's a man outside! I'm calling the police."

"What?" There was a long pause. "Frank, I'm watching the monitor now, there's no one out there."

"Do as I say! I'll be right there."

Poised to dial 911, he slowly circled the southern tip of the island, then crossed to the north side, eyes probing the shadows. His heart had begun to pound, a delayed reaction to his initial shock. He took a deep breath and removed the gun from the glove compartment. Felt its comforting weight in his right hand, as he steered with his left.

He stopped on the Bishops' swale, headlights trained on his own gate, then slipped the cell phone into his jacket pocket. He opened the car door, gun in hand, and cautiously stepped out. Everything seemed quiet. Only a neighborhood cat, skulking across the roadway, the green glint of its luminous eyes flashing in the moonlight. A seagull chortled overhead.

He scrutinized the pavement carefully, searching the grass and the bed of multicolor impatiens where he'd seen the intruder. No trampled flowers, no broken stems, no trace. He returned to the car, fumbled for the remote, then opened the gate, still trembling. He rolled slowly up the drive, watchful and alert.

Kathleen swung the front door open and gasped, hand to her throat, at the sight of him, the gun in his hand.

"I told you not to open it!" He swept by her into the house. "Lock it," he demanded.

"What on earth?"

He caught sight of himself, sweaty and disheveled, in the gilt-edged mirror in the foyer. He wiped his eyes with his gun hand. "Where are the girls?"

"Please, Frank. What's wrong?" She looked near tears.

He told her, but she remained unconvinced.

"There was no one out there," she protested. "I went to look when you called. I didn't see a soul." She glanced up and listened. "Did you call the police?"

He shook his head, then heard it too. Sirens. Their urgent wails streamed across the causeway toward them.

CHAPTER
EIGHT

Frank placed the gun on the glass-topped coffee table, then stood to await the police. Kathleen recoiled at the heavy sound of metal on glass.

"Please put that away," she said nervously. "You always hated guns, because of your father. I don't understand why you bought it. You know I don't want it in the house."

"They'll be here any minute now," he said.

"But you didn't call them." She wrung her hands. "So why would they be coming here?"

"Don't you see?" Frank said. "Somebody else, maybe the Bishops, saw him, too. They must have called the police."

Kathleen looked at him oddly. "Gardiner and Linda Bishop left town this morning, on a cruise." Did he see fear in her eyes?

"Kath . . ." He stepped toward her, then stopped to listen. The sirens seemed to pass the island and continue west. Some stopped, not far off. Others kept coming. He picked up the gun and opened the French doors. The draperies billowed in the breeze off the bay. Revolving red and blue lights bounced off the treetops over on DiLido, the next island. The sound of barking dogs carried across the water.

"They're going there," he said, puzzled. "Why . . . ?"

Kathleen remained silent, never taking her eyes off him.

He went to the phone, dialed the Miami Beach Police Department and asked the nature of the emergency on Di-Lido. "We're on the next island," he explained. "And something odd just happened here, right before we heard the sirens." Kathleen turned away in angry exasperation.

The operator put him on hold, then came back to say that units were investigating a shooting, and that if he had any information that could be related, a detective would be by to see him later.

He hung up the phone and turned to his wife. "There's been a shooting on DiLido. I'm going over there."

"Are you crazy?"

"No," he said quietly. "I've got to find out what's going on." He slipped the gun into his jacket pocket and left her standing in the doorway.

East DiLido Drive was blocked by police cars and fire rescue units. He locked the gun in the glove compartment and walked toward the hub of the action, a house in the middle of the first block north of the bridge. Neighbors, their faces shocked, spoke in hushed tones, watching from their lawns and front doors.

Someone lay sprawled on the grass near the brick driveway, next to a late-model Lincoln Town Car. Both front doors of the car hung open. The interior lights were on, the door chime dinging insistently. Why don't they close them? he wondered. How can anyone think? The medics had walked away, leaving the wrappers from sterile gauze pads and rubber gloves scattered on the ground around the victim. A uniformed officer unfurled a yellow plastic sheet and shook it out. Excitement and dread rose in Frank's throat as he moved closer.

The corpse was that of a woman. The cop ordered him back, but Frank stood his ground. A stubborn breeze thwarted the cop's efforts, lifting and sweeping back the sheet to expose her face. She still wore her glasses, though they had been knocked askew. An ugly bruise had purpled the skin beneath her left eye and her arm was twisted at an odd angle. Her blood glistened black in the distorted light. He stared, remembering the darkest day of his childhood.

"What are you doing, pal? You belong here?"

He looked up at the officer, startled. "I . . . I live on the next island. I called and they said a detective would come by to see me."

"You a witness?"

"No, but something happened, just before we heard the sirens." He felt confused.

"Okay, stay right there." The cop approached a detective and gestured in Frank's direction. The detective turned to look; so did another officer who had been stringing yellow crime scene tape across the roadway. Frank recognized him, one of the cops who had come to the house to search for his bedroom prowler. The patrolman leaned forward and spoke to the detectives, his voice low. They all shot another look his way.

Kathleen was right, Frank thought. He shouldn't have come.

A loud sob and a cry. "Oh, no. Oh, no!" For the first

time Frank saw a short balding man, hunched on the front steps of the house, ringed by rescue workers, neighbors and cops. The Lincoln blocked the man's view of the dead woman.

"My God," Frank murmured. Sherman Howe. He knew the man. The woman must be Margery, Sherman's wife. He had not recognized her on the bloody ground next to her driveway. He knew them both. She was a soprano, had studied in Rome when she was young. She had traded dreams of La Scala and the Met to marry and raise a family, but still sang in Christmas concerts and Miami Opera Guild productions. When the girls were small, he and Kathleen had taken them to see a production of *Hansel and Gretel*. Margery sang the role of the mother. The couple owned a hardware business. When they last talked, Sherman had said that with the children grown and gone, the house had become too big for them. They planned to sell, to move to a condo on the ocean, away from the traffic and excitement of South Beach.

Too late.

What happened? Frank wished Kathleen were with him. He turned to leave, to go home to her.

"Hold it, Mister Douglas. I'm Detective DeVito. You wanted to see me?"

The detective had a chubby, impatient face and a receding hairline, and held a small notebook.

"I thought . . . Something happened over at our place, on Rivo Alto . . . A short time later we heard the sirens . . ." Frank broke off, distracted. "Don't you think you should close those car doors? The lights and the door chimes will run the battery down."

The detective's eyes were curious. "We think it best to leave things as they are for now."

"I know them," Frank blurted. "I know the Howes."

"Is that so?"

"She was an opera singer, a soprano. I live over there." He gestured lamely toward home.

"You said. What was it that happened?"

"A prowler," Frank said weakly, running his hand through his hair, "the same prowler I've seen before."

"A white man? Tall, slim, apparently strolls in and out of your locked house at will? That him?"

"Right."

"Well, I don't think your prowler has anything to do with our investigation here. But thank you for bringing it to our attention." The detective turned away, exposing his bald spot and broad back.

"And there was this car, right behind me."

The detective hesitated.

"A Gran Prix with primer paint on the rear fender . . ."

The detective turned back to Frank. "Where did you see this car?"

"Behind me. Right on my bumper as I came home, onto the island."

"Occupied by?"

"Two guys in the front seat."

"You get a look at 'em?"

"They had the windows down, I saw the driver as they turned west . . . The prowler . . ."

"Toward DiLido?"

"That's right." He now had the detective's full attention.

"By any chance, did you get a look at the tag number?"

"It was hard to read. Had a blue neon border around it. Turquoise blue."

"Mister Douglas, we need to talk."

A small red sports car interrupted as it wheeled around the corner. Cops shouted as it braked hard just short of the yellow tape. The door flew open and a young woman in a crop top and a short skirt darted out, leaving the lights on, the engine running. She eluded officers and with a piercing scream, ran to the covered figure on the ground. A patrolman grasped her by both arms. Breaking away, she ran sobbing to the man on the steps. He stood up, feebly, and embraced her.

"Mommy, Mommy," the girl cried out. "What happened! My God, what happened?"

"She's gone," the father moaned, and she began to scream again.

"The daughter," the detective muttered. "She musta inherited her mother's lungs."

They talked in the brightly lit kitchen of a small, neat house on the dry side of the street, joined by a detective named Jarrett. He was thin and sharp-nosed with piercing eyes and a surprisingly gentle manner of speaking. "So this car was behind you as you were coming home," he said. "Where exactly were you coming from?"

"South Beach. From Joe's."

The detectives exchanged elated glances.

"Right, right, from Joe's." DeVito kept breaking away to spout indecipherable police jargon and numbers into his radio.

"What happened tonight?" Frank asked, bewildered. "What happened to Sherman and Margery Howe?"

"Okay." DeVito placed his two-way radio on the table and leaned forward. "We been having a rash of driveway robberies lately. People with luxury cars trailed home from upscale South Beach restaurants and night spots, then attacked and robbed at gunpoint in their driveways. The perps have been getting more violent. A coupla victims got pistol-whipped or shot at. Tonight your neighbors over here, the Howes, go see a six-o'clock movie at the Byron Carlyle, then stop for ice cream. They're driving home, from the north end of town. Them getting hit didn't fit the usual MO.

"But now we hear that at the same time, you're tooling home from Joe's, as were two of our prior victims, and maybe the bad guys are following you. But just as they're about to nail you in your driveway, you get spooked and haul ass. They back off and, whaddaya know, an easier target comes rolling into sight. Howe pulls into his driveway and gets outta the car to pick up the empty recycling bins out by the curb. While he's doing that, looks like the bad guys pull into the driveway next door and run close to the ground around the hedge to where the wife is getting outta her side of the car. She probably doesn't see 'em until they're on top of her.

"They get her purse, but apparently she puts up a struggle trying to remove her Rolex. A fatal mistake. She gets smacked in the face with a gun, then shot. We won't know until the medical examiner tells us, but it looks like the bullet mighta severed the main artery to her heart, because as she's still trying to fight them off, she goes into shock, evidently due to massive internal bleeding. It happens so fast the husband doesn't know what's going on 'til he hears the shot. He sees two figures run but doesn't get a good look at 'em. He goes to his wife as they cut through the hedge to their car. He thinks it was a Gran Prix, with blue neon around the plate."

"So the robbers, the killers, were in that car behind me?"

"You've got it."

"If not for the prowler waving me away," he whispered, "I could have been the one shot."

"No way of knowing."

None of this made any sense. "But why would robbers put neon on their car? Doesn't it make them stand out?"

"Never ceases to amaze me." DeVito glanced at his partner, who shook his head. "These turds decide to dress their car up to look sporty and contemporary. Next thing you know they're having a crack attack and doing something stupid.

"Now," he said, getting down to business, "think you would recognize the car if you saw it?"

"I might."

"Good, because a City of Miami unit has got a vehicle fitting the description stopped at Two and Nineteen. Wanna come with us to have a look?"

"What about the occupants?" Jarrett said softly. "Could you recognize them?"

Frank thought for a moment, remembering the lights, the profile. "Maybe," he said slowly. "It was just a quick look under the lights on the bridge. All I saw of the passenger was his profile, he had a funky plaited hairstyle. But the driver . . . I thought I saw a glint, something shiny in his mouth."

The cops looked pleased and got to their feet. Then Frank's watch began to chirp.

"What's that?" DeVito asked. "A beeper?"

"No, my watch. Think I could get a glass of milk? I have to take my medication now."

"Jesus, Mary and Joseph." DeVito rolled his eyes at his partner.

Jarrett sighed unhappily. "What are you taking?"

Frank unzipped his black bag. The detectives stared at the impressive array of vials inside.

"For my heart." He displayed his bracelet. "I'm a transplant patient."

"Oh. That's a relief," DeVito said, "as long as it's not something from a shrink."

The usually quiet street was still cluttered with official vehicles, alive with the business of sudden death, as they stepped out the front door. Kathleen was coming up the stairs.

"They said you were in here with the detectives." She looked frightened. The night was chilly and she wore a sweater over her shoulders.

"Robbers followed me, Kath. They killed Margery Howe."

She turned to the detectives. "He's had major surgery," she told them. "He has to take his medication."

"I've taken it," he said impatiently.

"Let's go home now." She reached for his arm.

"He's coming with us," DeVito said.

"Oh, no!" Her hand flew to her mouth.

"Nothing to be alarmed about," the detective said. "He's helping us out."

"We'll take good care of him," Jarrett promised.

"That's the car, the same car that was behind me," Frank said without hesitation as the detectives inched their unmarked past a dark blue Gran Prix outside a small grocery store.

The suspects were slumped in the backseats of separate police units.

"You stay put," DeVito said. "We'll have somebody take them out of the cage cars so you can eyeball 'em."

"Don't you have to have a lineup? Doesn't the law say—"

"You been watching too much television," DeVito muttered. "The law says we can ask a citizen to take a look at possible offenders standing on the street immediately after a crime. It's a different story the next day, or even a coupla hours later."

"Then," Jarrett said, "we use a photo lineup."

"Yeah," his partner added. "I can't remember the last time we had a live lineup. Too cumbersome, too expensive, too time-consuming. Ya hafta find everybody, lawyers, the prosecutor, a stenographer. The pain and torture, the worst part, is going over to the county lockup, trying to entice prisoners into helping us out. We need five to stand with one. Used to bribe 'em with a carton of cigarettes. Now they got the no-smoking policy at the jail. Last time we went in there looking for inmates to participate, they were spitting at us. Remember that, Murray?"

Jarrett nodded sorrowfully. "We don't even have a lineup room anymore."

"Now, Frank," DeVito said, "do us one favor? Just for the purposes of this investigation, let's forget this, uh . . . prowler. Let's try keeping him out of it. No point in mixin' apples with oranges here. We don't wanna hand some defense lawyer a red herring on a silver platter."

Frank nodded.

"Try to focus on anything you noticed that can't be changed, unlike clothing or hairstyle," DeVito said.

"It was only a glance," Frank protested.

Heads down, the two handcuffed men slumped sullenly against a patrol car beneath a streetlight. They looked small and slender, not at all threatening.

Frank leaned forward and wondered what they were thinking. The one with the plaited hair was obviously the passenger. The other muttered something under his breath, then grinned.

"That's it, see it?" The glint of a gold-capped tooth. "He was the driver. That's them," he said.

"Do me a favor," Frank said later. "If they talk to you, will you ask them if they saw anybody else, and let me know?"

"Sure," DeVito said. "We'll do that."

CHAPTER
NINE

Frank arrived home at nearly midnight, stunned at how an evening of simple pleasures had ended in death delivered by shadowy figures to the familiar surroundings of Margery Howe's own driveway.

It could have been him. Why had he been warned? No robbers or prowlers lurking in his driveway now, only a strange, apparently unoccupied car parked on the swale. Frank unlocked the glove box for easy access to the gun and flashed on his brights. Two heads popped up. Even in the glare of the high beams he instantly recognized his oldest daughter's heartbreakingly perfect profile.

He stepped from the Mercedes and strode up to the driver's side. The occupants were hastily adjusting their clothes.

"You must be one sick son of a bitch," he told Jay Bowden, his voice oddly calm, "hitting on teenagers at your age. I don't want to see you here again."

He leaned down, making eye contact with his daughter. "You," he said, "inside. Now."

"You've got the wrong idea, Frank," Bowden said.

"Don't want to hear it."

Bowden cleared his throat and tried again. "Shandi is an exceptionally mature young woman. She . . ."

Too weary and preoccupied to be furious, Frank walked away from Bowden's inane remarks, rounded the car and wrenched open Shandi's door. He thought he smelled the sweet pungent scent of marijuana.

"Daddy . . ." she protested, stepping out.

He pointed silently to the house, slammed the car door and stalked after her.

"Look who I found," he told Kathleen, who was waiting. The eyes of mother and daughter connected. Kathleen, he realized, knew all along where Shandi had been.

"Not only is your behavior disgraceful, it's dangerous," he told Shandi, who headed for the stairs. "One of our neighbors was murdered in her driveway tonight."

"Murdered?" Shandi turned on the bottom step and blinked. She wore a very short skirt and no stockings. "Who?"

"Margery Howe."

"The singer? Mom." She turned to her mother. "Is that true?"

"I'm afraid it is," Kathleen said.

"I am not a lunatic," he said. "In fact, I am considered a credible witness. Therefore, it is not necessary to confirm everything I say with your mother."

Shandi ran up the stairs.

"Here's your dinner." He handed Kathleen the long-forgotten brown shopping bag from Joe's.

"You hungry?" she murmured, taking it to the kitchen.

"No."

"Neither am I."

He called after her. "Where's Casey?"

"A sleep-over with her friend on Island Road."

"Looked like Shandi planned to sleep-over in Bowden's car out front," he said sarcastically.

She did not respond, so, exhausted, he went to bed.

Restless, he kept waking, expecting the dawn, then finding it was only twenty or thirty minutes later than when he had last checked the digital clock on his nightstand. Plaintive wails woke him at three A.M., a cat, pitiful and locked out. He lay there listening, wondering why Daisy, who usually slept in Casey's room, did not bark. The sounds stopped until he dozed. The cries woke him once more, then stopped again, as he realized that the wails sounded human.

He padded downstairs, alone in the dark, at 4:45 A.M., made a pot of coffee, then sat in the kitchen savoring the aroma and listening to the final hour of an all-night radio talk show. Lonely voices reaching out to other sleepless strangers in the dark. Frank had never felt lonely, even after his father's death. He had been too busy. His mother, hollow-eyed and too thin, had stopped cooking, stopped cleaning, and begun slurring her words, so he had carried on. It was he, at age eleven, who had scrawled a shopping list and pulled a squeaky-wheeled wire cart to the grocery. He who took buses to pay the electric bill so their power would not be turned off. He cooked and even picked wildflowers, pink and white periwinkles, to decorate the Jell-O and instant-cake-mix desserts he fixed for his mother, hoping to see her eat, hoping in some small way to make up for all she had lost. Hoping she would smile again. It was he who stayed awake when she was out all night, terrified that something evil had overtaken her too.

Despite the hour and his isolation, Frank did not identify with the solitary predawn callers. He had never been less alone. He felt an uneasy presence he had never been aware of before. He wondered if traces of his donor's personality and energy had been transplanted into his body along with another man's cells, heart muscle and genes. The idea seemed less ludicrous in this setting, sitting alone in the dark. But he had always loved logic, it had never let him down in the past.

At five-thirty A.M. Frank stepped out to see if the morning paper had arrived. It was not yet dawn and as he stood in the darkened driveway looking for it, a car pulled up to the gate. The two detectives.

They followed him into the kitchen.

"Quite a view ya got here." DeVito peered out at the city skyline across the bay. He looked rumpled, his eyes bloodshot. He'd lost his tie somewhere during the night. "We were passing through the 'hood here on the way back to the station."

"You mean you fellows haven't been to bed yet?"

"We been busy, talking to Willingham and Jackson, the cowboys from last night's little escapade. Didn't plan to bother you if there was no lights. Almost didn't see you prowling around your driveway in the dark." He cut his eyes at his partner.

"I was looking for the morning paper."

Jarrett looked interested. "Should be some kinda story. A reporter caught up with us late last night."

"Pushy broad," DeVito said, blowing his nose.

Frank poured them coffee. "So you talked to the killers."

"Yeah," DeVito said. "The passenger copped first, blames

the driver. Then the driver hears his partner is spilling, so he opens up. Now they can't blame each other fast enough.

"Said they were following you." He stirred sugar into his coffee. "Picked you up at Joe's. They were ready to rock and roll when you made the turn into your driveway. They pulled up real close when they spotted the gate, didn't wanna risk you getting inside and shutting 'em out. But then you floor it and take off instead. They figure you made 'em and think twice about the whole thing."

He raised his eyes from his coffee mug. "They didn't back off for no other reason. They never saw anybody else." He sipped his coffee noisily, then sniffed.

"Just thought you'd like to know."

Frank nodded and looked away.

"So just then," DeVito concluded, "what comes by but an older couple in a big Town Car, they hit the jackpot and your neighbor goes to glory."

Frank was serving bacon and eggs to the detectives, who were watching the *Today Show*, when Kathleen appeared in the doorway, clutching her bathrobe around her.

"I thought I heard voices." She sounded sleepy.

"Breakfast?" Frank used a spatula to slide more eggs onto DeVito's plate.

"Just coffee." Taking the cup with her, she disappeared back upstairs.

He joined her after the detectives left.

Kathleen sat at the foot of their bed, watching him dress after his shower. "There's a recipient support group meeting this afternoon. I think we should go."

He frowned as he fastened his watch. "What time is it?"

"Two o'clock."

He shook his head. "I doubt I'll be back by then, I'm running late now. And you know I'm not into those things."

"You're going to see that woman again today, aren't you?"

He turned to face her, his expression startled. "Yes. It's important to square her situation away as quickly as possible. She may face severe tax problems."

"But after last night . . . ?"

"What does last night have to do with it?"

"It's all part of . . ." She sighed. "I've been uneasy about this from the start. You know that. I'm worried, Frank. Your relationship with the man's widow is unhealthy." Her pleading eyes misted. "It's just that all of these things are happening to us so fast. I don't know how to handle them." She removed a handkerchief from her pocket and dabbed at her eyes. "I was able to cope when you were sick and facing surgery. But now I'm not sure where you're coming from anymore. It's as though you're not the same person. You look wonderful, you seem healthy, yet . . . We went through hell to be here for you, and now you go off on your own without telling us where you're going . . ."

"I'll finish it up soon, I promise."

She was using her handkerchief to scrub off her lipstick, then hugged him around the waist. He was in a hurry. "This situation is strictly temporary, you know that," he said kindly, then caught his breath.

She was unzipping his trousers, fumbling almost eagerly, releasing his penis. Cradling it in both hands, she ran her tongue around the tip, probing, burrowing it along the slit at the head.

His knees felt weak. Kathleen had never really liked oral sex. He couldn't remember the last time she had initiated it. She loosened his belt, slipped his trousers and shorts down below his knees and they swiftly changed places. He sat on the bed and she dropped to her knees on the thick carpet in front of him. It excited him to see his neat, immaculate wife in her impeccably crisp expensive designer blouse, shining hair pulled back so tightly that it looked taut at the scalp, like this, wild and wanton, emitting loud sucking noises and moaning under her breath. She gently massaged him, nibbling at the scar where they opened his groin to insert the catheter for his heart biopsies. Her lip always returning, taking him deeper and deeper. His hands were on her shoulders, the base of her neck, the back of her head. He closed his eyes and sighed aloud.

She knew him so well, whenever he came close, she slowed and teased and released him, licking and stroking and gently blowing, until he wanted to force himself back inside her mouth. When he finally released and fell back on the bed, she remained curled up between his feet on the thick carpet. His shorts and trousers were around one ankle.

He sat up slowly as she wiped her mouth with the handkerchief. "Hey," he said softly, and reached down to touch her crotch. "I want to kiss that little boy in the boat. Bring him up here."

She smiled, straightening her clothes. "No, I'm fine," she said. "I don't want to have to change again. No time." She consulted her watch. "I have to go drag Shandi out of bed or she'll miss class."

"That's not fair." He kissed her throat and reached under her skirt as she sat on the bed next to him.

"Sweetheart"—she caught his hand—"it's time to focus on your own life. Our lives."

He still wanted to pleasure her.

"In the family counseling sessions," she went on, "they

told us what to expect after your surgery. They said there might be personality changes, due to the medications . . ."

His afterglow was fading fast. "But, honey, that's just in the beginning before they take you off the high doses of steroids. My dosage now is a tiny fraction of that. My personality hasn't changed, Kath. I'm not beating my chest, bellowing Tarzan yells, or ripping down goalposts."

"Well, what about these . . . these hallucinations? Seeing people who aren't there?" Her tone was that of someone correcting an errant child.

"All I know is what's happened." He slipped his other foot out of his pants, hoping to retain some dignity. He did not want them dragging from one ankle on his way to the bathroom to clean up.

"Somebody, something, warned me away last night when I was about to be robbed, maybe shot." He tried to look credible, even though he now stood before her exposed from the waist down. "Call it what you will, guardian angel, apparition or premonition. I think it has something to do with the man whose heart they gave me."

"You mean you think it's him."

"I know how it sounds, but it would make sense, wouldn't it? That he would want to protect me—and his own heart."

"Oh, Frank. You've never believed in ghost stories and the supernatural." She looked stricken. "And you're still going to see her today?"

"I have to," he said, as he went into the bathroom and turned on the water in the sink. She was gone when he came out. The bed had been straightened, not even a crushed spot in the spread to show they had been there. He heard her voice down the hall.

*   *   *

Rory was at work in a flower bed, a trowel in her hand, when he pulled into her driveway. She wore a scarf over her hair, green garden gloves, denim overalls and a T-shirt. "The snails got the upper hand." She grinned ruefully, surveying the yard. "Didn't fertilize last month like I was supposed to, the allamandas are outa control and I forgot to cut back the poinsettias so they'd be red for Christmas." She smiled at him. "But slowly, surely, I'm gitting myself back in the groove."

"I see your green thumb, but what's with the nose?" A shiny green leaf protruded from beneath the bridge of her sunglasses.

"Oh," she laughed. "Nose protector. Didn't want to git the thing sunburned. Looks god-awful when it peels."

"And what is that?" A saucer was sunk into the ground, flush with the soil.

"That's for the beer."

"Beer?"

"Happy hour for the snails. I'll pour it full a beer right after dark. Snails love it, they suck it up, git tipsy and drown. Don't like puttin' out poison." She brushed off her overalls. "Don't like killing 'em at all, but when they get the munchies they eat every leaf on the place. Me and Billy used to hand-pick 'em, drop 'em in a grocery sack and relocate 'em to an overgrown lot on the waterway a coupla blocks over. Perfect new home for 'em, but one a the neighbors caught us in the act and raised hell. So now we just let 'em drink themselves to death.

"Thought you gave up on me," she told him, as they went inside.

Frank studied Daniel's picture close up while she changed to go to the bank. He felt nothing, no heartfelt connection. The man in the photo seemed to be an ominous stranger.

His thoughts that morning seemed inane in the bright light of day.

He delayed telling Rory what he'd discovered about Alexander's accounts until after they picked up her new checkbook and called her insurance agent to determine whether the life policy was gone as well. He listened with relief as the agent promised imminent checks to both the widow and Alexander's business partner. The delay was not unusual, the agent explained, in the case of suicide. The company had been awaiting final reports from their own investigator, police and the medical examiner's office. They were now complete and all was in order.

"Rory, I've got some bad news," Frank said, after the call.

"Are you all right?" Her big eyes grew huge. "You're not sick? Your heart . . . ?"

"No, it's you I'm worried about." He explained in detail the closed accounts, the emptied funds, the pension cashed in prematurely.

"This can't be right." She paced nervously, tossing back her hair. "There was stocks, CDs, the cash from the sale of the business, Daniel's retirement fund." She ticked them off, one by one on her long tapered fingers.

Her eyes dropped to the new checkbook on the table. "Where'd that money come from?"

"I transferred it there, from one of my accounts."

She shook her head. "I can't let you do that, Frank."

"You can pay it back when we find the money."

"Okay, as soon as the insurance check comes in."

"There's something else," he said solemnly. "Because of the capital gains on the sale of the business, the stock sales, withdrawal of the pension fund, you could be facing a huge tax liability." He leaned forward, intent, his voice earnest. "This is serious, Rory. Give me the leads and I'll follow the money, but I need somewhere to start. Do you have any idea what new ventures Daniel might have invested in?''

She remained silent for a long moment. ''He talked about maybe one of those gambling ships. But I was against that and I think he decided that way too. Then there was a wholesale flower import business he looked into, but it was all speculation, nothing concrete. He hadn't made up his mind yet.''

''Is there any other place that you know of where he could have stashed money or records?''

''Maybe his safety deposit box.''

''Why didn't you mention that before? Have you inventoried the box since his death?''

She shook her head. ''Couldn't bring myself to do it.''

''You have the key?''

They were still searching for it when Billy burst in from school.

''I know I've seen it since—''

''Are you gonna be my new dad?'' Billy demanded, watching suspiciously from a kitchen stool as they hunted through cabinets and rifled drawers.

Frank and Rory stared at each other.

''Nah, Billy. I'm already somebody's dad. I'm just here to help your mom.''

''Well, Mom, who is gonna take me to the Youth Fair?''

''We'll worry about that when the time comes. I'm sure you'll get to go,'' Rory said.

The boy went back to his milk and oatmeal cookies.

''Billy,'' Frank asked, ''have you seen a little key that belonged to your dad?''

''In a tiny red envelope,'' Rory said. ''Had a number inside the flap.''

He shrugged, head down.

''Billy? Billy, you answer me, out loud.''

The boy scrambled down from the stool and dashed for the back door, his mother hot on his heels.

"Billy, you come back here!"

He slammed out as she ran after him.

Frank followed them to the door.

"He's all right," Rory said, exasperated. "He's climbing up into his tree house. Probably to sulk. He's been overreacting." She returned and leaned against the kitchen counter. "The day before it happened, Daniel scolded him for some dumb little thing he did. Billy asked me last night if his daddy died because he was naughty and upset him."

"He thinks he's to blame."

"I need to work with him, get him into a little grief therapy maybe, just to get through this."

"You're right," he said, "a little therapy couldn't hurt."

"Guess we could all use some help," Rory said.

True, Frank thought as he drove home. He decided to please Kathleen and attend a group session or two. It would make her happy.

CHAPTER TEN

Kathleen looked harried.

Three-year-old Charlie whimpered for his mother. Giselle, five, had discarded her shoes and socks, and Randy, age nine, seemed intent on playing smash and grab with her Lalique crystal collectibles.

"Why would Sue Ann unload her grandchildren on us for the night?" Kathleen complained bitterly. "She knows this is not a good time for us."

"What better time? It was my idea." Frank hung up his jacket. "I gave them the theater tickets and said we'd baby-sit. I thought you'd love having nice little kids around for a change. I know I do."

He had intended no sarcasm but saw her react. They had not discussed Shandi yet, or the fact that she seemed to be flying free despite being grounded.

Randy and Giselle clambered all over Frank, while little Charlie remained shy and reserved. A sensitive, curly-haired tot, he was blonder than his older siblings, with huge, serious eyes fringed by impossibly thick lashes.

"Come on, gang." Frank had hoped Casey and Shandi would be home to enjoy and help with the children, but his daughters were nowhere in sight.

They played elevator.

He lifted little Giselle by her rigid elbows. "Second floor!" Higher. "Third floor!" Even higher. "Fourth floor!"

"Basement!" He swooped her back down.

Then Randy. "Second floor! Whoops, maintenance failure. Attention: This elevator is malfunctioning!" He jiggled the boy in midair, as all three youngsters screamed with glee.

"What is all this noise?" Kathleen emerged from the kitchen. "Frank, you shouldn't be lifting the children. Why don't you all go outside to play until dinner?"

"Care to join us?" he called after her.

"I have some letters to write." His eyes followed as she went upstairs. Then he turned back to the expectant children.

"Okay, gang. How about an environmental trek?"

"Yes, yes," they chorused. They had no idea what it was, but wanted it desperately. He could relate to that. He'd felt twinges of wistful nostalgia lately, as though mourning a lost love. But he had no lost love. Kathleen had been and was his one and only.

They tiptoed into the kitchen, past Lourdes, who pretended not to see them.

Charlie clung to Frank, thrilled, as they staged a commando raid on the bread box, stuffing dinner rolls into plastic grocery sacks, even swiping a few fresh shrimp intended for dinner, then escaped onto the terrace with their loot. They skirted the tiled planters overflowing with flowering shrubs, and filed out onto the dock.

"Fishies!" Charlie shrieked, pointing into the water. They rolled bread into tiny balls to feed the needlefish darting around the pilings. Screeching seagulls descended hungrily, raucously demanding their supplies. Stouthearted Randy never flinched as one of the pushy panhandlers swooped down and snatch bread right out of his hand. When the supplies were gone, Frank hauled up a rope that trailed into the water for show and tell about its encrusted barnacles, gunk and sea life.

Then they were off, around the north side of the house, where snails were dining on the spathiphyllum. The children watched the tiny mollusks retreat into their spiral shells.

"You know what snails like to drink?"

The children shouted out, "Kool-Aid!" and "Coca-Cola!" then giggled to hear that snails are beer drinkers. Giselle won the coconut-counting contest, and as they exited the gate, they all squawked back at a scolding flock of wild green parakeets.

From the bridge, Frank held Charlie up to see the huge cruise ships, the *Ecstasy*, the *Seaward* and the *Celebration*, in port, and the mirrored skyscraper where his office had once occupied the entire seventeenth floor. The sun was falling fast in a glorious blaze of fire.

Dusk settled as they circled the far side of the island. The water darkened and night sounds began. Frank felt content. If only he could relive his daughters' childhood years and enjoy more time with them. It's not too late, he thought hopefully. Kathleen was right about family priorities. Perhaps Rory's problems were better left in the hands of Dayton, an excellent accountant. His imagination might stop running away with him if he kept Daniel Alexander and his widow at a safer distance. He might even get a good night's sleep.

He inhaled the sweetly scented evening air as they meandered along, Giselle's small hand warm in his. Charlie on his left, Randy marching ahead, waving a twig he had picked up. Frank wanted to rush back to the house, to tell Kathleen to stop worrying, that it was over. He would call Dayton in the morning. Charlie began to lag behind. Frank turned in the growing darkness.

"Come on, son."

The tot peered anxiously over his shoulder, then hurried to catch up, short legs churning. Again he glanced back. Frank saw nothing but thick hedges, branches heavy with sea grapes and the lush upper limbs of huge orchid trees embracing like lovers overhead, shadowing the pavement below. Frank took the boy's hand and they strolled on. Charlie on one side, Giselle on the other. The boy began to balk.

"What's the matter, Charlie?"

"Let's go home." The child stared behind them again.

"You all worn-out?"

"No," he piped up plaintively. "I don't wike him."

"Who?"

"The man."

"What man?" Frank strained to see into the darkness. Night had fallen amazingly fast. "There's no man back there."

The other two turned and stared as well. "Nobody's there," Randy said mockingly. "Charlie's afraid of the dark," he chanted. "Charlie's afraid of the dark."

"Am not!" Charlie picked up his pace. "It's the man. I don't wike him."

"Why not?" Frank felt a chill. "We have good neighbors."

"He's fawowing us. He's mad," Charlie said, "wif blood on 'im."

"I think we're late for dinner," Frank said, "and I'm really hungry. How about you?"

When they arrived home he was carrying Charlie, and the others were nearly running.

"There was a monster!" Giselle cried, as they burst into the welcoming light and warmth of the house. Warm fragrant aromas from the kitchen mingled with good music from the sound system.

"A man," Charlie somberly corrected.

Kathleen looked accusingly at Frank, as though he had deliberately frightened the children.

"Charlie saw a shadow." The casual sound of his voice belied the dryness in his mouth, his faded appetite.

"A man," the tot insisted stubbornly.

Kathleen called after him as Frank started up the stairs to wash for dinner. "You should check your answering machine, sweetheart. When I passed your study earlier, I heard someone leaving a message."

He paused. He always left his study door closed. Nothing appeared to be disturbed inside. But he was certain she had been in there.

Rory's breezy greeting was his only message.

"Guess what I've got," she said playfully. "Billy came stragglin' in here when it started gettin' dark. I sneaked out while he was watchin' TV, and climbed into his tree house with a flashlight. Had to be quite a sight for the neighbors. Musta thought I finally lost it." She giggled at that, like a teenager. "Anyhow, I found an old cookie tin where the little termite had stashed a whole buncha stuff that belonged to his daddy. Swizzle sticks from the restaurant, some snapshots, stubs from Marlins games, key chains, a tie tack, aaannnnnd"—she stretched the word into two long syllables—"an itsy bitsy, teeny weeny key in a little red envelope. Lemme tell ya." Her voice dropped to a confidential tone. "Comin' down that tree in the dark was a damn sight trickier than climbin' up. Jist thought you'd like the latest inflight info. 'Bye."

He smiled. Then punched the play button again, stepped out into the hallway and closed the door. He had had extrathick, exterior-quality steel-cored doors installed upstairs years ago, when they renovated. He could not hear a thing from the hallway. He played the message a third time, assessing how it had sounded to Kathleen. He had no doubt that she had listened to it. The message was perfectly innocent. He sighed, hoping she had not imbued it with some negative spin. Neither had ever snooped on the other, as far as he knew. He had never lied to his wife. They had always been truthful and trusting. This was his fault, certainly not Rory's. But whatever Kathleen thought, he realized he had received more than one message this evening.

"Hey champion, this is Frank," he told Billy, who answered the phone. "Tell your mom I'll see her in the morning."

He scarcely slept. The children in the guest room did not disturb him; neither did Shandi, arriving home late from God knew where, nor Casey's TV blaring too loud and too late in her room. It was something else. When he closed his eyes beside his slumbering wife, he sensed they were not alone in the room.

When Frank stepped into the hall tying his bathrobe and intending to steal downstairs alone at dawn, a small face appeared around the guest room door.

"You sleep well, good buddy?" He held Charlie's hand on the stairs.

"The man kep' walking up and down. You hear 'im?" the boy asked solemnly, then looked up at Frank. "Can we watch cartoons?"

Frank dug out the waffle iron and cooked breakfast for the second morning that week. Randy and Giselle, even Casey, joined them, eager to demonstrate the "old-timey" dance steps learned for her first cotillion. Giselle and Charlie were fascinated. Randy snickered.

Frank watched and remembered dancing, holding his youngest daughter in his arms, when she was still in diapers, at some event that seemed not so long ago. When she was four or five, they had danced at a wedding, her patent leather Mary Janes planted square atop his polished dress shoes. Her next dance partner would be some pubescent boy with raging hormones. Where had the years gone?

He took Kathleen coffee in bed, asked when the support group met again, promised he would be there, then mentioned an early appointment.

"Is it about that call from last night?" she asked too casually.

"Yes," he said. "Everything's under control downstairs. Sue Ann will come for the children soon. Casey is with them now and Lourdes will be in shortly." He suggested she sleep in.

"Not on your life." She swung her pale legs off the bed. "Those little terrors are running around loose in my house. And if they go out, the little one will probably wind up face-down in the pool. Somebody's got to watch them."

"I could never do this alone," Rory said as they drove to the bank. "You have no idea how much your moral support means to me. I'm just sorry to be such a bother."

"No bother," Frank assured her, several times.

More sophisticated-looking than he had ever seen her, she wore a blue, businesslike dress, her hair pushed up and back, but was visibly nervous, twisting her long graceful fingers.

He felt eager, as though participating in a treasure hunt. He knew it was a long shot, but if Rory was lucky, the box could be stuffed with cash. It would not be rational for a businessman like Alexander to cash in his excellent investments and simply park the money. But who knows, Frank thought, suicide is not rational either.

They boarded the elevator to the safety deposit department in the Sunshine State Bank building. Rory filled out the access ticket and initialed his signature as Frank signed for admittance as well. She and the attendant disappeared into the vault, then emerged, with the attendant carrying a narrow steel box. The size, about two feet long and five inches wide, was a bad sign. Frank had hoped for something larger and tightly packed to the brim with high-denomination bills. The attendant ushered them into a carpeted cubicle with two chairs, placed the box on a built-in desktop and left. The door's automatic lock clicked loudly behind her.

They sat next to each other and eyed the box.

"Shall we?"

She nodded, chewing her lower lip.

"Hang in." He patted her hand. "Nothing's going to jump out. There's nothing we can't handle."

"You do it," she whispered.

He lifted the lid. No cash in sight. He spread the contents, mostly documents and manila envelopes, out on the desk.

Birth certificates for all three family members. Their passports. The marriage certificate for Aurora Lee St. Jean and Daniel Paul Alexander. The warranty deed on their house, along with the closing statements and title insurance. The wills were there, each naming the other sole beneficiary. A bank envelope containing eight silver dollars. A small sack of dimes and quarters minted when the U.S. government still used silver. Outdated incorporation papers from the restaurant partnership. Commemorative postage stamps that Alexander must have collected as a high-school boy. Laminated copies of Billy's birth notice and the obituary of Daniel's father. Eight fifty-dollar savings bonds belonging to Billy.

"Birthday presents from his grandma in Olive Grove," Rory murmured.

Two Indian-head pennies, a buffalo nickel and a 1938 Walking Liberty half-dollar. A pair of delicate amethyst earrings in a small velvet box.

"Daniel's mother gave 'em to me." Rory touched one gently. "They were her mother's. Figured there'd be hell to pay if I ever lost 'em. So I kep' 'em in here."

Where the hell is the money? he thought, frustrated.

Rory leaned across him to peer into the empty box. "That's funny." Puzzled, she riffled through the mound of papers and envelopes. "Where is it?" She sounded as agitated as Frank felt.

"What?"

"Daniel's pocket watch."

He frowned. They were looking for cash, receipts, bankbooks, not a watch.

"Antique. Solid gold. His great-granddaddy's. He was an adventurer, a hero, also named Daniel. When he was twenty-one he joined the gold rush in the Yukon territory. He rescued three people from a boat that capsized on the Klondike River. One of the men he rescued was the only son and heir of John D. Rockefeller. It was the father who gave Daniel Alexander the watch. Both men's initials, the date, 1897, and *Gratitude Is Greater than Gold,* are engraved on the back. It was passed down to Daniel's granddaddy, to his daddy and then to him on their twenty-first birthdays. It's family tradition."

"Sure you don't have it at Twin Palms?"

"No." She shook her head. "I looked for it after . . . Figured it was in here." She pawed again through the mound of documents.

"Maybe he left it somewhere to be repaired. Any unexplained receipts among his personal effects?"

She shook her head. "He was always so careful with it. It belongs to Billy now." She looked tearful. "It's tradition among the men of the family. Daniel's mama finds out it's gone, she'll rip me from here to hell and back."

"How valuable is it?"

She shrugged. "Don't know in dollars, but to the family, it's priceless, irreplaceable."

He wondered if the timepiece vanished with some sticky-fingered cop, rescue worker, or ambulance attendant in the confusion after the shooting. He had heard of such things happening. Or had Alexander liquidated it along with everything else? The history of the watch would command a much better price for it.

"It'll probably turn up," he said briskly. This was no time to obsess over a pocket watch, even a family heirloom. "We have more important problems to face."

"Oh, I know what you're saying." She gestured dismissively, her tone matter-of-fact. "Daniel's estate ain't worth a bucket of warm spit. Me and Billy are dead bang broke."

He replaced the contents in the box. "I'm starting to feel claustrophobic. Let's get out of here."

*   *   *

Rory hid behind her dark shades, unusually silent during the drive back to Twin Palms. His mind raced, trying to find some explanation for the missing assets.

Once inside the house, Rory started to cry. She stepped out of her high heels and slumped into a chair, tears streaming.

"I know it's a shock," he said quietly, "but all's not lost yet, we can still try to track the money."

She glanced up, confused, face flushed. "Oh, hell, you think I'm worried about the money? That ain't it! I kin always git a job. Sure, I cain't fly again, 'cuz of Billy, but I'll find somethin' . . . It's Daniel. Don't you see?" Her face crumpled again. "Now I know why. Somethin' happened. Daniel lost our money somehow. A bad business deal or some lousy investment. He was ashamed, didn't want me to know." Her shoulders shook. "He was so proud of being a wonderful provider," she gasped. "He sacrificed his own life to leave us the house and the insurance money. That was the last thing he could do for us." She gulped back a sob.

"He did it." She took a deep shuddering breath and clenched her fists. "Oh my God, Daniel! He did it! He killed himself! I never believed it until right now."

Frank leaned forward, put his arms around her and stroked her hair, enveloped in her sweet scent and her anguish, as she sobbed into his neck and shoulder.

"Why didn't he tell me?" She rubbed a fist at her nose and eyes. "We could have worked it out. We could have started over." Frank offered his handkerchief and she blew her nose. "It was his pride," she added furiously. "It had to be his pride and his goddamn ego."

She began to cry again, her pain as fresh as if Daniel still lay bleeding upstairs. Her raw misery was contagious, stirring up long-suppressed sorrows buried in Frank's youth, in the graves of his parents.

What if she begins to grieve all over again, he wondered, and stops opening the mail?

He leaned her gently back into her chair.

"I'll make you some tea."

"Hell, no. I need something stronger. There's a bottle of brandy in that cabinet."

He thought of his mother. "Billy will be home from school soon."

"It's only ten o'clock." She began to rise. "If I ever needed a drink, I need a big one now."

"Sit. I'll get it." His hands shook as he splashed two inches of brandy into a water glass.

She took tiny sips, her hiccuping sobs producing a strange echo-chamber effect in the glass.

He ached to help, but was clueless as to how, so he simply sat there.

Finally she sighed and handed him the empty glass. "I'd like that tea now," she said in a small voice.

They drank it in the kitchen. "How about some toast or soup?"

"No. You're so sweet." Her eyes and nose were red and swollen, her lipstick gone; a long lock of hair had come loose from the swept-up style and straggled down the graceful curve of her neck to the tender hollow of her throat.

She looked so beautiful, utterly vulnerable and so forlorn. He wanted to hold her, cheer her, murmur words of comfort.

"I should talk to Ron Harrington," he said instead, his voice brisk. "Daniel's partner. You say they were close, they built the business together. Daniel must have discussed his plans with him."

"Why?" she asked wearily. "What does any of that matter now?"

"If Daniel was cheated out of the money some recovery may be possible through legal recourse. If he lost everything in a legitimate business deal, you need that information for the IRS, otherwise you face big problems there."

He felt heat radiate from her body as she brushed his arm reaching across him for his empty cup. He could not leave her alone, but had to get her out of the house and into a public place he thought. He was only human. Her raw emotion had unleashed a surprising wellspring of feelings in him. He could not remember another woman stirring him as deeply. He insisted on taking her out to an early lunch. He opened the sunroof and drove leisurely. Who could wallow in despair on such a blue-sky day, awash in golden light, soaring gusts of wind and fast-moving white clouds? They drove to South Point Seafood House, a rustic wooden building at Miami Beach's southern tip.

They climbed the wooden stairs to the second floor, a private place to talk with the best views of sea and sky, and ships navigating the deep-water channel from the port of Miami to the open Atlantic. Diamonds twinkled all around them, reflections of light off the water.

He ordered some chowder, she nibbled at a shrimp appetizer, fretting again about the old pocket watch more than the money.

"If you're absolutely certain it's missing, we can circulate a description or a picture to antique dealers. They must have a trade magazine. A police report should be filed as well. We'll need an estimated value for a tax write-off. Any idea when it was last appraised?" He jotted a reminder in his pocket briefcase and looked up expectantly.

"Always the accountant, aren't you? I jist want to find

it." She paused. "Only family heirloom I ever had was a gold locket, belonged to my grandmother. The burglar took it."

"Such things are nice to have, but they're only things," he said. "A man once told me never to love anything that can't love you back. It was good advice."

"A wise man." She sniffed and lifted her chin. "Did you know your grandparents?"

He shook his head.

"On either side?"

"No, they all died in Hungary."

"Hungary? What were they doing there?"

He laughed. "I was born in Budapest."

She squinted at him curiously.

"My father's name was Imre Huszar. My mother's maiden name was Aranka Korsos. And my name was Janos.

"My parents were freedom fighters. They went through hell over there. Fighting the communists. The people made a brave stand. The cause was noble, but the Russians rolled in tanks, marched in tens of thousands of soldiers. Killed indiscriminately. Murdered young girls, executed teenagers. Went into hospitals and killed patients in their beds. My maternal grandfather was one of them. A communist reign of terror began. We got out through Austria, came to this country in fifty-eight. I was four."

"Janos!" The deeply etched dimples flashed. "How did you git to be Frank Douglas?" Crying had made her voice seductively husky.

"My dad was a determined man—hopelessly in love with America and its promise. Arrived as a penniless immigrant and started out salvaging and reselling junk from trash piles. Used to take me with him on his rounds. His first business was something called Hub Cap City. Then he opened his own small pawn shop. He never would have been successful, not in that business anyway. He refused to buy stolen goods and was a sucker for a sob story. His dream was for us to be the all-American family and *I* was to be the all-American boy. He wanted me to speak only English, so I wouldn't be different from the other kids in school. He applied for citizenship, pored through phone directories, newspapers and history books, picked out our new names and had them legally changed before I was enrolled. I became Franklin D. Douglas, after two of his heroes."

"Roosevelt? And . . . ?"

"General Douglas MacArthur."

"How neat!"

"I'm just lucky his heroes weren't Spike Jones and Fats Domino." He smiled. "He was enthralled by the American dream, the possibilities."

"And then he was killed," she whispered, hand to her mouth. "How horrible."

"More so for my mother than me. She was a lost soul. Hadn't learned much English. Even though she had become a citizen, her world revolved around my father. She was left alone in a strange new country, with no friends or family."

"What did she do?"

He shook his head, staring out at the silver and turquoise sea. "Looked for companionship in neighborhood bars. She died my first year in college."

"And look who you've become," Rory whispered. "I'm so lucky you were here when I needed you." She reached for his hand, then glanced up at the open sky. "Look!" A formation of pelicans glided smoothly toward the shoreline in a perfect V. "An omen," she said. "That's the sort of job I need. I love workin' with birds and animals. I volunteer at the Pelican Harbor Seabird Station, though I haven't done much since Daniel . . . I need to get back into that, it's good for the soul. Maybe I can find me a job in a related field. Lemme see. Zoo, vet, pet store, what else is there . . . ?"

"Dog catcher?"

She wrinkled her nose. "I'd take all the strays home."

"Park ranger?"

"Not baaaad. I would love that! Workin' out in the 'glades, defendin' wildlife. Probably has good benefits and I would get to wear a uniform!"

"Seriously," he said. "I know a lot of people in business downtown, I'm sure I could help you find a good—"

"An office gig?" She hooted in derision. "Pu-leeze, I want the badge, the hat and the airboat—and my own guard gator. I am serious. I'm gonna find out what I need to qualify."

Her resilient spirit, her plans for the future, cheered his heart.

The mail waited at Twin Palms. Tucked among the bills, the supermarket circulars and the Victoria's Secret catalog was an insurance company check for half a million dollars.

"Look at all them pretty zeros!"

"Don't go crazy," he cautioned. "Remember, you're broke. The tax man cometh. Not only will you owe taxes on that money, but you're still facing other major tax consequences."

"How kin anybody have this much money," she demanded, "and still be flat broke?" She pouted. "Kin I just hold it for a while?"

" 'Til we get to the bank." He checked his watch. "No point in losing even a day's interest on that kind of money."

"You're gittin' your twenty-five big ones back first thing," she announced. "Right off the top, plus the bail-out for my car."

"Let's just wait," he said. "No rush."

*   *   *

Ron Harrington had also received his insurance check, he told Rory when she called him at the Miami restaurant.

"No, I'm fine," she said, "just a little sore throat. An accountant is here helping me with Daniel's affairs. He wants to talk to you. I'll put him on."

"Frank Douglas here. I'd like to meet with you, Harrington, about Alexander's financial records."

"Rory didn't tell you?" The voice was tight and cold, with traces of a New York accent. "Danny and I were no longer partners."

"I'm aware of that, but we need your help to clear up some confusion."

"I sent all his papers over to Rory after Danny died." The man sounded harried and distracted. "I've got people waiting for me right now. Nothing I can help you with."

"I only need a few minutes of your time."

"Look, my sympathies are with Rory, her kid and her troubles, but there's nothing—"

"Well, we need your help, otherwise the IRS is gonna be all over us both. I just need twenty minutes, a few simple questions."

Harrington sighed. "How's Monday sound?"

"No window in your schedule before then?"

"Look, I tol' ya, I'm up against it right now, up to my ass in alligators here."

"What time?"

"Five, six o'clock. We're closed Mondays. I come in when it's quiet, to catch up on the paperwork. The place'll be locked up, I'll be in the back office. An alley runs alongside the building, there's a door. Rory can tell you where it is."

"See you then, between five and six. If you can see a way to make it sooner, give me a call."

"Sure. Gotta go, tell Rory I said chin up."

"Sure." He hung up and turned to her. "Is this guy always so warm, friendly and eager to help?"

"Oh, that's just Ron. Always uptight, stressed out. Pressure gets the best of him. Daniel was forever calming him down. That's why they were such good partners."

She kissed his cheek. "Thank you," she said solemnly, "for openin' my eyes and gittin' me on the right track." She clearly believed at last that her husband was, indeed, a suicide. And for the first time, Frank felt dead sure he was not.

CHAPTER
ELEVEN

"You know I don't like this stuff, don't play well with others," Frank protested as he started the car.

Kathleen patted his knee. "This is good for you, for us," she said earnestly. "An important step."

He eased down the driveway, past the splashing fountain, the blazing bougainvillea and the long chains of jade vine adorning the gate with its aquamarine flowers.

"Why do we have a house with no name?" he asked.

"Where on earth do you come up with these ideas?" Kathleen looked amused.

"I'm serious." He grinned at her.

"You mean like Tara? Mount Vernon? Or would you prefer Camp David? Or, wait, I thought our house did have a name. Remember? Back when we were renovating? What was it that you used to call it? Oh, I remember, the Incredible Money-Sucking Pit.''

The support group met in a bright comfortable room at the hospital. Chairs arranged in a circle, a wooden table at the back laden with napkins, paper cups, homemade cookies and a carrot cake brought by members. Bottled water, flavored teas and sodas chilled in a tub of ice.

A cheery young social worker in a sweatsuit doled out name tags, red for recipients, blue for family members.

He felt uncomfortable in this room full of strangers. Most wore bracelets like his. Not all had new hearts; some owed their lives to donated livers, or kidneys, even lungs.

They began with a moment of silence, for those to whom they owed their survival. He had no trouble remembering Rory and her dead husband; he'd been thinking of little else.

As members introduced themselves, they announced what vital organs they had had replaced, as though strangers' components functioning in their bodies had become integral to their identities. He felt embarrassed when they applauded him. What for? Surviving? Becoming one of a growing army of human beings kept alive with body parts from dead people?

A woman in her thirties wore red stretch pants and a T-shirt proclaiming *I Love My New Liver.*

She urged them all to do the same, to educate strangers about the critical shortage of organ donors. Frank shared the sentiment, but passed on the T-shirt.

"Now, any problems?" chirped Audrey, the perky social worker.

Hands shot up. Harry, a kidney recipient, related a long sad litany. His wife of four years, devoted and nurturing throughout his long illness, dialysis and surgery, had grown cold and left him since his recovery. The heartbreak of the pending divorce so affected his work that he lost his job as a radio station engineer. He had to lie about his health history in order to land even a lesser-paying job. Now living alone and depressed in a small apartment, he feared that his negative feelings and self-neglect might cause his new kidney to fail.

His medication could be contributing to his depression, Audrey advised. His dosage might need adjusting, she said, and suggested he see his doctor. Emma, a liver recipient, urged him to listen to self help tapes on positive thinking. Two members zeroed in on the fact that Harry had already been sick when he and his wife met and married. His illness, they said, might have made him attractive to her. When he survived, became healthy and no longer needed her constant attention, her interest waned. They suggested that the relationship was not a healthy one to begin with.

An advertising man, recipient of a kidney donated by his brother, was now on the list for a new pancreas. His doubts and personal problems spilled over, pouring out as he expressed his fears.

The stories went on, and Frank zoned out, a technique perfected during unpleasant medical procedures. They all would be dead without organ transplants, he thought, studying the others. He identified with their endurance. Survivors, all of them, but still strangers. He had never been a joiner. He always felt more comfortable alone or interacting with others one on one.

He had once tried to explain those feelings to Kathleen, describing himself as a "loner." He quickly dropped the word after she correctly pointed out that it was the one always used by former neighbors to describe serial sex killers or mass murderers. Frank genuinely liked people, he just didn't want them around him. He liked socializing, but on his own terms.

Those quirks, Kathleen insisted, were the crippling legacy of his childhood. No denying his early life had left its mark, but he disputed the negative interpretation.

So he didn't play golf, cards, or Trivial Pursuit. The game of life was what counted, and it was dead serious and too short, as he well knew. First he had worked his way through school, then succeeded in business; when his heart failed, survival had become his goal. Even the exercises he had always enjoyed, racquetball and running, were a means to an end, staying in shape, training to win. At this moment he would rather be hot on the trail of Rory's missing money.

Patience, he told himself, and gazed longingly at the door. Had there ever been a successful escape from one of these sessions? How much longer could they go on?

To his surprise, Kathleen suddenly spoke up.

"I would like to hear what you all think," she said, "about the advisability of initiating personal contact with your donors' families."

Audrey reiterated the program's policy of confidentiality, then opened the topic to the floor.

"Not a good thing." Andrew, a liver recipient in his fifties, waggled his index finger for emphasis. "I heard about one several years ago. The mother of the donor turned out to be a very domineering woman who had lost her only son. When she met the fella who received his liver, she wanted to run his life, stick her nose in his business. He and his family finally had to move to get away from her."

Others nodded. "There was a family we were told about," one woman said. "When the recipient visited to thank them, they asked for money, said they were behind in their house payments."

PULSE

"That's wrong," chimed in the woman in the red stretch pants and T-shirt. "It's like putting a price on human life."

"But don't you think," Frank asked, unable to resist, "that it's a small price to pay for life? That if there is a need, and you might be able to help them somehow, that it's the right thing to do?"

"Anonymity is best," the woman said flatly, as the others agreed. "Better to send an unsigned thank-you note through the program."

"Some people find it impossible to accept a gift without reciprocating." The social worker smiled sweetly at Frank. "We all have to learn how to take."

"And what about sleep disorders and psychological problems?" Kathleen tried to sound casual but fooled no one, he was sure.

"Commonly encountered by transplant patients." Audrey nodded.

The room murmured acquiescence. "We've all been through it," a kidney recipient said.

"The trauma of life-threatening illness, the stress, then finally going home. I cried every time I saw a face I knew," Andrew confessed.

"It's the medication, the steroids," said the soft-spoken middle-aged wife of a kidney recipient. "There was a gentle, mild-mannered little man in our first group. He loved his wife dearly, she was an absolute angel, nursed him through everything. Three days after she brought him home from the hospital, he chased her through the house with a butcher knife. She had to call nine one one."

"But," Frank said, "that all ends when the patient is weaned away from the initial high dosage."

"Medically, that should be the case, and that's a matter that every individual should discuss with his or her own physician," Audrey said, "but many patients indicate that psychological upsets often continue beyond that period."

Frank was uncomfortably aware of Kathleen leaning forward in her seat. "In what form?" she asked solemnly.

"Uncharacteristic mood swings, personality changes."

He felt humiliated and conscious of their stares. Kathleen had embarrassed him in front of strangers. "Maybe," he said, "those patients always had problems but were too sick to act on them. Maybe that fellow never really liked his wife."

Negative murmurs swept the room. Hell, he thought, what kind of support group is this?

"What about children?" he asked mildly. "Do recovered recipients often feel shut out of the family unit because their authority and parenting styles have been undermined by a spouse? Isn't it singularly important for parents to maintain a united front, instead of one conspiring with the children, keeping secrets from a spouse now eager to resume his, or her, role as a parent?"

The majority agreed this time.

Kathleen's face was brick red as Audrey cheerfully announced a break for refreshments. His wife avoided him, mingling with others, so Frank joined a small group of recipients at the back of the room. Turning away when two men unbuttoned their shirts to compare scars, he came face-to-face with Audrey.

"You must hear everything," he said, twisting the cap off a chilled bottle of Evian water. "Do you ever meet recipients who believe they experience a spiritual link to the donor or feel as though they have taken on some of the donor's memory or personality?"

"Ah, the metaphysical." She raised a skeptical eyebrow and smiled easily. "Patients do report all sorts of side effects while their medications are still being adjusted."

"But what if it has nothing to do with the medication? What if the mood swings actually are emotions and characteristics transferred from the donor?"

She chuckled. "In other words, if your transplant took place in Paris, you'd wake up with a taste for escargots? Or if your donor was a concert pianist, you'd suddenly play Chopin? I don't think so."

Kathleen remained silent until inside the car. "You know I'm the only full-time parent our girls have had for years," she said, her voice tight.

He turned the key in the ignition.

"First you were always at work, then you were always sick. Now you have the colossal gall to talk about parenting styles and embarrass me in front of all these people."

"I only brought it up," he said, backing the car out, "because you were embarrassing me. You know I don't like airing our private lives with strangers. For a minute there I thought you were going to ask their advice about our sex life."

"Maybe I should have."

"Oh, what's wrong with it?" Me and my big mouth, he thought. Now he'd stepped in it. What the hell did she mean by that? She refused to answer.

"This is what you wanted, Kathleen. You wanted to go to the damn meeting. Happy now?"

Weary as he was, he slept poorly again that night. Not only because they had quarreled, but because he felt a sense of urgency, time was running out. On whom? Or what? What the hell was happening? Someone, something, was there, waving a red flag just beyond his peripheral vision. What the hell was it?

* * *

He felt ready to burst out of the gate like a race horse by Monday afternoon. Tough and businesslike, that's how he would play it with Harrington. Was the man's initial reticence sinister, or was he merely protecting the reputation of a dead friend? He'd know when he looked the man in the eye. Frank had to convince him that Rory and Billy were the ones who needed protection now.

He put his laptop in the trunk, just in case. A light rain fell, snarling rush-hour traffic. A drive that would normally take twenty minutes took thirty-five instead. Frank was still early. A car veered sharply away from the curb and sped off as he approached, leaving a space open in front of the restaurant. A "Closed Mondays" sign hung in the front door, no lights were visible inside.

He pulled up his jacket collar against the chilly rain and turned in to the alley. The acrid smell of rotting vegetables in several Dumpsters made his stomach churn. Lights illuminated the Dumpsters and the side door. He pushed the button, heard the buzzer inside, but no one answered. The gloomy afternoon was about to segue unnoticed into night. He glanced toward the traffic sounds in the street. Standing alone in the alley, he realized, made him a sitting duck for any passing mugger. He hit the buzzer again, two sharp bursts.

The rain fell harder. He had intended to make a crisp, forceful impression. Looking drowned wouldn't do it. He leaned close to the door, a stubborn finger on the button. The only sound from inside was the buzzer's long bleat. A derelict paused at the mouth of the alley to stare at him, matted hair streaming, his baggy trousers secured by a makeshift belt fashioned from a rope. Swell, Frank thought. He grimly avoided the man's eyes, rapped his keys sharply on the metal door, and hit the buzzer again. They had an appointment, goddammit. He would not give up and leave. He glanced back at the derelict, who appeared about to approach him. Frank glared and shook his head. The man shuffled on. Maybe he should go to the front, Frank thought, and peer in through the plate glass windows. He rattled the doorknob in annoyance.

It was unlocked.

How stupid, he thought. He'd been standing in the rain all this time, and Harrington had left the place open for him. The interior was dark and he hesitated. "Harrington!" he called. "Frank Douglas here." He stepped inside and shook the rain off his jacket. He was in a kitchen area, surrounded by grills, walk-in refrigerators and freezers, and huge sinks. Dim light filtered in from the plate glass windows in the front dining room. Tables were stripped of linen, the chairs stacked. A light glowed in the back.

"Harrington?" The man had to be crazy, leaving the door unlocked. Anybody could walk in. He turned and twisted the dead bolt in the steel door behind him.

He called again, making his way toward the light. The only sound was his own breathing. He thought he saw someone and was startled for a moment, but it was only a starched waiter's jacket hanging empty on a clothes rack. The office door stood ajar, spilling light into a storage area stacked with crates.

"Are you there?" he said. The phrase echoed oddly in his head. He had spoken those words before, in a similar setting. Was the memory his, or someone else's? The wooden door creaked as he pushed it open.

Desk drawers were pulled out, the contents scattered. A wall safe gaped open. A man lay on the floor sprawled at a grotesque angle. A small rug had been tossed over his face.

He looked like a pile of crumpled and discarded clothes, except for the blood, exploded bone and brain matter.

"Papa?" Frank's knees buckled as the years fell away. He was eleven again. His briefcase dropped to the floor. "Papa?" Tears blinded him, but he had to see. He inched toward the body as he had done once before, the smell of blood making him tremble. He crouched to lift a corner of the small rug, twisting his head, straining to see the swollen features, the bulging eyes.

They were not his father's. He fell into a sitting position, head between his knees. He had to think, take control. He felt nauseous. He struggled to his feet and managed to make it to the door before he threw up on the wooden floor outside the office. Still gagging, his handkerchief over his mouth, he turned to stare back into the room. He should have come sooner, now it was too late.

He gasped, needed fresh air. Needed to call somebody. He lurched through the darkened restaurant and tried to wrench open the locked door. Hands shaking, he twisted the bolt and swung it open. A bright light from the alley blinded him for a moment. Someone stood there. A tall man, pointing a gun at his chest.

CHAPTER
TWELVE

"Stop right there, hands out to the side, and chill for a minute 'til I sort this out."

"He's dead," Frank gasped.

"Dead? Who's dead?" The young cop's voice changed. "What are you talking about?"

"Inside. The man's dead."

"Okay, put your hands flat against the wall." When he obeyed, the officer holstered the gun and frisked him. "Got any knives or needles on you? Anything I can stick myself on?"

Frank shook his head. The cop had jammed his foot against the inside of his instep, keeping him slightly off balance.

His heart pounded, his mind reeling between images of

what he had just seen and discovering his father the same way, thirty-three years earlier. Then, he had run blindly into the street trying to stop passing cars for help. Brakes had screeched, people had shouted. A policeman had come. But this cop was handcuffing him, speaking rapidly into a little microphone on his lapel, requesting backup "on the double."

A patrol car screeched up to the mouth of the alley moments later, then another. Two cops sprinting toward them amid a jangle of metal and keys. One wore a yellow rain slicker.

"I'm checking for a possible break and this guy comes charging out, ranting about a body in there." He turned to Frank. "Show me." Wasn't that what the cop said outside his father's shop? he thought.

One went around to check the front. Frank led the other two back through the shadowy kitchen, toward the office. His head swam and his legs were numb. What if they found nothing? he wondered. No blood. No body. Like the storm-tossed boat, the stranger lurking in his bedroom, in his driveway. Was Kathleen right? Was he crazy? They had all been just as real. Six feet from the door that stood half open, he stopped and shook his head.

"I can't." His voice broke. The police must have thought him squeamish, but he was apprehensive about what might not be there.

"Stay right there," the first cop said. He stepped sideways and peered cautiously into the office without touching the door. "Oh, Christ. He's right," he said to the other one. He stepped into the room for a moment, then emerged. "The guy's definitely dead." He turned to Frank. "Anybody else in the building?"

Frank shook his head. "I don't know."

The cops drew their guns and flashlights.

The first talked into his lapel again, asking for more backup, homicide, ID and a supervisor.

A homicide detective responded on another frequency. "We've got a forty-five, an apparent thirty-one at the Tree Tavern on Coral Way," the young cop told him. "Homeless guy flags me down, says he thinks there's a B and E in progress. I stop a guy flying out the alley door. Says somebody's dead inside. Victim appears to have multiple gunshot wounds to the head. Four or five casings. Looks like evidence all over the place." He paused to listen on the tiny earpiece.

"No, it looks more like a twenty-nine than a thirty-two, but I haven't notified robbery yet."

He glanced at Frank. "Yeah, he's not going anywhere."

"Who's the dead man?" a black detective asked him. Her inquisitive eyes roved over Frank's clothes, his expensive watch, his silk tie. The alley was roped off now. Bright camera lights and people were gathered on the far side of the yellow tape.

"I said, who's the dead man?"

Frank was startled into attention. "I don't know. Probably Ron Harrington."

"What do you mean, probably?"

"I never met the man."

"Kelly here says you appeared to be extremely upset. You were that worked up about it when you didn't even know the man?"

"My father. You see, my father . . ." After all these years, tears stung his eyes. "My father was murdered."

"Here in the city?"

"Yes," he whispered.

"Whose case is it?"

He paused, remembering. "A Detective Carpenter." He could see the man again, in his mind's eye, burly and balding.

"Carpenter?" She looked disgusted, voice accusing. "We have no Detective Carpenter." She turned impatiently to a patrolman. "Give this guy a seat in your car for safekeeping. We need to talk to him at the station."

"It was thirty-three years ago," Frank explained.

"Hey," said a graying detective, "I knew a Carpenter in homicide, retired 'bout twenty years ago when I was a rookie." He looked curious.

"You own a gun?" the woman asked. Her name was Constance Jewell, she said. Tall and broad-shouldered, she wore blue eye shadow and carefully applied tangerine lipstick. His driver's license was in her hand. The dispatcher had just informed her that Franklin D. Douglas had no outstanding warrants, no history, no record, not even traffic.

"Yes, I do, it's, it's in my car."

"Fired it recently?"

"This week, at the range."

"Lemme ask you a question." She gazed up at him with a heavy-lidded speculative look, as though about to proposition him. "Are you involved in this? Maybe you had a reason. Did you shoot that fellow in there?"

"Hell, no."

"Okay then. What do you think about this? I know it's inconvenient, but how about cooperating with us? We have a test that will pick up nitrates, traces of gunpowder, on your skin, see if you fired a weapon today."

He agreed to submit to a gunshot-residue test and to allow them to examine his gun, and they removed his handcuffs. He signed a waiver. A lawyer would advise against it, he knew, but he had nothing to hide. A technician swabbed his fingers and palms, one by one, then sealed the swabs in

174

vials. They seemed disappointed that his gun was a .38-caliber revolver and not an automatic.

"Call Detective DeVito or Jarrett from Miami Beach P.D. They know me," Frank offered.

"Call over there," Jewell instructed another officer, never taking her eyes off Frank. "See if they're working today and if they're on the air."

Two cameramen were filming as he and a patrolman walked down the alley and he climbed into the backseat of a squad car. The homeless man stared from the crowd.

"Am I under arrest?" Frank asked numbly.

"They just want to talk to you," the officer said reassuringly. He closed the door as a Channel Seven cameraman pressed his lens up to the window.

"So we meet again." DeVito pulled up a chair in a small informal interview room in the fifth-floor homicide office. The door stood open, with Detective Jewell in and out of the room as they talked.

"I've met people who were witnesses in more than one homicide in a week, but they're usually part of our crack-head population or some six-year-old kid who lives in Germ City, at ground zero in a war zone. You don't fit in, Frank. What's the story here? What's goin' on?"

He explained. He was helping Rory, a widow, to straighten out her husband's estate, and made a business appointment with Harrington. He gave them Rory's number to confirm his story. They called it several times, they said, but no one answered.

"Her husband was Harrington's partner."

"And what happened to him?" Jewell asked.

"He committed suicide, shot himself last summer."

The detectives exchanged glances. "So let me get this

straight," DeVito said. "The partner of your second murder this week committed suicide? Lemme ask you, Frank, you got some kinda nickname, like the Angel of Death?"

"You're forgetting his father." Detective Jewell leaned against the doorframe listening.

"Maybe I oughta get my lotto numbers from you," DeVito said.

"Shit happens, huh?" Jewell said.

They sent his gun off to the lab. The dead man, according to the wallet found in his back pocket with fourteen hundred dollars in cash, appeared to be Harrington, pending formal identification by the medical examiner.

Frank's name and the time of their appointment were noted on the dead man's desk calendar. His story checked out, clearly disappointing the cops who had hoped for a quick arrest. Based on Harrington's turned-out side pockets, the rifled drawers and the empty safe, they had called in a robbery detective and were discussing possibilities, known holdup men with violent tendencies.

If they are known robbers, Frank thought, why are they on the street? The helplessness and hopelessness of the entire system seemed overwhelming.

"We need to take your statement," Jewell told him.

"Can I do it tomorrow?" He was worried about Rory. Where was she?

Jewell shook her head. "We've got a dead body, we don't know what's going on. We need everything down on paper tonight."

He made the statement, took his medication, returned by the first cop who had frisked him, and promised to be available should they need to talk to him again. When they took him back to his car outside the restaurant, the reporters were gone and the crowd, aside from a few stragglers, had dispersed. Only the crime-scene technicians remained. Frank watched two emerge from the building. There was something troubling about them that he could not quite recall. He started across the street toward their van, but turned back to his car. He had to find out about Rory.

He arrived at Twin Palms in less than twenty minutes. The rain had stopped and the temperature had dropped. Stars shone, cold and hard in a gunmetal sky.

The station wagon stood in the driveway, lights on in the house.

He wondered how long she had been home and kept his finger on the bell.

"Who is it?" She sounded frightened, but threw open the door at once when she saw who it was.

She was still dressed, in blue jeans and a long-sleeved shirt over a Marlins T-shirt, her hair loose.

"You've been with Ron all this time?" she said brightly.

"Sort of." He rubbed his left wrist where the handcuff had bit into the flesh. "Where were you?"

She looked at him oddly. "Worked all afternoon at the Seabird Station, then picked up Billy from Jill's house. We went out for pizza, came home, and I had a nasty little encounter with something dead." She shuddered.

"What a coincidence." He followed her into the living room. "So did I."

"What?"

"You first."

"Well . . ." She switched off the TV and motioned for him to sit. "I was groping for the front door key in the dark and, wouldn't you know, dropped the mail on the stoop. A buncha magazines and those slick catalogs all scattered. When I slid my hand underneath to pick 'em up, I felt something slimy and dead on the doormat." She grimaced in mock horror. "Poor Billy musta thought I had a heart attack."

"What was it?"

"A great big ol' dead lizard. Tail half chewed off. I'm sure Hootie, the cat, killed it."

"Mine was messier."

Daniel Alexander watched from the mantel as he told her. In the dim light, Frank thought his smile looked malevolent.

"My God." Her hands flew to her throat. "Ron? You're sure?"

"The police seem certain it was him. At first they thought I killed him."

"Good God, no! What did tryin' to help me git you into? I'm so sorry, Frank."

"Now they suspect robbery." He wondered how much to tell her. Where had she really been?

"You think it was the insurance money?"

"He wouldn't keep that kind of cash around, would he?"

"He might have. Showing off. That was Ron. He liked to flash money, to impress people, especially women."

When he asked to see a picture of Ron Harrington, she brought out a scrapbook and turned to a photo of the partners in front of their first Tree Tavern Restaurant. Harrington appeared to be the man he had found. In the photo he and Daniel looked proud and happy. Who could have foreseen that within a few short years both would be dead?

"I'm not sure where to go from here," Frank told her. Harrington was long divorced, according to Rory, and had no widow he could talk to. "Maybe we can contact his lawyer and see if there is anything among his papers that might give us a lead."

It was late; he knew he should leave but needed to talk. He hated mistrusting her. She had seemed genuinely shocked by the murder. His heart went out to this widow, alone, with a young son. Why did he doubt her? He felt like two people with warring emotions. He had to talk to someone.

"Rory," he began, his voice uncertain. "Since the surgery, I feel like I'm never alone. I've had dreams, think I see things, sometimes hear a voice . . . not," he added quickly, "the sort of voices heard by paranoid schizos. But I've thought . . . maybe it was Daniel."

Her expression did not change.

"I suppose you think I'm crazy."

"Shoot no," she said calmly. "Daniel and I talk all the time."

"Well, Christ, Rory. Ask him what he did with the money."

"Well, it's not like precise Q and A, but when I need him most," she said softly, "he's always there. I kin hear him telling me not to worry, that everythin' will be all right, that I kin raise Billy by myself. That I'm strong enough to do what has to be done. He helps keep me going."

She took his hand. "Some a this," she conceded, "could be survivor's guilt. My aftercare counselor says it's only natural. We both feel it because we're alive and he isn't."

He shook his head. "But now," he whispered, his voice hoarse, "I'm sensing something else. Rory, I keep having the strong feeling that Daniel is alive."

"Of course he is." She touched his chest gently. "He's alive in you."

He sighed. No one would understand, or believe him.

"I went to a meeting," he said, leaning back, the intensity drained from his voice, "an organ-recipient support group, with Kathleen. It was a disaster."

"Maybe it wasn't the right kind of a meetin', not the kind of support that you need." She paused. "There are alternatives. You know I've tried different groups myself, trying to get a handle on things, looking for answers, solace or somethin'." She shrugged. "I've found one that might make more sense to you right now."

He sighed, wondering why women always believe that talking, even to total strangers, will solve everything.

"They're into other planes of existence, the struggles of restless spirits in transition." She looked at him expectantly. "Why don't you try one of their lectures?"

He declined. This was no time to become involved with charlatans hawking some out-of-this-world mystical hocus-pocus. Kathleen would be certain he'd gone bonkers.

Rory hugged him at the door and watched him drive away.

Exhausted, he was relieved to make the turn onto the island. It was after two A.M. Kathleen and the girls would be asleep by now. He yawned, eager to join them. He prayed not to dream that night. He rounded the curve, beneath the overhanging royal poinciana, and hit the brakes, startled. The gate stood open, the house ablaze in lights, strange cars in the driveway.

CHAPTER
THIRTEEN

The babble of voices broke off as he entered the foyer.

"Frank!" Kathleen sprang to her feet and rushed toward him. He opened his arms, expecting a hug. But she stopped short, in a confrontational stance. For a moment he thought she would rush him to pound his chest with her fists. The look in her eyes was wild.

"Kath, what's wrong? Are the girls all right?"

"What's wrong?" She turned to the others. "He's asking what's wrong!"

Sue Ann sat at the dining room table, a steno pad in front of her, a pencil in her hand. She looked embarrassed. Shandi sat next to her. A squat greasy-haired stranger wearing a black leather jacket and stubble on his chin was lounging in Frank's favorite armchair, a briefcase at his feet. Phillip Grayson, an attorney he had never liked and whose law firm he no longer dealt with, was on the telephone. He was in his shirtsleeves, tie loosened, as though commanding a war room.

"Never mind," Grayson barked into the phone. "He just walked in the door." He hung up and stared at Frank like the others, waiting.

"What?" He turned his palms to the ceiling. "What's going on?"

There was a squeal, and Casey raced downstairs in her pajamas. "Daddy! Daddy!" She hit him like a football tackle, hugging him around the waist, nearly knocking him off balance. He hadn't realized how weary he was.

Casey, still clinging to him, turned triumphantly to the others. "See, I told you he wasn't in jail!"

Uh-oh, he thought.

"Back upstairs!" Kathleen ordered. "You're supposed to be in bed!"

He quickly kissed Casey, who retreated to the stairs but then sat down halfway up to watch.

"Where have you been?" Kathleen nearly shrieked. "We've been beside ourselves! And you stroll in here like nothing's happened?"

"Hey, sport." Grayson feigned a relieved grin and stepped forward to pump his hand. "Good to see you. You had everybody worried."

The man in the armchair checked his watch and looked cheated. His eyes reminded Frank of the bill collector he had met at Rory's that first day.

Grayson looked cheerfully expectant. "Well, old man." He glanced around the room. "I guess you've got some explaining to do."

"No, you do. What the hell are you doing in my house

at this hour and who's that?" He jerked his head toward the stranger in his chair.

"Sorry," Grayson said smoothly. "This is Billy Marker from E-Z Bail Bonds. He was nice enough to come out at this hour."

"What is all this?"

Kathleen's voice had the brittle metallic edge of too much coffee, too little sleep and high drama. "How do you think I felt when I heard Casey screaming that Daddy was on television—in handcuffs?"

"Oh, good grief. That was all a misunderstanding. I handled it."

"A misunderstanding?" She clasped a hand over her heart, her rings winking in the light. "Are you saying that no one was murdered, that no one is dead, that you weren't thrown in a police car like some common criminal?"

"I don't think 'thrown' is the right word. I had a business meeting with a man. I got there and found him murdered. The police were only following standard procedure since I was the one who found the body. It was a rotten experience, all right? It'd be nice if I got a little warmth and sympathy at home."

"What was the nature of the business you had with the victim?" Grayson asked.

"Nobody has answered my question." Frank pointed at Grayson. "What is he doing in my house?"

"I didn't know where to turn." Kathleen's voice quavered. "I've never experienced anything like this. I called Phil and he came right over. He's been absolutely wonderful."

"We've been calling the jail and the police department, trying to track you down, Frank," Grayson said. "They said you walked outa there hours ago. When you didn't surface and nobody heard anything, we figured the cops were lying.

I was about to try to get a writ. We had Billy here to get you out of jail as soon as possible, if it was a bondable offense."

"Thank you all for the vote of confidence." He nodded to the group. "I've had a long day." He headed for the stairs. He wanted them to go home. He wanted to make amends with Kathleen in private.

"This doesn't sound good," Grayson said solemnly, "with all that's been happening and that incident over on DiLido the other night."

What had she been telling him? Frank stopped at the foot of the stairs, his hand on the banister. "Of course it doesn't sound good. But this is Miami, for God's sake. Things happen."

"Not to people like us," Kathleen shot back.

"This is really embarrassing, Dad. You were on every TV station," Shandi said. "Everybody we know saw it."

"Woulda been nice of you to call home, old man." Grayson shook his head sadly that anyone could be so thoughtless.

Frank fantasized about decking the man right there. Had his daughters not been present, he might have tried it.

"You really oughta come down to my office in the morning."

"You are not my lawyer." He continued up the stairs.

"Where were you?" Kathleen demanded.

"There were things I had to take care of. All right?"

"This all has to do with that Alexander woman, doesn't it?"

"We can discuss that later, Kath."

She exchanged "I told you" glances with Grayson.

Frank looked at his watch. "Thank you all for coming, the bar is closed, the party's over."

Sue Ann was already out the door. Frank stood, arms folded, staring down the others. Grayson picked up his jacket.

Billy the bondsman lurched out of the chair. He detoured on the way to the door and handed Frank his business card. "Just in case," he said.

Grayson draped a protective arm around Kathleen in the foyer. Frank heard him ask if she would be all right and to call him in the morning. She tearfully thanked him.

As the door closed behind the lawyer, Frank turned and climbed the stairs, his arm around Casey's shoulders. "Thanks, punkin," he said. "Sounds like you were the only one around here with her head on straight."

"Did you see the body, Dad?" she asked eagerly.

"Yeah," he said. "I did."

Kathleen never came to bed.

In the dream that woke him, he was struggling to hold a door closed against a storm. On the other side somebody shouted, pleaded and pounded. Above the storm and the cries, he heard something else. His mother weeping.

Realizing he was alone, he padded barefoot down the hall to the guest room. The door was locked. He knocked, then knocked again. "Kath," he called softly, "open the door."

No response from inside. This was the first time in twenty-one years that either of them had chosen to sleep alone. He felt eyes watching. Daisy, curled up outside Casey's room, had raised her head. The dog stared mournfully at him, as though he were a stranger in his own home. He went to his study, called to leave a message for Lucca, then returned to bed. Another woman's erotic embrace haunted his dreams. Together they writhed in passion. He stretched toward the light to see her face, but recoiled. Their naked bodies, wet and slippery, were not drenched in perspiration. It was blood.

*　　*　　*

Sue Ann was at the office bright and early, chipper and cheerful as usual.

"Sorry about last night," he said. "Kathleen shouldn't have bothered you."

"No bother. I'm just glad everything's okay." She paused. "It is, isn't it?"

He assured her it was, as Lucca appeared on the TV monitor entering the outer office.

"Glad to see you, boss." Framed in the doorway, larger than life, he was tanned and tieless, crisp white shirt open at the neck. "Caught your TV debut last night."

Sue Ann stood rooted, listening, so Frank said he was hungry and asked her to pick up some bagels from the shop down on the mall.

"Whatsamatter, boss, you don't trust your secretary?" Lucca asked after her reluctant departure.

Frank shrugged. "Just wanted a little privacy." He told the detective everything that happened at the Tree Tavern and asked his professional opinion.

"Big Red is at the bottom of this somewhere, right?"

"I wanted to talk to him about her finances."

"Figured it was something like that when I heard the name of the restaurant. He was the partner, huh? You are ruled out," he said, slouching in a leather chair, "or soon will be, I presume. I mean you wouldn't give up your gun and submit to a GSR test unless they'd come up clean. Right?" The question in his eyes was real.

"Of course. I just wish"—Frank clenched his fist—"that I'd gotten there sooner."

"Oh sure, you'da walked into it and I'd be sending condolences to your widow. You were lucky. Twice now, huh? Must be nice to lead a charmed life. I wouldn't try for three if I was you. Everybody's luck runs out sometime."

"I want to know what the hell is going on."

"The homeless guy who blew the whistle sounds interesting." Lucca looked thoughtful. "Wonder if he mighta noticed you because he'd seen something else going on there earlier. The detectives are buying robbery, huh? That location is off the beaten path for most of our busy inner-city robbers. And his pockets were turned out, but the killer missed a wallet loaded with cash. No medics had been there, right?"

"No." Frank looked puzzled. "I found him first."

"Sometimes paramedics are so damn efficient," Lucca explained, "that they go through a victim's pockets looking for a name to complete their paperwork. They leave, detectives show up, see turned-out pockets and jump to the conclusion that it's a robbery-homicide when what they've really got is something else.

"You say his hand was in his jacket pocket, and somebody had covered his face with a throw rug. Humph. I'd hafta see the scene photos, but it don't sound like robbery to me."

Frank leaned forward. "What makes you say that?"

"Hand in his pocket sounds casual, not like a guy uptight, in a panic, staring down the muzzle of some holdup man's gun. Sounds more like somebody he was comfortable with took 'im by surprise. And the throw rug. In my experience that's usually somebody who had some kinda relationship with the victim and doesn't like the dead guy looking at 'im. Then there's the overkill. He's shot, what, four, five times in the head? Your typical robber shoots a victim once or twice, then splits, but to shoot somebody in the head that many times . . . Whoever it was was either mad as hell, making an example or determined to be absolutely sure.

"Were the weekend receipts on the premises, or had he made his bank deposit?"

"Don't know, but he may have had a lot of cash around.

Rory said he liked to flash it. And he had just collected a million-dollar insurance payoff on Alexander."

"The plot thickens. Who knew about it?"

"We did, and whoever he told."

"It'll be interesting to see what the city comes up with, if anything."

"There is something I need you to check out."

"Sure, boss. Want me to give the detectives a call?"

"Not on this case."

Lucca's dark eyes flickered in surprise.

"It's Alexander. I want you to check out his death."

"We did that."

"He liquidated everything, every last dime, in the six months or so before he died. I can't trace the money so far. He took it all in cash. We went to his safety deposit box. Nothing. Except that an antique watch, a family heirloom that he prized, is missing. I don't think he's dead."

"Ain't you living proof of that, boss?"

"A gut feeling keeps telling me that somehow, he's alive."

"Then whose heart you got, boss?"

"I don't know."

"Okay, you wanna know? Go ask your buddy, Big Red. Say you're right. Say they fake his death in an insurance scam. Say his partner is in on the deal. Then she's gotta be an accessory. The wife knows, she's gotta be in on it."

"I don't see how she could be."

"How much money is missing?"

"Maybe two, two and a half million. Could be more, no way of knowing how much he had in the ground. The restaurant business is notorious for secreting money, manipulating cash register tapes. Many successful restaurants don't report a lot of their profits to the federal government. The money stays in the ground."

Lucca raised a shaggy eyebrow. "One way or the other, Red's lying. Guy doesn't blow that kinda dough on wine, women and song in less than a year without the little woman getting some clue that everything ain't right.

"If he didn't blow the money, why would people with that kind of dough commit murder and fraud for only a million?"

Sue Ann appeared on the monitor, reentering her office, a paper sack in hand. She must have broken all existing speed records, Frank thought, to and from the bagel shop.

"I want you to take a new hard look into Alexander's death, with an open mind, no preconceived notions. Then you tell me if he's dead or alive."

"She cremated him, huh? That's convenient. At least that's what the suicide note asked for. Did she do it?"

"I'll find out."

"Only way to know for sure, boss, would be to dig up the son of a bitch. You must have better things to do with your time and your money. I thought you were gonna take a little vacation with the wife and kids. Ain't that a better way to spend your money? But if you're really determined to throw it away, I won't argue. I'll take it." Sue Ann rapped at the office door, then opened it.

"Whaddya think about them fish, boss?" Lucca smoothly shifted gears. "Danny boy goes down with a bad knee and it's bye-bye, Super Bowl."

"Didn't know you were a Dolphin fan," Sue Ann said.

She popped back in after Lucca left.

"I'm supposed to remind you about the appointment with your cardiologist at one-thirty."

"What appointment?"

"He's expecting you."

He was not really surprised to find Kathleen in the waiting room outside Dr. Lassiter's office. She coolly kissed his cheek.

The receptionist ushered them in quickly. Frank decided they must have been hastily squeezed in between appointments or that Lassiter had given up lunch to see them. He thought it odd that nobody asked him to disrobe or seemed to be planning any tests.

"I wanted to see you, Frank. We're all concerned."

"About what? My regular checkups have been fine."

"We've invested a lot of time and care in you, Frank. Everybody's pleased about what a success story you've been. So it's crucial to address any problems quickly before they become serious."

"I'm really all right," he said earnestly. The heart was sound, he knew it.

The doctor looked dubious, peered over his spectacles, then glanced at Kathleen. "How have you been sleeping?"

"I don't seem to need a lot since the surgery. My donor must have been a light sleeper," he joked, his grin weak. He was not willing to discuss what happened when he did sleep.

"Your medication can sometimes result in unusual or inappropriate behavior, hyperactivity, even risk taking." Lassiter slowly closed the file folder in front of him. "What we're going to do, Frank, is hospitalize you for a few days, for a total evaluation."

Frank kept his voice calm. "I think it would be a mistake to tinker with my dosages now that I'm doing so well."

The doctor rose, rounded the desk, and gave Frank's shoulder a friendly squeeze. "Well, let us just have a look at you for a few days, maybe have you talk to some people, get things back on an even keel. I've arranged for you to be admitted this afternoon." He smiled reassuringly at Kathleen, who pushed back her chair.

"I've packed a bag for you, toiletries, all the things you'll need," she said brightly. "It's outside with the receptionist. Brought that new novel you've been wanting to read. I got a ride over here. We can drive your car to the hospital and I can take it home."

"I am not going into the hospital," he said flatly. The doctor and Kathleen exchanged glances. "This is ridiculous. I've spent enough time in hospitals. You don't try to fix something that ain't broke. I'm fine. I'm on an even keel."

"The mind is as important as the body, sweetheart."

"I'm fine," Frank said. "I'm not going anywhere."

"I strongly advise it," the doctor said sternly. "Just a few days."

"I refuse to discuss this." He got up and walked out.

"Frank, please," Kathleen called after him. He did not stop.

He was waiting for the elevator when she came trotting down the hall, lugging the bag she had packed. "Wait, Frank," she said, breathless. "I need a ride home. I don't have my car."

He didn't answer on the way down to the lobby. Tampering with his medications could be dangerous, even send him into rejection. She nearly ran to keep pace with his angry stride.

"How could you try to railroad me into the hospital?" he asked as he drove her home.

"It's for your own good," she protested. "I'm worried sick about you, sweetheart. You've become obsessed with this Alexander woman to the point where it's endangering your life and your reputation. Your family has become low priority.

That is totally out of character for you, Frank. Seeking her out was a dreadful, terrible mistake."

"How can you be so selfish?" He suddenly remembered one of the many small apartments he and his mother had shared, the one with rats, and the bathroom in the hall.

"Me?" she yelped indignantly. "Selfish?"

"Yes, you. Remember all the planning I did when I was sick, to ensure the future for you and the girls if I died? I had that luxury. Nobody did that for her. They cut out her husband's heart and gave her back the shell, an empty container. She saved my life, and others who also received his organs. If you remember, I know firsthand what widowhood and poverty can do to a woman. I saw it kill my own mother. I could never rest if that happened to you. Why do you begrudge what little I can do for them? The peace of mind, the redemption it would bring me? Are you that self-absorbed, that selfish?"

He felt her smoldering silence.

"You and the girls mean everything to me," he said, his voice shaky, "and I promise you, once this thing is wrapped up, we can all go away, relax and spend some time together."

"What thing? What the hell is it that you're 'wrapping up'? What has this woman got you into? At this rate we'll *have* to leave town before you're finished. What are you doing to our reputations? If wanting our family to mean more to you than a stranger is selfish, then I confess. I'm guilty. I'm selfish, even though I serve on a number of important civic and community boards. I've worked very hard and I'm about to be appointed to a prestigious position. How do we face people, how can we hold our heads up? You've changed so . . ."

"I've done nothing wrong, Kath. I haven't changed. I'm the same man you married."

"The man I married was a CPA, for God's sake."

Back at the house he took the valise, marched upstairs and angrily unpacked it. Kathleen was on the phone when he went back downstairs. She quickly hung up and disappeared into the kitchen.

He picked it up and hit redial.

It rang twice. "Grayson, Hoberman and Adams. Law offices," a chirpy young voice sang out.

He hung up, stalked out the front door, got in his car and drove out the front gate.

He used his car phone to call the office and check his messages. Sue Ann sounded surprised, caught off guard. "Where are you? How did your doctor's appointment go?"

She knew, he realized. She was in on it.

"Fine," he said casually. "Couldn't be better. I'll be in soon."

Expecting him momentarily would take some fun out of her afternoon of soap operas. Twice since his return to work, he had surprised her glued to a tiny Watchman in her top drawer. Maybe his daughters had been neglected when he worked too hard, then was sick too long. Maybe the family unit had closed seamlessly around them and their mother, excluding him. He could understand, but he felt genuinely betrayed by Sue Ann.

He found himself driving toward Twin Palms. He called. It rang half a dozen times and a strange voice answered.

"Pelican Harbor Seabird Station."

"I must have the wrong number. I was calling Mrs. Alexander."

"Hold on, she's right outside."

She came on the line sounding breathless. She'd had her calls forwarded. "Come on by," she said, and gave him directions.

He had passed the place a thousand times but had never turned off the Seventy-ninth Street Causeway, past the Marine Patrol Station down behind the radio tower on a narrow spit of land jutting out into the water.

She waved as he parked. She wore a simple white blouse and carried a metal bucket. A playful bay breeze ruffled her long hair, the dampness tightening ringlets around her face. The patter of little feet sounded behind her. She was trailed by two pelicans, a cormorant, a tall white egret and two cats followed by a flock of squawking seagulls.

He smiled for the first time that day.

An odd-looking bird staggered after her, attempting to nibble at the hem of her cotton slacks. "What the heck is that?"

"We call him Lurch. Isn't he beautiful? You can see how he got his name by the way he walks. He's a black-bellied whistling tree duck. S'posed to live in Texas, along the Rio Grande. At least that's what all the bird books say. Apparently he can't read.

"Look." An incoming formation of pelicans wheeled in wind drafts over the bay. "They have hors d'oeuvres at the seafood restaurant west a here at two o'clock, that's when the kitchen help tosses out their fish scraps. Then they come here for dinner. We feed the needy and chase away the greedy. The adults can gobble up to four pounds of fish a day."

Some two dozen pelicans, many minus a wing, hobbled about, eying her pail. "We have about thirty-five permanent pedestrians.

"The surgical patients are in that pen over there," she said, "bein' rehabilitated. They'll be released when they're strong enough. Those others . . ." She squinted curiously at him. "How much do you know about pelicans?"

"Only that their beaks can hold more than their bellies can."

She laughed, and led him past a row of pens. The door to one hung open, inside were several nests fashioned from dried twigs. "They're ancient creatures. Haven't changed in forty million years. They mate for life," she said. "Like people. Both parents build the nests, tend the eggs and feed the little ones."

Two fluffy, blue-eyed white chicks stared up greedily from separate nests, their rosy pink beaks opening and closing in anticipation of being fed.

"The babies each need up to a hundred and fifty pounds of fish during the three months they're in the nest. The parents come back with their bellies full and feed the babies by regurgitating. To make 'em do that, the babies snap at the parents, at themselves, at each other and at us. They just bite and bite unmercifully at our ankles, 'Feed me! Feed me! Feed me!' Anything for attention. Anything to make their parents barf. Just like human children, at least mine anyhow."

"Mine too," he sighed. "Can't tell you how often I've wanted to throw up lately."

"They just want you to feed 'em." She smiled engagingly.

He wished it were that easy.

An older woman, a volunteer, emerged from the office to report a distress call. "They've got a pelican in trouble over by the restaurant, in the water, all tangled up in fishhooks and lines."

"Harry and Darlene, who operate the station, are up at Haulover on another rescue," Rory said. "I'll go," she told the woman.

"Maybe I can help," Frank said. "We can take my car."

"Oh, sure," she said. "As if you want that fancy set of wheels smelling like a fish market."

They loaded gloves, a long-handled net, a bucket of fish and what resembled a large cat carrier into her station wagon and drove across the bridge.

A young couple, a busboy and a waitress, were throwing fish fillets off a wooden dock behind a house near the restaurant, trying to keep the injured pelican close to shore. He was handsome, with a long white neck and yellow head, but definitely in trouble. A large metal hook deeply embedded in his wing was connected by leader wire to a treble hook that pinned the sides of his pouch together. Unable to eat, impossible to fly.

"How the hell did he get into that mess?" Frank asked.

"Fishermen," Rory muttered. She stretched out flat on the dock, and extended the net, hoping to scoop up the bird as the couple lured him closer with fish. He was ravenously hungry but unable to swallow because of the hook. Frank crouched beside Rory.

"If we get him," she warned, "whatever you do, don't grab his wing, they snap so easy. Never, never grab a bird by the wing. We don't wanna hurt him worse than he is. Jist hold the carrier and let me handle him." She expertly maneuvered the dip net, but the bird eluded her at the last moment, paddling just out of reach.

Suddenly a huge dark shadow materialized in the blue-green water, two, then three. Everyone gasped, including the people who had gathered to watch.

"What the hell are they?" Frank said.

"Tarpon." She shoved her hair back, still clutching the net. Nearly six feet long, the marauders were in a feeding frenzy, fighting each other for the free fish being tossed to bait the wounded bird. "Well." Rory sat up on the dock. "Ain't this a revolting development."

Frank enjoyed the irony. Sportsmen with expensive gear

hire high-priced professional guides, charter deep-sea fishing boats, cast off before dawn, endure sunburn and seasickness and rarely sight such fish.

The pelican, now more spectator than participant, had paddled even farther away.

Rory slipped off her sandals. "I'll go in after 'im and try to git him back over here so you can net him."

"With these huge fish? Wait a minute."

"They're no problem, that's the problem," she said, indicating the spectators. "Nothing like a pack a strangers rushing you when you're trying to get an injured wild thing into a carrier." She asked the restaurant workers to keep people back and handed Frank the net. "Don't let nobody steal my shoes."

"Wait, you can't . . ."

She dove off the dock in a perfect arc.

The tarpon scattered as she surfaced, bright hair feathered like the sun in blue water around her. She swam with strong strokes, trying to circle out beyond the pelican to shepherd him toward shore. But the bird was a hell of a swimmer and both moved out into the dark blue open bay.

Frank thrust the net toward the wide-eyed young restaurant worker. "Here. If we get him, don't grab his wing. Understand?"

"*Sí*, yes," he said.

Frank peeled off his shirt, kicked off his shoes and hit the water. The chill stunned him for a moment. Then he swam toward them. This was the first time Frank had been in the water since surgery, except for lazy laps in the heated pool at home. But after the initial shock he felt invigorated. Rory watched him, treading water.

"Okay," he called as he got closer. "I'm gonna dive, come up out beyond him and try to steer you both back in. How about those shallows south of the dock? Maybe we can get him ashore there.''

"Let's do it," she sang out.

He swam beneath the bird, who had stopped and was floating, watching Rory. When Frank surfaced and flicked the water from his eyes, he was about fifteen feet from the pelican, facing west, toward the one-story seafood restaurant, a woodsy shore with mangroves and scattered houses against a distant backdrop of silver cityscape, brilliant blue sky and blazing sun. Behind him lay the shimmering bay, Miami Beach's pastel towers and the blue-green Atlantic stretching east to Africa. For a moment he felt that he, too, was part of it all. Earth, water and sky.

He splashed noisily. The bird fluttered in alarm and began to move toward Rory. She angled away, arms open wide in the water, and they slowly steered him toward a shallow, stony beach.

"I'll get 'im. I'll get 'im." Her dripping clothes clung to the sleek curve of her hips and her long legs, the wet cotton of her shirt hugging her breasts as she emerged from the water. She snatched a floating green stalk and thrust it toward the bird. As the creature lunged for it, she grasped his upper beak, held it closed, reached around and drew him close. Her body pressed against a closed wing, the other cradled in her arm, she lifted him from the water.

"Watch the fishhooks! Watch the hooks." Frank summoned the busboy with the carrier and borrowed the boy's pocket knife to slash the wire binding the bird.

Rory released him safely into the box and the door snapped shut. Then she whooped, laughing triumphantly. "We did it!" They collapsed in each other's arms. "We did—"

He cut off her words with a kiss. The air chilled his dripping body, but her mouth was as warm as the sun and salty.

The light glinted like fire off the water, burning the moment forever into his memory.

Her eyes, the color of the water, were startled, the way he felt. They quickly moved apart and picked their way barefoot across the rocky shore, through tangled weeds and stickers to the dock.

Bystanders cheered and applauded. A tourist who watched the rescue wrote a check on the spot, a fifty-dollar donation to the Seabird Station.

They delivered their patient to the station's infirmary. Caged emergency cases and intensive care patients lined the walls: a critically ill gannet, a five-pound white seabird, brought in by a lifeguard; an adult pelican fitted with a plastic orthopedic boot; a baby pelican found wandering in South Beach traffic, feeble and shrunken; and a beautiful cormorant who had flown in on his own, trailing two feet of steel leader wire that protruded from this throat. X rays revealed it was attached to two large hooks embedded in his stomach.

X ray after X ray clipped to lighted boards exposed monofilament line, wire and hooks in birds' bellies.

"Why," Frank asked, scrutinizing them, "can't they make biodegradable line and hooks that stomach acid could dissolve?"

"They could, if they wanted to," Rory said. "You try making somebody listen."

Harry and Darlene, who founded the station, had returned. Frank held the bird on the table as Harry removed the hooks and took a temporary stitch in the wound beneath the wing. He could feel the creature's heartbeat and its downy, snow white neck, not like feathers at all, but as soft and as glossy as a rabbit's fur.

"That's as much as we can do for him now," Harry said.

"The doctor will clean the wound tomorrow, pack it with antibiotics and insert a drain."

Frank left as the couple worked on the pelican rescued at Haulover. A ten-inch gash in its throat was so deep that when it tried to eat, the fish would slip through the wound. Rory walked Frank to his car. Her hair was still damp, her big eyes sweeping the panorama of sky, clouds and water. "All this tends to make you forget everything else, don't it?" she said.

He had come to inquire whether she had cremated her husband. How could he?

"Better get outa those wet clothes," she said, as a Volkswagen pulled up. The driver climbed out, carrying an injured seagull in a shoe box. He was a teacher, he said. The children at his school had lured the bird with bread, then broken its wing with rocks. He and Rory disappeared inside the building.

"Sorry, Daniel," Frank apologized aloud, alone in the car as he drove home. "Sorry for lusting after your wife." How could this happen? Then he decided that it was only natural to be attracted to the wife of his heart, if Daniel was dead, if the heart beating in his chest was really his.

Frank made it into the house unseen, but in the upstairs hall encountered Shandi coming out of her room.

She looked at his trousers, still wet around the crotch and the zipper. "Oh, Daddy." She looked stricken and ran downstairs.

CHAPTER
FOURTEEN

Kathleen kissed him good night, held his hand, and returned to their bed, but he felt no intimacy. He lay beside her, fearing sleep, fearing she would sense his disturbing dreams of another woman. In all of them he knew he had been betrayed, yet still longed for her intimate whispers in the dark, the shiver of her sharp fingernails raking his back. The state of his marriage would improve only when whatever drove him lay at rest at last, when he had exposed the truth and buried the past.

He did not see Rory after what had happened. He thought of her, and Billy, often in the bright light of day. Then the call he awaited finally came. Kathleen looked pale when he said at dinner that he had a meeting. He did not explain, but left them still at the table, pretending not to see their expressions, the looks they exchanged. He could fix that later.

* * *

Lucca wore a red tie and held a thin file folder.

"Surprise!" he announced jauntily. He dropped the folder on Frank's desk and slumped resolutely into a chair, legs stretched out in front of him.

"The guy who blew his brains out with Daniel P. Alexander's gun, in Daniel P. Alexander's house, after putting away some of Daniel P. Alexander's whiskey, waasss—Mister Daniel P. Alexander!"

He swallowed. He had been so sure . . . "I wish I could be as certain."

"Well, if you ain't, you should be. He only happened to fit Daniel P. Alexander's physical description, was wearing his clothes, his wedding ring, and had Daniel P. Alexander's fingerprints! To say nothing of the fact that Mrs. Daniel P. Alexander discovered her dying husband and identified him to the medics and the cops as, guess who?"

He looked Frank straight in the eye. "You've got it. Daniel P. Alexander."

"I don't know . . ." How can it be? he thought.

"Boss, you ain't gettin' my message here. If it walks like a duck and quacks like a duck . . . it's Daniel P. Alexander."

Frank toyed with a silver paperweight in the shape of a windjammer. "But you told me once to never ignore my gut feelings."

Lucca sighed. "He was cremated, by the way. The ME records show he was released to Biscayne Crematorium. Oh, one other thing, you'll see it in my report. Your man Harrington, he was no Boy Scout. Had himself a couple little scrapes with the law back home in Connecticut."

"Like what?" Frank leaned forward, focusing on Lucca's words.

"Strictly white collar. Worthless checks, unauthorized use

of a credit card, failure to pay child support, a little skirmish with the IRS. Nothing serious, never did any hard time."

"So what do we do now?"

"We?" He snorted. "Boss, you are a PI's wet dream. Like I say, you ain't getting my message. Most private investigators live by the golden rule, which is: A case is never closed while the client's still got gold.

"Cops want to wrap a case up fast, PIs are exactly the opposite. They can always find a way to keep an investigation alive. Another interview, another computer check, one more phone call, another day to research old court records, four more hours to write it all up in the wordiest way possible. It all boils down to bucks. Like the Energizer Bunny, they'll keep on going and going and going. They'll milk a case until the cows come home.

"That's them. It ain't me. In all good conscience, I can't keep taking your money for this."

"All I know, Lucca, is that something is not right. Where is the money? Why was his partner murdered? If Daniel Alexander is dead, was he murdered, too? Where the hell is the watch that should be in his safety deposit box?"

"Look, boss, I don't know what kinda shit that broad, Big Red, is feeding you . . ."

"She is not 'Big Red,' this . . . this distorted image you have of her. Stop calling her that, Lucca. You don't even know her."

"And you do?" The detective studied him speculatively.

How could Frank explain to this larger-than-life detective, who demanded proof of everything and believed nothing, that the problem here was not Rory, it was inside him. It was he who wanted answers to questions he was afraid to ask.

"Whatever happened," Frank said wearily. "I don't think she knows."

"She's lying," the detective said derisively. "That's the bottom line."

Once he was like Lucca, Frank thought. Rational, logical, a believer in the bottom line. Who was he now? What did he believe in? "She's gentle," he said, "a good mother, she volunteers to rescue seabirds . . ."

"I don't give a good goddamn if she's Mother Teresa, she's lying, boss. You're letting your emotions get the upper hand. Trust me. Up to now I've done everything you've asked, but I sure as hell can't work out your emotions for you. This is why I don't do domestics."

Lucca got to his feet. "I enjoy working for you, boss. Hope you call me again when you need something. But not on this one. Deal?" They shook hands.

"Is there . . . anyone else you can recommend?"

"Jesus, boss!" Lucca's face screwed up in frustration. "You don't listen! Go talk to Red. You can figure it out for yourself." He turned to leave, then stopped. "Or," he said, his voice kinder, "go see somebody, see your doc, have him write you out a 'script for something that'll help you relax, mellow out. Look, you've got your health back. You've got your family. You've got everything. Enjoy it. That advice is free. I'll bill you for the rest."

When Lucca left, Frank called Rory, he had to see her. She had plans, she said, but invited him along.

Her dress was soft and sweeping in a creamy yellow. Billy was sleeping at his grandmother's. "What is that?" he asked after they were in the car. "Your perfume, what is it?"

She looked embarrassed. "Came outa the little brown bottle in the kitchen. Vanilla. It's related to the orchid," she added.

"I knew it," he told her. "It smells like cookies and ice cream.

"And nobody tests it on baby bunnies' eyes," she said.

They were nearly late and had to hurry. Frank smiled wryly when he saw that these New Age seekers of inner light, spiritual connections and realms of consciousness met in a brightly lit bank building, in an atmosphere of money, mortgages and worldly pursuits. Did the starched-collar bankers detect a scent of incense in the morning?

Estate-planning seminars were apparently conducted in the same room during the day. Rows of metal folding chairs faced a well-lit podium. He overheard snatches of conversation related to self-hypnosis, meditation and dream therapy. Despite his lifelong skepticism, he felt a sense of anticipation, or was that because Rory sat to his right, eyes alight and uplifted, hair pushed back, to reveal the graceful curve of her neck and her high cheekbones?

Lights dimmed at the sound of a Buddhist temple bell. As its resonance lingered, a dark, slightly built man stepped to the podium. Unlike Frank's image of a mystical guru, the man wore a well-cut business suit and hair only slightly longer than his own.

"Listen," he commanded, in a voice rich and mellifluous, "to the sound of serenity. The universe is listening. Things spiritual are spiralling forward exponentially, as rapidly as scientific discoveries. We must be part of the process . . ."

His topic was spirit and self, the eternal links between mind and body. Those gathered were to "hold hands, close your eyes and travel to that infinite well of wisdom deep within yourselves, where the answer to every question lies."

Rory's hand was smooth and tender, not so the bony paw to Frank's left. Arthritic and misshapen, it belonged to a shrunken and watery-eyed old man who smelled of corned beef and pickles.

Frank wondered if somebody would lift their wallets while they all traveled to their inner wells. He sneaked a sidelong peek at Rory, her face serene, her breathing even. Sucking in a deep breath, he tried to retreat into his mind as the speaker urged. Images of Lucca and his unsettling words blocked him, but Frank wrestled the big detective aside to wade more deeply into the rushing river of his consciousness. Shudders rippled down his spine. Something waited along that remote and misty bank. A pleading stranger instead of an inner child. Angry, demanding and full of anguish. Frank shuddered again. Rory gently squeezed his hand and he felt the chair beside him creak as the old man turned to stare. The air-conditioned room had become far too cold, yet perspiration blossomed at Frank's temples and beaded across his forehead.

His eyes flew open as he fought the urge to flee. He needed fresh air. His startled eyes caught those of the lecturer, who paused. "You are always safe within yourself." The man spoke as though directly to him. "Cherish the divine being inside you."

Bullshit, Frank thought. That was no divine being. Something foreign and frightening prowled the deep wilderness of his mind.

"Life is so simple," the lecturer was saying. "It is we who make it complicated. Make me your stepping-stone as you journey to eternal light through the long dark night of the soul."

The meeting ended in polite applause and the room cleared except for a few stragglers. Frank and Rory remained in their seats until everyone else had gone. An older man was carefully packing the temple bell into a straw-filled box as Rory approached the lecturer. They spoke briefly and she signalled Frank to join them. She left them alone near the podium, at a small table stacked with tax work sheets and investment-planning brochures, things he could understand.

"I have a problem," Frank began, surprised that he felt comfortable confiding in this stranger. Probably, he told himself, because the man is crazier than I am. He spoke about his surgery, the intruder, the dreams, the sightings, the night Margery Howe was killed, his own feelings. The assistant who packed the temple bell approached, but the speaker dismissed him with a gesture.

He was nodding as Frank finished. "Cellular memory," he said. "It is not unusual for transplant patients to experience the presence of the donor. Many report spiritual links with those whose organs they received." The man's eyes glowed. "Science has brought us to this new plateau. I spoke earlier of the inexorable connection between mind and body. Perhaps the link now exists between his mind and your body."

"That is not the official line from those in charge of the transplant program," Frank said. "Suggest something like this and they want to change your medication and call in a shrink."

The man smiled, genuinely amused. His teeth shone, white and perfect. "Many in the medical profession are hampered by their practicality, their scientific mind-sets." Leaning forward, he whispered, "This spirit has clearly demonstrated that he is not hostile to you. You must listen to what he is trying to communicate."

"I've tried, but I can't understand. My God, this is all foreign to me. I don't sleep. My mind can't shut down at night. He won't let it."

"Stop resisting. Open yourself to him. Listen to him. In

meditation I have often encountered restless spirits in transition, many are confused, unaware that they are no longer in this life. Some are angry, full of fury, unable or unwilling to ascend to the next phase of existence because of unfinished business. Perhaps the shock of a sudden, unexpected departure from this life . . .''

"They say he committed suicide," Frank said. "Death doesn't come unexpected to a man who puts a gun to his own head."

The speaker shrugged, smiling serenely. "Heed his message. Learn why he is angry, in distress. Do not resist. Surrender, help him, so he can move on and travel toward the light."

"It would explain so much," Frank said, as he drove Rory home. "But it sounds like a bunch of New Age mumbo jumbo."

"It isn't," Rory said softly. "Whether you believe or not, it's all there, in the Bible. The New Testament is full of dreams and visions, extrasensory perception, contacts between this life and the next, miraculous healings and out-of-body travel.

"I know ESP is a fact. Didn't you ever know exactly what somebody was gonna say before they said it? Or that the phone was about to ring and who was calling? Or think of people you haven't seen in years and then cross paths with them the next day? My mama had a vivid dream about her daddy. He lived eight hundred miles away, but she woke up at three A.M. and saw him standing, plain as day, at the foot of her bed. He hadn't even been sick, but she knew right then he was gone. That was the exact time he had died. And when my grandma died in the hospital, her old dog, Tigger, came to the back door and just howled and howled. He'd never done that before. The hospital called twenty minutes later. She was gone. Things like that happen to everybody."

She invited him in, brewed tea and served angel food cake. The tension between them was palpable. That kiss at the water's edge had changed everything. His lips tingled when he looked at her. He knew she felt it too. Billy's absence resonated from the walls.

"I better go." He checked his watch.

"Yes." She smiled and got to her feet. "You'd better."

She hugged him lightly, soft hair brushing his cheek, the way one hugs a friend. He opened the door, turned to say good night and something flared like a spark. They collided spontaneously, like a force of nature. They were insane, possessed.

Her hands were in his hair, his under her skirt. "We can't do this," he said.

"I know." Her eyes were closed.

He opened her dress, exposing her breasts, hoarsely whispering, "Yes, yes."

"This can't happen."

"We won't. We can't."

Her skin felt hot, on fire. Her thighs opened.

His felt an urgency he had never experienced. "Upstairs?"

"No." She hesitated. "We can't."

Of course, he hated himself. The bed she had shared with Daniel. His mouth found her breast. Fondling, cradling them together, his tongue moving back and forth from one taut nipple to the other.

Plump tufted sofa pillows, pushed away, slid to the floor.

He was scarcely aware of Daniel Alexander, watching from the mantel. Their anatomies had been designed for this purpose, a perfect fit. The connection was more than physical, he felt every neuron in his brain, every nerve ending in his body. After decades of lovemaking with only one woman, he intuitively knew exactly how and where to touch this one. The blood-borne chemical hormones did their job and his pulse beat accelerated. If my heart can survive this, he thought, unable to hold back any longer, it will survive anything.

They lay there afterwards like storm-tossed survivors, limp and exhausted. Her fingers stroked his forehead, tracing his brows, his mouth, then the scar on his chest, her hand coming to rest over his still-racing heart. "You're still excited. Is it always like this?"

"It takes my heart longer now to speed up and to slow down." He held her, her head resting on his shoulder. "But no, it's never like this. I didn't plan this," he swore. "I never . . ."

"I know," she said softly.

He drove home picturing her alone in her bed in that house. What had he done? How had an evening focused on the spiritual become so physical? He scrutinized his image in the rearview mirror at a stoplight. How could he look the same? Why did everything he felt now conflict with all he knew about Daniel Alexander?

"I'm surrendering," he said aloud. "I'm not resisting. Tell me what to do. I surrender, I surrender," he repeated, over and over.

Kathleen was in bed when he got home, only pretending to be asleep, he was sure, as he quietly undressed. He felt her eyes, watching him in the dark.

CHAPTER
FIFTEEN

By the time dawn streaked the sky, he knew that Lucca was right about one thing. Rory was the place to start. He waited an hour, then called her from his study. She sounded warm and happy to hear his voice. Hers stirred him, replaying images from the night before, but he kept his tone impersonal and businesslike. They needed to talk. She said she would be there.

Kathleen asked no questions but her smile devastated him. He went to the office, as though to work, reread Lucca's reports, made notes, and listed names. Rummaging in his desk, he found the voice-activated tape recorder he once used to dictate memos between business meetings. He inserted fresh batteries, tested it, and drove to Twin Palms.

Rory obviously expected a hug, but he brushed by her

instead and placed his briefcase on the table. "Okay, let's get to work. Sit down."

"You're like a different man this mornin'." She looked puzzled, her voice still soft and tender. "Have you eaten breakfast?"

"Make some coffee. We'll need it."

When she brought his cup, she kissed the back of his neck, her hair spilling onto his shoulder. Instinctively he reached up to touch it, but caught himself. "Sit down," he said.

He punched the record button on the tape machine. "Tell me exactly what happened, moment by moment, the day Daniel died."

Her eyes widened.

"Tell me everything. Don't leave anything out."

"Why are we doing this?" she whispered.

"To get to the bottom of it. Start at the beginning."

"The bottom of what?" Her voice remained calm, but for a moment there was a wild, unsettled look in her eyes. "My husband committed suicide."

"Something is wrong with that scenario. You said so yourself when we first met."

"But I've accepted it, finally. I don't want to go there again," she pleaded. "We—"

"When we find out what's wrong, what doesn't add up, then we will know where the money went. You want to find the money, don't you? Your future, Billy's."

"Sure." She sounded uncertain, eyes hurt.

"Tell me what happened."

"I came home and he was—"

"No!" he snapped. He regretted saying it more forcefully than he intended, but went on. "Start when you woke up that day. No, no, better yet, the night before. What happened the night before? Was anyone else in the house?"

"No. Just us." She stared at him, long fingers plucking at the tablecloth.

"Go on," he urged. "What happened?"

"Well, he came home earlier than usual. He was happy. Not ecstatic, but happier, more relaxed, than I'd seen him in weeks. He brought chocolate éclairs. Wanted to open a bottle of champagne at dinner. My aftercare counselor said that is often the case with suicides. Once they make the decision to take their lives, they're no longer confused or in pain, they're actually relieved and in good spirits, which, of course, makes what they do more shockin' to those around them.

"I thought he might be in a good mood because he had made a decision about his future, what career path to take. He was laughin' during dinner, tellin' stupid jokes he had heard at the restaurant. Billy acted up and was sent to his room."

"What did he say he was celebrating with the champagne?"

"Nothin'. Us. Sometimes he did that when he was feelin' romantic. It had been a while since he had."

"What next?"

"That's it. We took the éclairs and the rest of the champagne to bed with us." Her voice trailed off, eyes empty, hands folded in her lap, like a schoolgirl at confession.

For an awkward moment, he wondered what to ask next.

"What time did you go to sleep?"

"I don't know," she snapped, rising to her feet. She began to pace a short distance, back and forth. "Late, probably about one-thirty or two."

"Any arguments?"

"No, not at all."

"What time did you get up next morning?"

"Billy woke us about eight-thirty. He was hungry and excited. We were goin' to the Museum of Science to see the dinosaur exhibit. We'd been plannin' it for a long time. He had saved his allowance for one a them dinosaur model kits. Then we were goin' on down to Dadeland to shop for school clothes. He needed sneakers. Then we were gonna see a two-o'clock Disney movie at the Dadeland theater.

"I asked Daniel if he wanted to come with us, or meet us later for the movie, but he said he was tired, gonna relax for a while, then run some errands and work on a few projects around the house."

"What else happened before you left?"

"Nothing."

"Did you eat breakfast? Did you say good-bye?"

"Of course."

"Tell me."

"Billy wanted pancakes," she said, sitting down again, "but there wasn't time. We had to run or we'd never make the movie. We all had cereal and bananas. Then we took off."

"Where was Daniel?"

"Right in there." She cocked her head toward the kitchen. "Readin' the newspaper. He came to the front door, I saw him and waved as we pulled out of the driveway."

"What were you wearing?"

She sighed, slumped in her chair, hand to her forehead. "A cotton sundress, a flower print, and sandals. Took sweaters in the car 'cuz it's always so cold in the movies."

"What was Daniel wearing?"

"Ol' jeans he'd pulled on to come downstairs, and a T-shirt."

"What was the last thing you said to each other?"

"What?" She looked startled.

"As you left. What did you say?"

Her voice quavered as he checked the tape to be sure it was rolling.

"I asked him to take some things out of the washer when it stopped and put 'em in the dryer. He said, 'Sure. Have fun.' That was it. We never talked again."

"What happened next?"

"We saw the dinosaur exhibit. Stayed longer than we thought. Then drove down to Dadeland. Traffic was horrible, parkin' god-awful once we finally got there. Billy and I had this big discussion in the shoe store about why an eight-year-old boy did not need one-hundred-dollar Michael Jordan tennis shoes. I called the house once to git Daniel's thoughts on the shoes and to make sure he put the clothes in the dryer, but there was no answer. I thought he was outside or maybe runnin' his errands."

"What movie did you see?"

"We didn't. By the time we were done shoppin', no way could we make it to the movie theater in time. I promised Billy we'd go the next day. We stopped for French fries at McDonald's and came home." She swallowed.

"So you got home earlier than you expected?"

"By two hours or so." She raised her eyes to his. "If only I'da come back even sooner, I could have stopped him. His car looked like it was in the same place that it was that mornin'. We brought the packages in from the car. I didn't see him around. I called out to him, but he didn't answer. His coffee cup was still sittin' on the table. When I checked the utility room the clothes were still in the washer. I was irritated by that and called out to him again."

"Was the front door locked when you came in?"

"I used the key. I guess I would have noticed if it wasn't."

"Was the alarm on?"

"No, we only used it at night when we went to bed, or if we all went out. With Billy and the cat in and out every five minutes, that kitchen door is always openin' and closin', so we didn't turn it on during the day."

"What happened next?"

She looked past him out the window. "I called him again . . ." Her voice broke. "And he didn't answer. I picked up some of the bags, Billy's new shirts and trousers, and went upstairs. The door to Daniel's study was closed. The house was quiet. Billy was down in the kitchen working on the dinosaur kit. I went to Billy's room and started to put his things away, but then I started gettin' curious about where Daniel was and went down the hall to the study. I opened the door."

"Show me."

She shook her head.

"It's important."

"Why are you doin' this to me?" she asked plaintively. "After what—"

"I have to know everything." His words were demanding, his voice even, but his mind reeled with excitement, as though the elusive scent of truth was finally in the air, at last.

He followed her slowly up the stairs. She was breathing heavily like someone in pain. "I opened the door." She turned to him, eyes pleading.

"Do it." He ignored a sudden need to touch her, to comfort her.

Sniffling, she turned the knob. "The blinds were drawn. I saw the blood first. It was everywhere. I screamed and ran to him, then I saw the gun. I think I screamed again. He was barely breathing, but I felt a pulse. I would have fainted, 'cept I heard Billy, pounding up the stairs hollering, 'Mommy! Mommy!'"

"What did you do?" His voice was a whisper.

"I came out, slammed the door behind me." She closed the door and turned back toward the stairs. "Caught Billy there, at the landing. I was hysterical, I half carried, half dragged him downstairs to the phone. I dialed nine-one-one. I couldn't let go of Billy for a second for fear he'd run upstairs. He was already struggling with me, hollerin', 'What's the matter! Where's my Daddy!'

"When he heard me say, 'Send an ambulance, my husband's been shot and I think he's dying,' he started screamin' and kickin' even worse.

"I called Jill, the mother you met here that day, the car-pool mommy. I was gonna drag Billy to the neighbors across the street, but we hardly know those people, an older couple, and I didn't want him with strangers. Jill got here in two minutes, brought her next-door neighbor. She may have a big mouth and her idea of a hot meal is Pop-Tarts, but when you need 'er, she's there." She hugged her arms as though the memories had chilled her body. "They took Billy and was pullin' away just as the rescue squad drove up. Thank God for small favors.

"I was so relieved to see 'em. As bad as it looked. I still thought they could save him."

"How bad did it look?"

"What do you mean?"

"What did Daniel look like?"

Her body shrank like a wild creature about to run. He caught her by the shoulders. "Tell me, please."

"I don't care about the money! Leave me alone!" She wrenched away, directing her fury toward the empty study. "Daniel, you son of a bitch! How dare you do this to me! You've ruined my life!"

"Tell me."

"Blood was everywhere," she sobbed. "He was drenched in it. Some caked, some dried, some fresh and oozing out with other stuff. His face was distorted, huge and swollen. Discolored. All black, purple and puffy around his eyes. The bullet went in one side and came out his face. It was like it wasn't even him anymore.

"But they were radioin' and on the phone and workin' on him. I thought maybe it was 'cuz they could save him. They made me wait outside the room. Then they said the rescue copter was coming in to airlift him to the trauma center. Next time I saw Daniel they had his entire body in one of those blood pressure suits with a big bandage around his head. The helicopter landed on that vacant property down at the corner. The treetops looked like a hurricane was stirring 'em up. They stopped traffic. Strangers were watchin'." She paused to blow her nose into a tissue she had fished from her pocket. "I'll never forget that day. I couldn't go with 'em. I was gonna drive, but a police officer took me."

The recorder clicked off. Frank flipped the tape and they went downstairs to finish. She sat, hands again clasped in her lap, her expression unutterably sad.

"They told me later that Daniel was being kept alive by artificial means. I kept askin' if there was even a ten percent chance that he might make it. They said no chance, his brain had been destroyed. He was brain-dead."

"Did you see him in the hospital?"

"Oh yes, I sat with him for the longest time, talkin' to him. Beggin' him not to die. But I finally believed the doctors. You can jump-start a heart, but you can't jump-start a brain. I woulda brought Billy in to say good-bye, but there was nobody to say good-bye to. Nothing but tubes and bandages and machines. I didn't want Billy to see his dad that way." She blew her nose.

"They couldn't take his eyes," she said softly. Palm fronds shimmied in a soft breeze outside the window. "They'd been destroyed. But they were searchin' the national registry for organ recipients." Her eyes met his for a moment and her voice dropped. "For you."

He thought of himself at that time, in his hospital bed propped up by pillows, about to drown in his own unpumped blood, gasping for air, his life and hope nearly gone.

"I never saw the note he left on his computer screen until later, with the detectives."

"What was Daniel wearing when you found him?"

She gave him a reproachful look. "A sport shirt and a pair of navy slacks."

"So he changed after you left. What else was he wearing?"

"Shoes, socks, his wedding band. What does any of it matter?"

"Where are the clothes he was wearing when it happened?"

"Gone. Ruined, bloodstained. They cut them off him. They did give me his weddin' ring."

"And Daniel?"

"Cremated, as he asked in the suicide note . . ."

"Convenient," he muttered. This was not right. Somehow he knew it wasn't. She had to know that, too.

"What are you saying?" She stared in disbelief.

"You're not telling me something, Rory. What are you hiding?"

"You're right." She sobbed again, shoulders shaking.

He resisted touching her. "Tell me." He stood over her chair, his voice harsh. "Say it."

"We weren't . . . Daniel wasn't . . . We weren't the marriage made in heaven. It wasn't perfect."

"What do you mean?"

"Things were real rough between us, beginnin' when Billy was about four. Daniel worked nights, was never home except to sleep. He'd go out with his friends after the restaurant closed. I wanted more children, I wanted to play house. I'd wake up at four, five A.M., and he wouldn't be there. The business was hard. He'd be hyper and busy all evenin', the people around him all out for a good time. He said it was hard for him to wind down just like that, to go home and go to bed. We had a big blowup. I thought we weren't gonna make it. Went to counselin' last year for six months. Part of the agreement was for him to git outa the restaurant business and into somethin' more normal so we could have a family life. That's what we were doin'. I thought it was workin' out. I thought he was happy. I had no idea. I'm so mad at him for not talkin' about it, but I'm mad at myself for not seein' it and doing more.

"If only I'd come back sooner. I could have stopped him. I could have been there, offered more help. If only I had, he wouldn't be gone now."

That's it? Frank thought. There had to be more. "What else didn't you tell me? What else are you lying about?"

"Nothing."

"I'm sorry I put you through this." He sighed and sat silently for a moment, his head in his hands. "Rory, Daniel's death, the missing money, Harrington's murder, they're connected, all parts of a puzzle, and sooner or later I'll find the piece that puts it all together."

"But what if there's nothin'? What if Daniel wasn't happy, lost the money, couldn't go on and that's all there is? I can finally accept it now. Why can't you?"

"I know there's more. Trust me."

He left her standing at the door, pale and exhausted. They did not touch.

The rescue squad dispatched to Twin Palms the day Daniel Alexander was shot had come out of Station Eight on Oak Avenue. Frank called Station Eight and asked for Lieutenant Sheldon, whose name was listed on Lucca's report.

"I'm a friend of the family, helping out," Frank explained when Sheldon came to the phone. "I'm in the neighborhood. Could I just stop by the station for a minute?"

"You a lawyer or working for one?"

"No, just a friend."

"Sure, if we don't have a call before you get here."

Another member of the rescue team that day was also on duty when Frank arrived. The third was on vacation. They talked in the immaculate kitchen area where a burly fire-fighter stirred potatoes and carrots into a huge Dutch oven simmering on the stove. Whatever was already in the pot smelled great to Frank.

"Beef stew," the lieutenant said. "We're getting ready for lunch." The sounds of men playing pool came from another room.

"The guy had no chance," the lieutenant said candidly, when Frank asked about Daniel Alexander. "But we work closely with the organ procurement team. He looked to be a prime candidate, so we notified the hospital, put on a com-pression bandage, the suit, did all we could to keep him going. The family should have peace of mind. It's not like he was writhing in pain or coulda made it if he'd been found sooner. I mean, the guy was leaking brain matter."

"So he never spoke, never regained consciousness?"

"No way. He was a dead man. Never knew a thing or had a thought after he pulled that trigger."

They remembered little about the scene, the house, or even Rory, other than to recall that next of kin had been present.

"All I 'member is it was upstairs," the other firefighter said vaguely, "and I rode with him on Air Rescue."

"We see so many," the lieutenant explained. "But even if it had just happened this morning, we probably couldn't tell you what the inside of the house looked like, what anybody was wearing, that sorta thing. We get so focused, it's like tunnel vision. All we see is the victim. It's really intense."

"We went into an apartment once," offered the other firefighter, "we're supposed to wait 'til the cops arrive. But some woman was screaming that her pregnant sister had been stabbed, so we go charging in, start working on the stabbing victim and never even notice the guy crouched in the corner still holding the knife, 'til the cops show up and shoot 'im. At first we thought they were shooting at us."

Frank experienced an unexpected surge of emotion when he shook their hands. He owed them an immense debt. They were unsung members of the far-reaching team that had saved his life, as unaware of him as he had been of them.

"Thanks," he said simply, "for everything you do."

The morgue was the next stop, an imposing fortresslike structure, six blocks long, at One Bob Hope Road. Only in Miami, he thought ruefully, would the last stop on the way to the cemetery dominate a short street named for a comedian.

The sunny, carpeted reception area revealed no hint of what lay elsewhere in the building, in its walk-in coolers, surgical suites and laboratories. Cherubic and friendly, with wispy white hair atop a round pink face, Dr. Vernon Duffy was the medical examiner who had handled the case.

"This fellow was probably intoxicated at the time he shot

himself." The doctor perused his own notes. "He still had traces of alcohol in his system when we got him. He'd had plenty of time to metabolize it. Let's see, he lay there wounded for X hours, perhaps two or three, before being found. Then he lasted for Y hours in the hospital. Let's see, about fifteen. So X plus Y equals seventeen, eighteen hours." He calculated rapidly. "His blood alcohol was probably up to about a point three when he shot himself. Not unusual. Suicides will often use alcohol to bolster their courage."

"There's been some concern on the part of the family," Frank lied, again assuming the role of helpful friend, "that perhaps he was not a suicide, or perhaps it wasn't even Alexander."

The doctor lifted an eyebrow. "What do they base that on?"

"Physical appearance . . . Apparently the dead man's face was extremely distorted and swollen."

The doctor consulted his file. "Yes. This fellow's aim was a bit high, which is why death wasn't instantaneous." He pushed some photos across the table.

The face in these pictures did not resemble a human being, much less the handsome man he had seen in photographs. Frank closed his eyes and gripped the table edge for a moment to hold himself steady, as something inside him howled in painful recognition. He fought back nausea.

"The bullet angled up from above the right ear toward the front," the doctor was saying, "involved the frontal lobes and exited the left side of the face. En route it fractured the orbital plates." He raised his eyes up over the half glasses he used for reading. "Those are the thin bones above the eye sockets. Those fractures caused severe bleeding around the eyes and the eyelids. The swelling of his brain had impaired respiration to the point that he was near death when he was discovered." The doctor paused, studying him. "Are you all right?"

"Yes." Frank averted his eyes from the photos. "I can see that he was unrecognizable."

"That's from swelling and edema."

"But he was positively identified?"

"Let me see here, yes." He focused on another paper in the file. "Through fingerprints. The state of Florida had them on record. Mister Alexander had a concealed-weapons permit, which requires printing."

"What about dental records?"

"No," he said. "We always do fingerprints. But he came in here from the hospital, was taken there from his home. The police had filled out a report and the detectives were satisfied that this was a noncontroversial case. A further check involving dental records wasn't necessary."

It was too late in the day to go to police headquarters, he thought, so Frank returned to his office. As he walked down the hall, the door opened and Kathleen stepped out. They were both startled.

"There you are." She kissed his cheek. "Sue Ann," she called. "Look who I found out in the hall."

He asked what she was up to.

"I was shopping in the neighborhood," Kathleen explained, babbling, "and I thought I'd come by and take you to lunch."

He checked his watch. "It's four o'clock."

"A late lunch," she said sheepishly. "A very late lunch. Just wanted to spend some time together."

She left in a hurry, for a woman eager to spend some time with him. He wondered what that had been about, but had little time to dwell on it. He wanted to review his notes and tapes, had calls to make and messages to return before five. He opened his desk drawer and saw his checkbook was missing.

"Sue Ann?" She appeared in the doorway. "Where's my checkbook?"

"Out here, I was balancing it and putting the numbers together for your quarterly taxes." She marched in to return the large leather-bound book.

"Thanks." He watched her leave the room.

He leafed through it page by page. No blank checks missing. What was going on? She normally handled the task on the first and the fifteenth. This was neither.

He pushed the intercom. "Sue Ann, what did Kathleen want?"

There was a pause. "You," she chirped. "Guess she misses ya."

CHAPTER
SIXTEEN

Frank would be too obvious in the Mercedes, so he asked Kathleen to swap cars for the day. She was groggy, still unaccustomed to his new routine of rising before dawn.

"Why?" she mumbled.

"I'd just like to drive yours."

"But why? You never wanted to before." She punched her pillow and rolled over heavily, but did not close her eyes.

"I thought you liked the Mercedes. I'll leave you the keys."

"Some other time, Frank."

"No, I want to take your car today."

She groaned, then sat up, exasperated. "Okay, but I've got to get my stuff out of it." She padded down the stairs, protesting all the way.

He was at the front door ready to go when she returned, squinting against the rising sun. Birds sang in the gumbo-limbo tree outside and the morning smelled fresh and promising.

She carried a sheaf of papers, an accordion folder and a slim leather briefcase.

"What have you got there?"

"Files from the museum board and the Arts League Council. Some proposals for the Art in Public Places committee." She turned away and headed upstairs with them.

He stood waiting for a moment. She had made no move to kiss him good-bye. " 'Bye," he said to the back of her blue bathrobe as she reached the head of the stairs, then disappeared down the hall. He wanted to go after her. What was he doing? What has to be done, he told himself.

He wore neutral colors, a different pair of sunglasses, a distinctive style with mirrored lenses, and took along a newspaper, a legal pad on a clipboard and an old Marlins baseball cap. She was not likely to spot him in another car.

He was early. Rory's station wagon still stood in the driveway. He parked down the street, across from the vacant lot where Air Rescue had landed. He lowered the windows a few inches, yanked his baseball cap down over his face, hunched down in the seat and watched.

Normally the warmth from the sun would have made him drowsy. But he felt alert, on edge. He had never spied on a woman before.

Rory emerged at 7:10 A.M. She wore some sort of oversized T-shirt that skimmed her hips. Her long legs were bare. He held his breath, fighting the voyeuristic pleasure that made him hard as she bent to pick up her morning newspaper. She tossed her hair back, slipped the paper out of its plastic sheath and scanned the headlines on the way back inside.

Twenty minutes later, she and Billy emerged. He was dressed for school. She wore white pants and a striped top. She looked model-slim, too thin. He thought of his mother and wondered if this new widow was eating properly. Mother and son were finally in the car. She backed down the driveway. The brake lights flashed. Some discussion. Billy bounded out again. So did she, leaving her door open. Back into the house. He re-emerged carrying his lunch box. She did too, hurrying him, then stopped, scooped up a kitten that had escaped in the confusion and carried it back into the house.

Finally both were back in the car; it bounced out onto the street and drove right by him. He saw her head turn toward the vacant lot across the street. She never even glanced his way. He waited five minutes to be sure they wouldn't be back for some other forgotten item, then climbed out of the car wearing the cap, carrying the clipboard and a pen.

He knocked at the door directly across from Twin Palms, a small, well-shaded house with a circular drive.

"Sorry to bother you so early." He smiled at the tiny, dark-eyed woman. The couple was elderly. The husband used a cane and sat in his bathrobe watching the *Today Show*. Invited in, Frank was surprised at how freely strangers speak to anyone carrying a clipboard.

"She's a nice girl and they had a cute little boy," the woman said. "Busy all the time. Wish you could bottle that energy. You should see that young fella pedal his bicycle up and down here. Had to tell him once not to speed through our driveway on it."

"We didn't know anything happened until Pearl heard the helicopter," the man said, both hands on the cane between his knees. "Never even heard the rescue truck."

"It happened in the heat of the summer," the woman

added. "We had everything closed up, with the air-conditioning and the TV on. Didn't see or hear a thing until the commotion with the helicopter. Poor girl. Never had anything like that here before."

"Musta had his reasons," the old man said.

He heard the same story at every house on the block. Windows closed to the heat, nobody heard the shot, few heard the sirens. All at home heard the chopper. Nobody saw anything unusual prior to that. No one recalled seeing Daniel Alexander that day, until he was rolled down the street, his head bandaged and medics holding his IV bags.

Stubbornly, Frank refused to give up. He thought Rory intended to work at Pelican Harbor after car-pooling the kids. What if she had changed her mind? He called her house from Kathleen's Catera.

"Pelican Harbor Seabird Station," someone answered. He hung up. She had forwarded her calls.

He walked around the block to try the house that backed up to Twin Palms. An overweight man in his forties answered in a T-shirt and shorts. Unshaven, he wore a neck brace and an open shoe on one foot.

"One of your neighbors died last summer and I'm just checking out the circumstances."

The man's eyes looked knowing behind thick glasses. "Insurance, huh? I'm dealing with that myself. Come on in. What company?"

Frank gave the name of his own insurance company.

"You talking about my backyard neighbor, the fellow lived right behind me?" He sat down and gingerly raised one foot onto a small stool.

"That's right."

"The guy had some wife there. She's really something."

He smirked. "Was out there just the other night climbing up into her kid's tree house."

Frank glanced toward the rear of the house before taking a seat. A wide picture window revealed the yard with just a chain-link fence separating it from Rory's. The large fixed window was flanked by two smaller ones that cranked open. All provided an excellent view of the back of Rory's house, her windows and the tree house. A pair of binoculars sat on an end table next to an armchair. Frank was not the only one spying on Rory.

"Her name's Rory, right?" said the man, as though reading his mind. "I didn't know it until I saw the story in the newspaper, about her husband killing himself. She's really something," he said again.

Frank wondered how much of Rory the man had seen. A stack of girlie magazines sat on the floor beside the armchair.

"Been noticing my neighbors a lot more in the last year and a half. Been outta work since I got into a wreck a year ago last April. Got rear-ended by a semi at the big curve on the Palmetto. Busted my foot, hurt my neck and spine. Lucky to be alive. You don't know how that feels. It's been hell trying to get the insurance company to settle for a decent amount. Looks like we might have to take it to trial."

"So I guess you were home that day, housebound."

"Yup. Heard the whole thing. Except the newspaper got it all wrong."

"Oh?"

"Said she was out, came home and found him. She was there when it happened."

Frank couldn't breathe for a moment. "How do you know that?" he asked.

"Heard the shot. Didn't know that's what it was at the

time, but I heard it. Heard her voice, just before. She was there."

"It was pretty hot back in July." He thought his heart would stop beating. "Didn't you have the windows closed? The AC running?"

"I always keep them two back windows open, even in the summer." He shrugged sheepishly. "I like to hear what's going on in the neighborhood."

Rory, Rory, Rory, Frank thought, a lump forming in his throat. Lucca was right. She had to be the dangerous woman in his dreams. She was what his heart had been trying to warn him about.

"She come out on the back porch a coupla minutes after it happened, went in the garage."

"You saw her? What was she wearing?"

"Well, I couldn't tell you that. Had a cast on my foot at the time and I was sitting over there at the dining room table, didn't have a view. Couldn't move fast enough to get a decent look. But I heard her voice, she come out the back door, slammed it and went in the garage. Just caught a glimpse."

"How can you be sure it was her?"

"Can't miss that red hair. And she's the only woman lives there. I've heard the mother's voice, the old lady. Raspy, she visits a lot. Must be his mother. Cries every time she comes now. Wasn't her. The way I figure it, the kid is out, her ol' man comes on to her, wants some, she ways no. They argue. He can't take the rejection anymore and boom!"

"They fight a lot?"

"Had a coupla good ones a few years ago. Saw him haul off and smack her once. They been pretty quiet lately, until this."

"The reports state that she and her son left the house

about nine-thirty that morning, came back a little after two and found him shot."

He shook his head. "She was back about noon. I heard their voices. Thought maybe they were fighting again, just before the shot."

Frank felt sick to his stomach. "You must be mistaken about the time."

"No way. No doubt about it. Reason I was at the table, I was eating lunch. Put a coupla burgers from McDonald's in the microwave. I always eat lunch watching the news at noon, Channel Seven. I'm eating lunch, watching the news, hear the voices, hear the bang, then she came out. Don't know what she did then, can't see their driveway from here, that's for sure. Couple hours later I hear her call his name, then her and the kid screaming and hollering, then here comes the sirens, then the whirlybird. That's how it was."

"Did you tell that to the police?"

"They didn't ask. Don't ask, don't tell. All it gets you is a lotta trouble. I think maybe she's got a new boyfriend now. Had something going on the other night, but they stayed pretty much in the front of the house." He gazed fondly out the window into the green adjoining yards. "I'd been wondering if the widow was lonely these nights. They say them redheads are hot."

Frank resisted the urge to confront her at the Seabird Station. What would it accomplish? She had lied all along, was good at it and had a reason. She would only continue to lie. He had believed her. The man he had just spoken to had obviously crossed the line between nosy neighbor and Peeping Tom, maybe worse. His glasses were thick, but his hearing was not impaired. His words had the ring of truth.

He had been acting too quickly, without thinking things

out, letting emotions drive him. What had Kathleen said? Totally out of character, that was it. He had to control whatever drove him and take command, as he had done with Rory the day before. He would follow through, precisely, methodically, the way he had always proceeded in the past, until the pieces fit. The bottom line was waiting, out there somewhere.

Miami police headquarters, a redbrick stronghold, lies in the heart of Overtown, the city's most violent neighborhood. Frank had been there before, in darkness, in the company of detectives who rolled their steel cocoon unobstructed into their own private steel-gated parking garage at the rear. Their coded key cards provided instant passage through locked security doors. A private back elevator had whisked them up to homicide. Without a cop, the building was an impenetrable fortress. Now he was an outsider, a citizen seeking answers. The public parking lot was full. Frank finally found a spot on the street and walked into the front entrance in broad daylight.

Signs instructed him to place his briefcase on a conveyor belt and remove his keys from his pocket to pass through the metal detector.

He remembered the old station, a squat two-story structure still standing on Eleventh Street, abandoned now except for the ghosts of past pain and anguish in this violent and changing city. He had gone there with his mother, after his father's death. Hailed as state of the art twenty years ago, this "new" station already appeared run-down and deteriorated. The lobby lighting was poor, the floor scuffed and shabby. Was there a city left, he wondered, in which the most-used public building was still a library or a concert hall? Not in Miami, perhaps not in this country, not in this lifetime.

A disinterested cop at the front desk directed him to the

Public Information Office to fill out interview request forms. The clerk there only half listened, shaking her head. Request forms are issued only to members of the media. Shuffled back to the front desk, he persevered, amid a growing sense of horror that these were the people responsible for protecting him and his neighbors. He eventually learned that to talk to Officer Frank Valdez, to Homicide Detective Joseph Thomas, and to ID Tech Denise Watson, he must first obtain the permission of each of their supervisors. He finally persuaded the front desk officer, who seemed pained at any request, to read him their phone numbers off a reference card he had obviously been issued for that purpose.

Frank stood at the battered public telephone in the lobby, aware that the party who left him on hold was nearby, somewhere within shouting distance, on the far side of a wall or door. How did Lucca always manage to slice through the bureaucratic bullshit? The man was worth every dime. The commander of the ID bureau was out of the building, but through persistence, Frank finally reached the other two.

"Oh, yeah, I remember that one," said Valdez, who had been the first policeman at the scene. They sat in an office in patrol. "Good-looking redhead, right? Yeah. She boo-hooed all the way to the hospital."

He recounted the details. "You could see the guy was as good as gone, but they were trying to preserve the organs. I don't know if they did."

"They did," Frank murmured.

"Or if she would be inclined to give permission. A lot of 'em don't, ya know. Some people don't believe in it. She was pretty out of it. Kept asking if I thought he was gonna make it. What am I gonna say?" He shrugged. "I told her he was in good hands. I needed to get all the info for my report before letting her go ballistic on me. You know, some of 'em really lose it."

Valdez remembered little more than what he had written in his report. Rory had seemed credible to him. He had never been called to that address before, though he had patrolled the zone for nearly a year. "I woulda remembered her," he said emphatically. "Yeah, that was a nice neighborhood." He sounded nostalgic. "Not much happening there. Where I am now, in Northside, we've got nothing but robberies, shootings, drug deals and cheap hookers."

The shift changed. Valdez went home. Homicide Detective Thomas arrived a short time later. The man wore a dark suit, a tie and a genial demeanor. He reminded Frank of a funeral director.

"The wife pestered the hell out of us," Thomas said, lighting up a cigarette. "Called every day for a while. Wanted us to keep investigating. Insisted he couldn't have done it, that it had to be homicide."

Why did she badger police when she was lying? Frank wondered.

"Happens a lot. Don't know if it was denial, guilt or greed in this case."

"Greed?"

"Sure, the life insurance factor. He had a big policy. She's the beneficiary. If his death was ruled accidental, or homicide, she'd collect double indemnity. Maybe face value of the policy wasn't enough for her. The stigma is another factor. She'd get a lot more sympathy from friends, relatives, the world at large, if her husband was murdered or accidentally killed. The insurance company pay off yet?"

"Just recently."

Thomas was aware of Harrington's murder. Thought it

interesting but doubted there was a link. He was more than satisfied that Daniel Alexander had committed suicide.

"We did everything. The crime scene tech took swabs for a GSR test, to see if he'd fired the gun. In a case this cut and dried we often don't even process them. I mean the guy left a note. But because the widow was so insistent, we ran it through the lab."

"What was the result?"

"Positive, traces of nitrates on his right hand. The man was right-handed, shot in the right side of the head." He shrugged.

Two down, one to go, nothing new so far. But he knew, something told him, the answer was there, somewhere in that building. The commander of the ID bureau was back in his office.

"I'd be glad to let you talk to ID Tech Watson," he said, "but she's not here."

"When will she be in?"

"She won't. She's no longer with the department."

"Where has she gone? Where does she work now?"

"We're not permitted to give out that kind of information."

Watson was not listed in the telephone directory. Frank drove back to the office, trying not to think about Rory, her lies, her smile, or was it someone else's? Confused, he focused on the task at hand. If Watson owned a house or a condo, he could locate her through property tax records. An urgent inner voice warned him, don't stop, keep going, keep going. His head ached, he was weary, but if he rested, he would only have more time to think about what he had done to himself, to Kathleen and their marriage, how stupid he had been.

Sue Ann gave him his messages. "Oh, and somebody's called four or five times. Wouldn't leave his name. Wants to talk only to you, said he'd keep trying."

She stepped into his office with a letter for his signature, looked over his shoulder and saw he had accessed the Dade County Property Tax files on his computer. "See a piece of real estate you're interested in?"

"Just browsing."

He scored immediately.

Denise Marie Watson. Owner of a single-family residence at 749 NE Ninety-fourth Street in Miami Shores. Two bedrooms, one and a half baths, 1,478 square feet, built in 1949. Assessed at $94,300. Taxes $2,264. The only real estate in her name in Dade County. He jotted down the address.

The phone rang a short time after Sue Ann left for the day.

"Frank Douglas? Jay Bowden here."

Frank sighed audibly. "What's on your mind, Bowden? I'm busy."

"Yeah, I hear you are. I have a business proposition I think would interest you."

"I have no interest in anything you're involved in." He was about to hang up.

"As a father, I think you'd be very interested."

"Spit it out."

"Not on the phone. We need to talk in private, strictly confidential."

"My secretary leaves at five. Five-thirty tomorrow, here at my office?"

"I'll be there. Keep this between us. It's better for all parties concerned that you don't mention this at home."

What the hell could the son of a bitch want? How could he stop Bowden if the man wanted to marry his daughter? The possibility revolted him. He didn't need this now, with all the other pressures he felt. If he insisted that Shandi finish college before making a commitment, could he make it stick? Would Kathleen support him?

Frank made small talk with Shandi at dinner that night, studied her face and saw no clue. She went off afterwards, casually saying she had books to return to the library. The library was considered an exception to her "house arrest." He watched her slight figure on the TV monitor, walking quickly down the drive to where a car waited. She carried no books, not one.

He wanted to rush after her, but waited to hear Bowden out. He would not afford an argument or accusations now, he thought, realizing that Kathleen must have sensed his guilt. She avoided his eyes and attempts at small talk about the girls and their friends.

"Is Shandi still seeing Bowden?" he finally asked, as they got ready for bed.

"What?"

He knew she had heard him. He repeated the question and she shrugged, changing the subject, launching into a recitation of some minor calamity concerning a museum zoning matter and people he neither knew nor care about.

"I shouldn't bore you with all this," she finally said, voice soothing. "You need some rest." She brushed his hair back off his forehead, tucked him in like a child, then went into the bathroom to floss her teeth.

He heard the clang of the pedestrian gate at nearly two and stole out of bed. All he saw from an east window was the glow of taillights pulling away, but he was sure it was

Bowden. He heard Shandi come in and go directly to her room, no stop-off in the kitchen. He heard her shower.

Shandi was still asleep when he was ready to leave next morning, though it was later than usual. Casey was outside, sitting on the edge of the pool, dangling her feet in the water, when he stepped out, clutching his coffee cup.

She squinted up at him in the bright morning sun. She wore shades, minus the usual plastic nose protector. "You wearing sunscreen, punkin?" He stroked her wet hair, pulled back in a ponytail. "Where's your nose protector? Don't wanna scorch that cute little snout."

"Couldn't find it." She shrugged. "Mom says I don't have to put on sunscreen until ten o'clock."

"Well, you're gonna need that nose, it's the only one you've got." He placed his cup on the patio table, plucked a leaf from the hedge and tucked it up under the nose bridge of her sunglasses. "Voilà," he said. "The schnozz is saved."

"Cool." She grinned up at him, stroking the smooth surface of the leaf with her index finger.

"What is that?" Kathleen had trailed him out, still in her bathrobe and slippers. She padded closer to Casey.

"Mother Nature's nose protector."

"What are you doing?" She snatched it off Casey's face as the girl blinked in surprise. "What if she has a reaction?" Kathleen asked, her voice accusing. "She could be allergic!"

"It's not poison oak, for God's sake. Casey's never had an allergic reaction in her life. It's from the hedge."

Kathleen shook her head. "Frank, where on earth do you get these crazy ideas? And you," she sternly addressed Casey, "you should know better."

"Me? What did I do?" Casey yelped. "Why is it always me?"

"That's enough," Kathleen said sharply.

"Why am I always the one in trouble? Nobody ever yells at Shandi no matter what she does! At least I didn't get my butt tattooed!"

"Tattooed?" Frank said.

"Young lady!"

"She did! I saw it!" Casey darted inside to examine her nose in the hall mirror.

Frank turned to Kathleen. What are we doing? he wondered. They had never bickered.

She misread the question in his eyes. "It's some sort of little thing, a rosebud, I think," she explained offhandedly. "Apparently it's a current fad among all her friends . . . Thank God it's where nobody will see it."

He didn't dare say what he thought, instead sat, silent, at the patio table and gazed miserably at the horizon.

Casey opened the French doors. "Daddy, the police department's on the phone. They said you can come get your gun."

"Good," he said. He heard Kathleen's sharp intake of breath before he turned and went inside to take the call.

No problem finding the small one-story house on Ninety-fourth Street; somehow Frank knew which one it was even before reading the numbers on the mailbox. Painted white, with a white tile roof. No flower beds, no trees, no fence. A "Sold" sign had been planted in the center of the neatly kept lawn. The place looked empty. He called the realtor.

"The buyers closed two months ago," she said. "They're planning some renovations, they need to get a variance, something about the setback on the south side. If you're interested in that neighborhood, I can show you something else. I've got several—"

He said he was interested in the former owner.

"I think she was relocating. I have no idea where she is now."

She had no forwarding address for Denise Watson; neither did the Miami Shores post office. He returned to the house and walked through the backyard. He knew this place somehow. The old hose rolled into a coil, the shallow stoop, the vertical blinds at the window. He felt as though events had taken place behind those blinds, inside those rooms, that he should, but could not, remember.

He glanced over the fence as a car backed into the driveway next door. A chubby middle-aged blonde in baggy slacks waved and began to unload groceries. She was disappointed to learn he was not her new neighbor.

"Denise worked for the police department," she said, opening her hatchback. "She wasn't the most friendly, but it was nice having somebody with a badge on the block, made you feel more secure. Worked odd hours, kept to herself. Sometimes she worked nights and slept days. Got mad as hell at my kids for making too much noise. They were *only* playing. Didn't like the dog across the street either, he barks a lot. Nick, her boyfriend, lived with her for two, three years, but they split up. Guess she took it hard and decided to move on to greener pastures. He took off, then so did she. Never even said good-bye. Maybe if she knew you were gonna show up, she wouldn't have left." The woman smiled and balanced a grocery sack overflowing with bags of snacks, Cheez Doodles, chips and cookies. She accepted his offer to help lug the bags into the house. The floor was cluttered with toys and the refrigerator papered with cartoons and messages from family members.

"Don't know where she went. Probably another police department. Her life revolved around that work. Not that she didn't take care of herself. Went to aerobics classes every day, wore those cute little tights and outfits. And liked having her nails done. Had designer manicures. Sculptured acrylic nails with artwork on 'em, little stars and moons and things. Wore 'em real long. Don't know how she ever washed a dish. Guess she didn't. Hope the new people next door have kids."

She promised to look for pictures taken at a neighborhood barbecue and gave him Denise Watson's old unpublished phone number. "Don't see how it will do you any good."

She was right. Dialing it from his car led to no new number, only a message that it had been "disconnected at the customer's request."

He called a media lawyer he knew, to ask a question, then returned to police headquarters, through the metal detectors, back into the bureaucracy. Eventually referred to personnel, he requested that they forward a message to Denise Watson, asking her to contact him.

"Can't do it." The man behind the desk didn't try to conceal how much he enjoyed saying no. "We have no forwarding address ourselves. If we should hear from her"—he shrugged—"which I doubt, we'll be glad to pass along your request."

What kind of police department can't even find their own employees? he wondered. "Then I'd like to see her personnel file. That's public record."

His request created confusion and a referral to the legal department where he cited the state's public records law.

"Usually only members of the media file these requests," the department's legal advisor told him.

"The media represents the public. I'm a member of the public. No reason I can't see a public employee's file."

The lawyer agreed. "But we'll have to review it first to delete anything that could violate the employee's privacy."

Frank waited thirty minutes while someone in another office dabbed Wite-Out over private information such as the old phone number and old address that he already had. Finally the file, his last hope, his only hope, was surrendered to him.

He opened it, alone in a small conference room off the legal office. Denise Marie Watson, born January 7, 1970. Joined the department May 11, 1991. Title: Miami Police Department Crime Scene Technician II. Her job was to examine crime scenes, to collect fingerprints and other evidence to assist police and prosecutors.

Her picture staggered him. He held it in both hands, staring at the fresh-faced young woman in the official ID photo. Her hair was thick, curly—and dark. So were her deep-set eyes. The delicate rosebud mouth, her expression grave, yet knowing, triggered an unexpected sense of longing that made him want to weep. He tried to distance himself, to examine his emotions in businesslike fashion. Perhaps it was the knowledge that someone who appeared so young and innocent was a foot soldier in the hopeless war on crime. Perhaps it was because he had missed lunch and was hungry. His heart told him it was something else. Hand shaking, he turned the page.

According to her routine evaluations by supervisors, Denise Marie Watson excelled in report writing, the collection of firearms evidence and ricochet examination. Her ratings in crime-scene sketching, photo techniques, initiative and attitude fluctuated between good and satisfactory. Obviously ambitious, she had attended seminars and advanced courses in fingerprint collection, the handling of trace evidence, death scenes, bloodstains and bullet holes. She had even completed a course on the reconstruction of decomposed bodies from skeletal remains.

She had been injured on the job only once. A severe ankle sprain suffered when rotted floorboards collapsed as she photographed and processed a homicide scene, the case of a homeless derelict slain in a crumbling, condemned building.

She had won commendations from prosecutors for her meticulous evidence collecting in the notorious River Cops case, in which a rogue band of cops drowned several drug traffickers and stole their cargo, and a letter of merit from the chief for community service and "acting as a role model" as a participant in the Big Sisters program. Included in the file was a letter in a childish scrawl from her "little sister." The schoolgirl wrote to thank the chief for allowing Denise to take her on a tour of the station and to watch the K-9 dogs train.

Letters of appreciation from citizens and crime victims who praised her work were clipped together in a thick stack. Frank sighed, riffling through them. Two elderly sisters who lived together were pleased and grateful that Crime Technician Watson did not spill black fingerprint powder all over their rugs and sofa like the thoughtless technicians who had responded to their two prior burglaries. A homeowner cleaned out by burglars praised her professionalism and competence, calling her a credit to the department. About to flip to the next letter, Frank gasped, then froze. The signature at the bottom was Daniel P. Alexander.

Denise Marie Watson had responded to the burglary discovered by Daniel and Rory when they returned from their skiing vacation eighteen months before his death.

Daniel had been impressed enough by her work, or her, to write a complimentary letter. Trying to conceal his excitement, Frank asked to use the Xerox machine, and for fifty cents a page, he copied everything, important or not, even her picture.

Despite his rush to leave, he had to battle more bureaucracy and red tape at the property bureau. For Christ's sake, he thought, they had called him to reclaim his gun, but now dull-witted clerks fumbled about looking for it, then took even longer to obtain authorization for its release.

Frank cursed traffic as he drove back to the Beach. He had almost forgotten his five-thirty appointment with Bowden. It was nearly five when he arrived at the office. Sue Ann, just leaving, was not as chipper as usual.

"How are you?" she asked with real concern. Her eyes had an odd, troubled look, as though he were ill.

"I'm fine," he said.

"Want me to stay, anything you need to dictate?"

"No, go, go," he said, wanting her out of the office before Bowden arrived. "Has Kathleen called?"

"No." She looked guilty. "Frank, I don't want to wind up in the middle of any problems the two of you might have."

What was she talking about? He had no time to ask. "I wouldn't expect you to," he said briskly. "I would think you'd remember who signs your paychecks."

She nodded. "We go way back. We're like family. I enjoy working for you. My grandkids adore you."

Her tone and her searching look was unsettling. What the hell is this? he wondered, then checked his watch: 5:24. "See you in the morning," he said, and closed the door.

He unlocked the outer office after she left and waited for Bowden, who arrived precisely on time.

Frank forced himself to shake Bowden's hand and offer him a seat. He studied the man and tried to stay civil. Bowden now sported a mustache. He wore a black T-shirt under a white jacket, apparently affecting an outdated *Miami Vice* look. His hair was long and he wore a heavy gold bracelet on one wrist. Frank wondered bitterly if the man's bottom was tattooed as well. Was his daughter, that little girl so bright and beautiful from the day she was born, out of her mind? Was she stark, raving mad?

Bowden's eyes swept the room like a furtive character out of a B movie. "We're alone?"

"Nobody else here. What was it you wanted to see me about?"

Bowden's fingers explored his mustache as though he was unaccustomed to it being there. "You're aware that I've been seeing Shandi?"

"That's hardly news."

"Right, and I'm sure you know that I left the security of my teaching gig to take on the title of creative director of the new Green Glades Playhouse."

Frank nodded.

"We're in the process of putting the first season together, and believe me, Frank, it's a struggle." Bowden sighed dramatically and shook his head. "Not easy at all. We've lost some important funding that may cost us matching funds promised by the city. We've had landlord problems and a thousand other snags and setbacks that I won't bore you with now."

"Good."

"Frankly, one of the things that attracted me to Shandi in the first place was how supportive you and Mrs. Douglas were of the arts, how generous you were with our little drama department when she was in school."

"And all along I thought it was her beauty and talent you found irresistible."

"Oh, that too! That too." Bowden smiled.

The image of Rory—or was it Rory?—and him naked together flashed across Frank's consciousness with sudden power, then he imagined Shandi and Bowden and his skin crawled. He felt queasy. He wanted to end this meeting.

"What's on your mind, Bowden?"

"Here's the deal." The man casually crossed his legs as though they had all the time in the world. "It's obvious that because of our age difference, past student and teacher association, or whatever, you're not entirely thrilled at the idea of your daughter and me as an item. I can understand that." He held up one hand as if Frank might protest. "If I were a father, I'd probably feel exactly the same, you know? Daddies are very protective of their little girls. That's understood.

"So I've come up with a solution that would make us both happy. Because of my current situation, struggling to get this artistic venture off the ground, I'm willing to sacrifice. In other words, you help me and I help you."

"What's the bottom line?"

"You make an anonymous donation, and I let her down easy, tell her I met somebody else." His eyes were bright, his expression sly.

"What if I don't feel charitable?"

"Oh, I think you will. I mean, anything could happen. Shandi's crazy about me. You know how spoiled she is, always has to have what she wants when she wants it, exactly how she wants it. She might even decide to do something crazy—like elope."

"I have faith in my daughter's intelligence, Bowden. She's strong-willed, but she would never do anything that she knows would hurt her mother and me."

Bowden did an exaggerated double take, as if to say Frank shouldn't be so sure. "If you care to run that risk"—he licked his lips—"be my guest. But, in all modesty, I think that I pretty much call the shots in this relationship right now. You know how emotional young girls in love can be."

Frank wanted to dive across his desk and choke Bowden's tongue out. Instead he tried to look thoughtful.

"As for Mrs. Douglas, a lovely woman, I wouldn't want anything to add to the stress you both have been undergoing."

What had Shandi told this guy?

"Well, I will have to talk to Kathleen. She handles all our contributions to the arts."

"Ohhh, I wouldn't want to burden her with this," Bowden said quickly. He looked annoyed, as though running low on patience. "I understand you're pretty quick with a checkbook yourself when the mood arises."

What the hell? "What do you mean?"

Bowden smiled so widely that pink gums gleamed above his teeth. "You know." He lifted an obscene eyebrow. "Your contribution to the widow's fund? See, I'm practically a member of the family already."

No one knew about the money he had transferred to Rory's account. Yet news of it had spread from Kathleen to Shandi to this two-bit chiseler. Outrageous, he thought. Sue Ann and Kathleen. How dare they spy on him!

"I would never stand in the way of Shandi's happiness," he said, fighting to remain calm. "If you're what she wants, and the feeling is mutual . . ."

Bowden's smile faded. "I think that my idea would be more beneficial to everybody concerned."

"How much of a contribution are we talking about here?"

Bowden's relief was obvious. "Healthy, very healthy, maybe somewhere in the neighborhood of seventy-five thousand?"

"Seventy-five thousand!"

"I know it's three times your donation to the . . . widow's fund, but we're talking family here, and you have no idea how much capital it takes to mount a production."

"What would such a sizable donation guarantee?"

"Well, under the circumstances, you obviously would not want your name listed on the program as a donor." Bowden looked much happier now. "But it would guarantee no contact. Zilch. *Nada.* Shandi shows up, I walk away. She calls, I hang up. No ifs, ands or buts. *Finito.*"

"Wouldn't that be cruel, wouldn't she be hurt, without an explanation?"

"She'll bounce back fast." He sounded confident. "Happens all the time." Bowden nodded sagely. "Girls that age get over it in a hurry."

"Hmmm," Frank said. "I'll have to sleep on this before I can commit."

Bowden's eyes registered alarm. "I don't think you'd regret it, Frank. My solution is best for all of us. If you'd like to just give me a part of the money now . . ."

Frank shook his head. "I need to give it some thought before I write a check."

"What's to think? I'd rather not wait," Bowden said, "and I'd prefer cash."

"Here, the same time tomorrow." Frank got to his feet and extended his hand.

"The sooner, the better," Bowden said.

When he was finally alone, Frank locked his office door, checked his watch and announced the time and date aloud. He unlocked the cabinet, hit the stop button, then eject, removed the videotape from the machine, slipped it into its cardboard casing and scribbled the time and date on the label.

No time to ponder his betrayal by those he trusted most. He called Lucca.

"How ya doing, boss?"

"I need you to find somebody," he said urgently. "I've learned something important."

He reported the link between Denise Marie Watson and

Alexander, excited, convinced that this would change the detective's mind.

Lucca snorted. "You call that a link? A finite number of people work for the city and there are an infinite number of calls. A lotta those people go back to the same addresses more than once."

"And then disappear, with no forwarding address?"

"People leave police work, leave Miami, if she did indeed leave, all the time."

"But the letter?"

"The man was a letter writer. People who work for the department solicit those letters, like to pad their personnel files with 'em."

"No. No." Frank was on his feet now, pacing around his desk, phone to his ear. "This is it! Lucca, this is a piece of the puzzle! Harrington's murder is connected, too. I'm sure of it."

"Hold it, hold it, hold it right there. Jesus Christ. Come down to Planet Earth for a minute here. I ran into some of the detectives from the city the other day. Asked about Harrington. They're looking at robbery, an inside job. Plan to run some of his employees on the lie box. When he cashed that fat insurance check he took a major chunk in cash, apparently stashed it in that two-bit safe in his office. Apparently it was common knowledge among his staff. They're looking at a dishwasher and a waitress who both came up with minor records. They're working a coupla angles. Guy was apparently a ladies' man, or thought he was. Had been doing a coupla the broads working for him. The ME says he apparently got lucky not long before he bought it. Could be a woman involved. Apparently he was flashing green all over the place."

"Rory said he liked to do that, but—"

"Rory! Boss, if you are banging that broad, you're nuts! Didn't anybody ever tell you not to get involved with anybody who has less money or more problems than you do? Stop thinking with your dick."

"That has nothing to do with this! I'm telling you, Lucca, Daniel Alexander did not kill himself. He—"

"Listen." The detective's voice dropped to a guttural growl. "You are making yourself and everybody around you nuts. You got your old lady ready to throw a net over you."

"What are you talking about?"

"You heard me, boss. Look, I already said more than I should have, but listen to me. You better straighten out your act damn fast or life as you know it is in for some big changes. See ya." Lucca hung up.

CHAPTER
SEVENTEEN

He fought panic. He was close, too close to allow anyone or anything to stop him now. He reread the pages from Denise Watson's file, then drove back to her former home, still empty, still waiting.

The house next door was noisy and full of children. The chubby blonde woman opened the door wearing fresh lipstick and a bright blouse. "You're in luck," she told him. "They were in the first place I looked."

She had found only one good snapshot of Denise among those taken at the barbecue. Smiling inscrutably at someone or something over the photographer's shoulder, she wore long, shiny earrings and held a drink in her hand. It was not her smile or her low-cut blouse that left Frank reeling this time, it was another face. A man hovered protectively at Denise's elbow, nearly out of focus. Tall, lean and dark-haired, he wore jeans and a western-style shirt. He held a can of beer in one hand, a cigarette in the other.

"Who is that, the man with her?" Frank asked hoarsely.

"Oh, that was Nick, the live-in boyfriend, the one who left. Nick . . . can't think of his last name. Bolton, I think. Nice fella, had an accent, from Texas or Oklahoma, I think. Somewhere like that. Supposedly was a heck of a football player in high school and college. Hard to believe he was an athlete, always had a cigarette in his hand." She squinted at the picture. "See, you can see it there. Said he picked up the habit in the service. Nice fella, he got along with everybody, but he was crazy about Denise," she said nostalgically. "Surprised me that he finally left her. But she was always on him 'cuz he wasn't ambitious enough. Can't remember what he did for a living. Had some kinda job, but it didn't bring in enough for her. He wasn't a bad fella," she said absently, shuffling through the rest of the pictures of the neighborhood party. "Put Tabasco sauce on everything." She wrinkled her nose. "Even on my homemade baked beans with barbecue sauce. Denise said he even poured it on his eggs. But he got along with everybody," she said again, glancing up from the pictures. "You know him?"

"I'm think I've seen him," he whispered.

Information had no listing for a Nick Bolton; Frank did not expect to find one, but checked anyway. He went back to Denise Watson's file for the name of the only other person who might help him now.

He called Kathleen from the car. "I may be a little late for dinner, sweetheart. Why don't you guys go on without me?"

"Where are you? What are you doing?" Her voice, too

bright, too casual, tightened his stomach. He did not know her anymore.

"Checking out a piece of real estate," he replied, just as casually. "I'm thinking of getting in on a development deal here." Lie number one, he thought. "I'll be home soon."

The dying rays of the setting sun spilled a bloodred stain across the rooftops of Overtown, no-man's-land during the last riots. He found the address, half a mile and a million light-years from police headquarters. He took a chance and left the Mercedes at the curb. He had no choice. He knocked on a grimy door that opened onto the street, praying that she was still there.

A mountainous black woman inched open the door and eyed him suspiciously.

"Is LaKisha Henricks at home?"

"Whatchu doing here? Whatchu want her for? She eight years old."

Behind her were skinny children, all arms and legs, all ages and sizes.

"Please, it's important. I'm here to talk to her about her big sister, Denise Watson, from the police department."

The woman closed the door, slid off the chain and opened it.

"We ain't seen her in months." The woman's bulldog face wore an offended expression. "She done took off, jes' like that chil's father. They s'posed to get her another big sister." She looked Frank up and down and scowled. "Not a big brother. I'd just as soon they never gave her no big sister, 'stead a one that just go off and break her heart again."

"I'm sorry about that. Is LaKisha here?"

"Yeah," she muttered, and turned her back.

He followed her inside.

A TV blared. The children in the tiny living room were

mostly male. The oldest, about eleven or twelve, gave Frank a hostile stare.

"LaKish. Com'ere. This man wants to talk wit you."

Winsome and dark-skinned, LaKisha was small for her age, with pink plastic barrettes, pigtails and a gap-tooth smile.

"My name is Frank Douglas," he began. "I guess you miss Denise."

She looked up shyly from beneath her eyelashes and nodded.

"You used to have fun together."

"Yeeah." She dragged out the word and put a finger in her mouth.

The other children gathered around, noisy and curious, distracting LaKisha, who seemed to withdraw.

"Can I talk to her alone?" he asked the mother.

"You show me where you be alone around here," she muttered.

"How about out back?"

"It be getting dark." She shrugged. "Antwan," she told the older boy, "you go wid 'em." She glared at Frank. "And you watch 'im."

They sat on a broken back step, facing a garbage-strewn courtyard littered with discarded pieces of furniture. Antwan stood like a sentry, several feet away, arms crossed, watching.

"You can talk to me, LaKisha." The child quietly studied the pitted concrete. "What did you and Denise used to do together?"

"Go places sometimes." She spoke in a small, barely audible voice.

"That's nice. Did she come say good-bye to you before she left?"

She shook her head, pigtails bobbing. "She say she goin' away. But she don't be saying good-bye."

"What did she say?"

LaKisha shrugged and fiddled with one of her braids.

"Did Denise tell you where she was going?"

"No."

"When is she coming back?"

"Don think she be coming back."

"Do you know where she might be now?"

She shrugged again, stealing a sly, self-conscious glance at her brother.

Frank's heart sank. A dead end. He had come for nothing and had so little time.

He sighed and got to his feet. "I know a girl who would be a nice big sister for you. Actually she's not much older than you, but she could teach you a lot and maybe help with your schoolwork. Her name is Casey. Do you know how to swim?"

She shook her head.

"Well, it's time you learned. Casey could teach you." He took her hand, small and warm. "There are some things I have to finish first, but then I'll work on it. Thank you very much for talking to me."

They went back inside, the boy sauntering behind them.

"Satisfied?" the mother demanded.

He thanked her and headed for the door, hoping to find his car where he left it. The girl's mother still fumed and muttered. "She act like it don't matter. But it do. Every day she be out there looking for the mailman. Looking for the postcard. That woman done promised her, but it don't never come."

"The mailman?"

"Yeah."

He glanced at the girl, who was still obsessed by the errant braid. "LaKisha, Denise said she'd write to you?"

"Yeeah. She say she be sending me a postcard."

He swallowed hard. "From where?"

The girl looked annoyed, scrunching up her face as though it would help her to remember.

Please, he thought.

"She say she gonna send me a postcard from Seattle. It dint come yet."

"You're sure she said Seattle?" He crouched in front of her, intent.

She nodded solemnly. "She say when she get there, she'd send me a postcard."

"Thank you."

He turned to the mother at the door. "This is important," he said. "You think she's telling the truth?"

"If LaKish say Seattle," the mother said, "it be Seattle. She ain't learned to lie yet. How you think she'd know 'bout Seattle if Denise didn't tell it to her?"

"Would you happen to have a picture of Denise?"

The woman scowled, then scrounged through a drawer until she found it. Denise and the little girl, standing in front of headquarters, apparently when they took the tour of the station.

He promised LaKisha he would bring it back.

He knew what he had to do as he drove home, then wondered what was happening there. Throw a net, what exactly did that mean? It occurred to him that Kathleen had been dogging his steps when he was there. If he went out on the patio, she followed. If he went upstairs, she was behind him. Not to be with him, but to watch him.

He joined his family, already at dinner, acutely aware now of their attitude toward him, the pity in their eyes.

How had it gone this far? Twice he saw Kathleen check her watch, expecting someone, or a telephone call.

He had no appetite and ate little. He felt too tense. He said he was tired, thought he'd take a shower, do some reading and retire early. Kathleen followed him upstairs. While he undressed, she disappeared into her office down the hall. He stepped into the master bath, turned on the shower full blast, then slipped back out into their bedroom. The bedside phone set had one line lit, hers.

He didn't dare pick it up. She might hear him.

He padded down the hall in his bathrobe, his bare feet sinking into the carpet's thick pile. Her door was slightly ajar. He heard her voice. He stood with his ear to the door, listening. If one of the girls came upstairs now, he would be caught red-handed.

"He'll probably never forgive me," Kathleen said fretfully, "but it's the only way. Phil said I have to protect myself and the girls, as well as Frank. And he's right, of course. I know, I know. I just want to get tomorrow over with. I'm so nervous. We've been through so much together in the past year. This is the last thing I ever thought I'd have to do. But the sooner the better. No, no, Ann, you haven't seen him, heard him. There's no doubt it's the right thing. There's no other way to get him under control. I mean, who knows what he'll do next? It's absolutely nerve-racking."

His stomach churned. Someone on the stairs. He hurried back down the hall and into the master bedroom just in time.

"Mom?" He heard Shandi in the hall.

He stripped off his robe and stepped into the shower. He let the water run hot, soaped and scrubbed his skin furiously, teeth clenched in outrage. Whatever was happening was tomorrow. She had been talking to her sister, Ann. Why didn't

Ann try to talk some sense into Kathleen? This was his house, his family.

He was so close, but who would listen to him now?

"Your skin is so red. Was the water too hot in the shower?" Kathleen asked. "You could have scalded yourself." Her cool hand touched his forehead. "You feel almost feverish."

He lay in bed watching her.

"Kathleen . . ."

She brushed her hair, watching herself in the mirror. "Yes, dear?"

He wanted to confess how flawed a man he was, to ask her forgiveness, to explain why he had to finish what he had started. "Was that you on the phone just now?" he asked instead, "when I came out of the shower?"

"No." Her eyes met his in the mirror. "It must have been one of the girls."

She tucked him in again, as though he were a child.

She was restless. It took a long time, but when he was certain she was sleeping, he slipped from their bed. Her office door was locked, something she had never done before. He used the master set of keys from his study.

Her desk was also locked. He found that key almost immediately, tucked beneath her desk blotter. Her daily journal, a shiny red book, lay in the top drawer, along with files and copies of affidavits. Kathleen was thorough. She had always been thorough. The grounds for her action were neatly delineated, laid out like a shopping list.

Franklin D. Douglas
• Recent heart transplant patient, on medication.
• Experiencing bad dreams, hallucinations, hears voices.

- Obsessed with the belief that his heart donor is still alive, has become inappropriately involved with the dead man's widow.
- Depleting family assets, gave more than $25,000 to a stranger.
- High-risk behavior, witness in a murder, discovered the victim in another murder, interviewed as suspect in the latter (present newscast video as evidence).
- Paranoid behavior, recently purchased a handgun, despite a lifelong aversion to weapons, and displayed the loaded firearm at the home he shares with his wife and two young daughters, installed security cameras and alarms at home and office, calls to police, retained a private investigator.
- Due to mental state, may not self-administer his life-sustaining medication as directed. Due to this and all of the above, he presents a danger to himself and others.

Persuasive. Had Frank read all this about a stranger, it would convince him that the individual should be committed.

His hands shook as he shuffled through the files. Kathleen had been seeking sworn affidavits from other parties. That had to be how Lucca found out, he was sure. She must have approached him, seeking either an affidavit or information about the work he had been hired to do. A black line was drawn through Lucca's name. He apparently did not cooperate. But Dr. Lassiter had, advising hospitalization. Sue Ann's name was followed by a question mark.

With or without an affidavit from his secretary, there appeared to be more than enough to persuade a circuit judge to issue an immediate pickup order in an ex parte proceeding. The room felt icy cold, the chill coming from within him. Kathleen's notes, her crisp copies of legal papers, made it clear what to expect. Deputies would find him, then take him in custody to either Highland Park or Dodge Memorial, expensive, private locked-down psychiatric hospitals.

A note from Phillip Grayson assured Kathleen that should the court balk, resulting in some unforeseen delay, she could resort to the Baker Act, an emergency procedure. Local police would take Frank into custody and involuntarily commit him to Jackson Memorial Hospital's psychiatric unit for a seventy-two-hour evaluation. "Not as pleasant an atmosphere as the private hospitals," Phil wrote, "but a very viable alternative."

Fury overtook him. Grayson must be enjoying this. How many people had the son of a bitch told? How much was he charging Kathleen? How could she listen to him?

He arranged the papers back the way they were, locked the drawer, the door, and crept back to bed. Kathleen still slept, her back to him. He wanted to shake her awake with bellowed recriminations, reasonable explanations, and pleas for remission of sins unmentioned on her misleading and damning list. He took deep breaths and he tried to think clearly. He had to get through the night first, then find a lawyer, a damn good lawyer, in the morning. How could this happen now? Time was running out, he had none for a court battle trying to prove himself competent, a battle he might initially lose. He had more urgent priorities, what he owed to the man in the photograph. Follow the trail, find the answers now, something told him, or no one will ever know the truth.

What if they came for him in the morning? He could be led off in restraints, in pajamas, in front of his daughters and his neighbors. But no, had the order been signed, he thought, they would have come already. The hearing must be set for this morning. He still had a few hours.

He was drinking coffee in the kitchen when Kathleen

came down. "What are you doing today?" He smiled, afraid that she would see what he knew in his eyes.

"Early meeting, the museum board." She smiled ruefully. "What are your plans?"

"That real estate proposal, probably spend the day in the office on the phone. It looks good."

Kathleen dressed in an elegant business suit, then went into her study. She emerged snapping the locks on her slim leather briefcase. He noticed she had taken great pains with her makeup this morning. Even wore mascara. Did she hope to impress the judge, or Phillip Grayson?

Shandi hugged him tightly before leaving for class. "Love you, Daddy."

He read it in her eyes. She knew.

He kissed Casey when the van from school honked outside. "'Bye, punkin," he whispered. "Be good."

"'Bye, Dad."

She ran down the driveway without looking back. She didn't know.

"Kathleen?"

She turned, her face a mask.

"Why don't we just both take off, the hell with everything else. Spend the day together. How about it? You and me."

She paused. "Tempting, sweetheart, but no can do. This meeting is important."

They walked out to their cars together. She kissed his cheek. He followed her Catera out to the causeway and tooted his horn as she turned west, toward the city. He turned east toward the Beach and his office. The moment she was out of sight he braked, made a U-turn and doubled back to the house. Upstairs, he dragged a duffel bag from the back of the guest room closet where they stored the luggage. He moved swiftly through their bedroom and bath like a thief, sweeping toiletries, his toothbrush, underwear, shirts and socks into the bag. He wanted to take sweaters and a warm jacket, but that would leave a clue. He could buy garments as he needed them. Nobody could stop him now.

He left the house in a hurry, stowed the bag in the trunk and stopped for a moment in the driveway to drink in the bougainvillea and the sweet scent of the island, a blend of salt air, flowers and fresh-cut grass. He wondered when he would see it again, then got in his car and drove out the gate.

He went to the bank first, carried his briefcase inside and filled out a withdrawal slip for twenty-five thousand dollars. While he waited for the teller to bring the money, it occurred to him that he and Daniel Alexander were becoming more and more alike. Both bought guns, both made love to Rory, and both walked out of banks with cash-filled briefcases. To where? That was the question.

"Sir?" The teller looked troubled, nervously adjusting his glasses. "Could you step this way?"

"Look, I'm in a hurry," Frank said sharply. He checked his watch. "I just want to make this withdrawal."

"That's what the manager would like to speak to you about. There's a problem."

The manager, a woman he had done business with for twenty years, was embarrassed. His accounts, she said, both business and personal, had been temporarily frozen by order of the probate court, pending a competency hearing. The papers were on her desk.

She threw up her hands. "I don't know what to tell you, Frank. I'm sure you'll straighten this out. I'm sorry."

He felt light-headed as he walked out of the bank. He called the pharmacy on Alton Road, then drove there. "Did a stupid thing," he told the pharmacist, who had a two-month supply of his medication ready. "Lost the bag I carry my pills in. Thought I'd stock up. We may do a little traveling this month."

He had to stock up, here, now. His prescription could be traced.

"You don't want to run out of this stuff," the pharmacist said cheerfully. "Gotta tell ya, you look great. Nobody would ever know."

Frank handed over his American Express card. The man ran it on the machine. Frank fidgeted, checking the time. The pharmacist came back, his expression odd.

"Mister Douglas, there's a problem with your card."

"What? It must be a mistake. There shouldn't be anything wrong."

"I put it through twice." He looked uncomfortable. "The company said to confiscate it. There's been a stop put on it."

"That can't be right."

But it was.

Kathleen was thorough. She and Grayson had been busy. He searched his pockets, but found only a few hundred dollars. It wasn't enough. "Will you take a check?"

"It's against store policy," the pharmacist said slowly, "but hell, I've known you all these years. I know you're good for it."

This was a man who had once opened his store at midnight to fill a prescription for Casey, then a sick and feverish baby. Frank smiled gratefully and wrote the man a bad check, committing a felony. Under the circumstances, he thought, he could always plead insanity.

He called bank officers he knew personally at two other institutions. His accounts there, too, had been frozen. One told him that it appeared that Kathleen was instituting a procedure to be named sole guardian of their assets.

"It's a mistake," he assured them. "It will be straightened out." Bank machines ate his two remaining credit cards when he attempted to make cash withdrawals.

He called her from a phone booth.

She answered at once. The hearing must have been brief.

"What have you done?"

"Darling, where are you?"

"Kathleen, you know me better."

She paused. "No, I don't, sweetheart. But"—her voice took on the soothing tone she so often used lately—"everything is going to be all right. It will just take time. This is for your own good. We've got some wonderful doctors, they're—"

He hung up.

"Good morning," Sue Ann chirped. She looked relieved to see him.

He brushed by, into his office, then watched the monitor. She picked up the phone immediately. He took the videotape of his conversation with Bowden from his desk, slipped it into a manila envelope, then rummaged without success through the drawers for cash. Unlike other men he knew, he had never kept a secret cash stash or a private credit card. Kathleen and Sue Ann knew everything, had everything.

Sue Ann was off the phone. He hit the intercom. "Would you bring me the McAllister file?"

"McAllister?"

"That shopping center deal we did about five years ago?"

"Right." He watched the screen as she walked into the small file room. He stepped out into her office, took the petty cash box from her top right-hand drawer and emptied it. Three twenties, a ten, a five and small change.

"Where are you going?" she asked as she returned with the file.

"Just out for a bagel, be right back."

"I'll get it for you," she offered eagerly, but he was already down the hall.

He emerged from the elevator and walked through the lobby toward the parking lot. Two brown-shirted deputies were walking in his direction; one held an official-looking document in his hand. They stopped at his Mercedes; the one with the document checked the tag, then spoke to the other, who nodded.

Frank fought the urge to run. They didn't know him by sight. Half a dozen other passengers had disembarked from the elevator with him. He turned to a woman a few steps behind him. Plain, in her thirties, slightly overweight, she carried a postal meter, a bulky purse over her shoulder and an armload of oversized envelopes.

"You know," he said, speaking cheerfully though his stomach churned, "we pass nearly every day and never say hello."

"That's true." She smiled, obviously flattered. "Everybody is always in such a rush."

"One of these days," he said, "we should stop to smell the roses and share a cup of coffee or a sandwich. Here, let me take that." He took the heavy meter from her and pushed open the door.

"Thank you," she said. "I've noticed you, too." They walked out, chatting, into the sunny parking lot, a couple. "I'm from Arkansas," she offered, "a small town where you know everybody and they know you. I was just saying the other day that Miami is the strangest place, everybody is from somewhere else. It's not a community, it's just a crowd. Nobody's friendly."

He laughed a bit too heartily as they passed the deputies on their way into the building. "Ain't that the truth."

He walked her to her Chevette, parked three slots down from his car, and set the meter on the front passenger seat.

"I'm glad we crossed paths today," he told her, hoping the deputies were aboard the elevator by now.

"See you soon," she called as he walked away. She waved as he slid into the Mercedes and wheeled out of the lot. There was only one place left to go.

CHAPTER
EIGHTEEN

The dimples deepened as Rory opened the door. "Hey," she murmured. "I didn't know if you were ever coming back."

He had no idea what to say. He closed his eyes as she hugged him.

She stepped back after a moment and studied his face. Her smile faded. "What's wrong?"

He couldn't trust her. But without her, he was lost.

"I'm in so much trouble."

"You? What?"

He told her what Kathleen had done. Her reaction was shock and indignation.

"Froze your bank accounts! Cut off your credit cards! Is she crazy! Let me call Kathleen right now," she demanded.

"I'll explain. Tell her it was all my fault." She hesitated. "She doesn't know, does she? That we . . ."

He shook his head hopelessly. She surely suspected.

"You were only helping me. I'll give back the twenty-five thousand dollars right now! I wanted to give back the money!"

"It wouldn't change anything." He paced the room as she sank into a chair watching him. "It's only a small part of the picture. This is turning ugly, fast."

"Hire a good lawyer and we'll stop it all before it happens."

"There's no time to do that now. There's something else I have to do first."

"What could be more important? You can't—"

"I'm close to the truth, Rory." He stopped in front of her. "Remember that puzzle we talked about? It's real and I'm this close to solving it." He watched her eyes, bewildered and innocent.

"Do you remember a woman named Denise Watson?"

She denied it.

He explained who Denise was, then opened his briefcase and spread out the pictures. "You remember her now?"

She studied them intently, then shrugged. "Can't say for sure. I 'member that the person who came out to dust for fingerprints was a woman detective, or whatever, and she was talkin' to Daniel 'bout security and alarm systems. Fallin' all over him, but that wasn't unusual. Women always found him attractive. She wore a badge and a police ID hangin' from her belt. But I was so upset and bumfuzzled that day, comin' home from vacation and everythin' gone, they coulda sent Charlie Manson out and I wouldn't've noticed."

"Daniel is alive," Frank said, "and I'm sure she's the key."

She caught his hand as he replaced the photos in his briefcase. "You are so wrong about Daniel. If you were right, you wouldn't be here right now. He's dead," she said sadly. "He's gone. You may have some cockamamie theory, but you are no mental case. You're the sanest, most levelheaded member of the opposite sex that I know." Her voice sounded wistful.

She got to her feet and leaned against him, her head on his shoulder. Her hair tangled in his fingers. It was soft and fragrant, her body warm.

"What do we do now?" she murmured.

Her use of the word *we* made him weak with relief, despite his suspicions.

"I have to go find Denise, prove to you and everyone else that he's alive, then come back and straighten out my own life. But I've only got about two hundred and seventy-five dollars cash." He stepped back to watch her face. "I need a loan."

"So you can find Denise?"

He nodded.

"Where is she?"

He tensed. "In another city."

"How did you find that out?"

"It wasn't easy."

He could see her react to his evasive answers.

"How long will it take?"

"It could be just a few days, maybe a lot longer depending on my luck."

She went to the phone and punched in a number. What was she doing? He edged closer. Would he have to yank the cord from the wall?

"Mother Alexander? Hi, it's me. Sorry to bother you. But I'm running like crazy here 'cuz I'm gonna have to be out of town for"—her eyes darted back to Frank—"two weeks or so."

He frowned and shook his head. "No, no," he mouthed. She ignored him.

"You've been wantin' to spend some time with Billy. Would you take him? It's . . ." She turned to Frank, who signaled for her to hang up. "It's family business. I'll explain it all later. Right away, this afternoon. Okay, I'm sorry you can't. He'll be so disappointed, but I can send him up to his other grandma. Oh, then you can? Wonderful. I'll bring him over right after school."

"What are you doing?" he demanded when she hung up.

"You said you didn't know how long it would take us."

"I never said 'us.' You can't come with me."

"I say we follow the yellow brick road, find the wizard and ask for answers. I know it isn't true, Daniel's not alive, but I have to go, to see it through just like you do. If nothin' else, just to be there when you see what an ass you've made of yourself."

"I have to go alone."

"You don't trust me? After everythin', why?"

"I have a reason."

"Such as?"

"A witness who puts you here, who says you were here in the house that day at noon, when the shot was fired."

"That's a lie!" she said furiously. "Who told you such a thing?"

He shook his head.

"If that was true," she demanded, "why would I beg the police, you, everybody, to keep investigatin'?"

"Double indemnity?"

She looked stunned for an instant, then slapped his face,

a sudden, stinging blow that brought tears to his eyes. "How can you say that?"

He knew she would never give him the money now. "Where were you," he asked calmly, "when Harrington was murdered?"

"You think I had something to do with that?" Her face reddened and her voice broke. "The police came here, to ask me about you. You were the suspect, not me."

"A woman may be involved."

"If you knew Ron," she said, her voice cold, "you'd know a woman was always involved. He even made moves on me when Daniel's back was turned."

"Did you kill him?"

"No. Did you?"

"No." They stared each other down. "I wish I could trust you, Rory." The hell of it was, he thought, that he believed her. Was it because he wanted to, because his gut instinct told him she was truthful or because she was so good? If she was lying, this was an Academy Award–winning performance.

"You can." A tear skidded down her cheek.

The man who spied on her could be the liar, or mistaken.

"You must know I wouldn't lie to you." Her lips parted slightly, her eyes locked on his. She had backed him into a corner, literally.

He waited nervously outside the bank and watched her emerge carrying the briefcase, her graceful long-legged stride, bright hair lifting in the breeze. She slipped into the car and kissed his cheek. "I got fifty instead of twenty-five," she said. "Just in case. And we have my credit cards, too."

"No cards," he said, pulling out of the parking lot into traffic. "When I disappear, Kathleen and her lawyer will probably report me missing, deranged and dangerous. The police may really start to look for me. Either way, she'll hire an expensive private detective to track me down. Your place will be their first stop," he said, thinking aloud. "If you're with me, you can't leave a trail either. We probably have only a couple of hours to work with here. I don't know how long it will take when we get to . . . where we're going. Damn! They'll check the airport, and I can't buy a ticket under a phony name because of the security procedures. They want picture ID before you board." He sighed in exasperation. "We can slow them down temporarily by leaving from Fort Lauderdale Airport. They'll check Miami first."

"No need," she said coolly. "They'll look for your name on a manifest, not Daniel's. You can use his driver's license." She studied his profile. "Wear your shades, comb your hair over to the left and you can pass for him. The check-in guys at the curb are too busy to check IDs that close."

Using Daniel's identification had never occurred to him. "Good! Then we leave from Miami. Bring some pictures of Daniel, and his passport, just in case."

"His passport?"

"Just in case."

"Daniel had an American Express card. We can use it for the tickets," she said. "It hasn't been used since . . . but it hasn't expired. We can't pay cash."

"Why?"

"The profile. The airlines use it to identify terrorists, hi-jackers and drug smugglers. Cash raises a red flag. We don't want airport cops pulling us aside for a closer look at your picture ID."

Despite his reservations, sharing almost everything brought him immense relief and helped him think. What would he have done, he wondered, if she, too, had thought him crazy?

Billy was due home soon.

"I don't think I should be there," he said, as they approached her street. "Billy might say something to the wrong person. It's too risky."

"You're right," she said, "he's so talky. Don't know where he gets it from. What— Hey, you missed the turn."

"No, I didn't."

He'd glimpsed a green and white Metro patrol car parked on the swale at Twin Palms, a uniformed deputy halfway up the walk.

Kathleen and Grayson were thorough, and quicker than he thought.

He drove to a shopping center in the heart of the Grove, into a towering parking garage behind a multiplex theater, and found a slot near the elevator in the gloomy half darkness of the fifth level. There was a cab stand at street level. He scribbled his car phone number on a slip of paper.

"If the deputies are still there, have the cabbie make a U-turn like he's looking for an address, get out around the block and walk up on foot. I don't want them nosing around here after asking him where he picked you up. Call me with the credit card number and I'll make the reservations. Meet me back here at the car in two hours."

"That gives me barely enough time to pack a few things and get Billy to his grandma," she complained.

He reached for the briefcase as she jerked it out of his reach.

"No way!" she said. "How do I know you'll be here when I come back? Enough a this *Mission Impossible* shit. The briefcase goes with me. I'm holdin' the money. I never trusted car phones anyhow, they're not all that private. I'll call the airline and book us on the next flight out." She studied him in the shadowy interior of the car. "But to do that"—her voice dropped—"and to know what in God's name to pack, you have to tell me where we're going."

He thought about snatching the briefcase and pushing her out of the car. "How do I know you'll be back?"

"Because I'm tellin' you so. You can bet your ass on it."

"I am." Was he making a huge mistake? "Don't tell anybody, don't even promise Billy a postcard from Seattle."

"Seattle." He couldn't read her eyes in the dim light. "Make it two and a half hours," she said.

She left the Mercedes and walked toward the elevator, swinging the briefcase. He could have stopped her, could have taken the money. What's another felony when you are certifiably crazy? Instead, he clung to hope, that she was someone he could trust, that she was innocent. He sat frozen in place. The elevator opened, she stepped inside and turned to face him, holding the briefcase in front of her. She blew a kiss as the doors closed.

Fifteen minutes dragged like an hour. He walked into the adjoining mall, used the men's room, bought a soft drink and sat on a bench in the shadow of a two-story escalator, eyeing the crowd, trying to think, hoping not to see anyone he knew. He considered buying a movie ticket, taking refuge in a darkened theater, but another story unreeling on the screen would be torture when he was so obsessed with his own. If she did not come back, he thought, he could pawn his watch. He had not been in a pawnshop since his father's death, but he could find one. He didn't have the papers on the Mercedes. Criminals ship hundreds of stolen cars out of the country through the Port of Miami every day. One of them might buy it, but how do you find people like that? His experience had all been in legitimate business. Why had he told Rory about Seattle? He pictured her calling Kathleen, Sue Ann or the cops so they could stop him, for "his own good."

Could Rory betray him after the intimacy they had shared? Kathleen had, and he had loved her for half his life.

Not too late to find a phone and call a lawyer for help. But who would help when he had no proof? He tossed the empty drink can into a trash bin and checked his watch. She was not due back for more than thirty minutes. If she did not come, somebody would. Somebody he would not be happy to see. He walked briskly back to the parking garage to move the Mercedes. He would conceal it on a nearby street, then watch for her on foot. That way, if things went wrong, he could get lost in the crowded mall. As he stepped off the elevator, his car in sight, he saw Rory's Sable cruising slowly. She appeared to be alone.

The station wagon disappeared, then circled back, as he watched. She leaned forward, searching the shadows, as the car moved at a crawl. He sprinted up beside it and rapped on her window.

She cried out, startled, then lowered the window.

"You scared the hell outa me! Where the blazes were you?"

"You said two and a half hours."

"So shoot me, I'm early. Next flight leaves at eight-ten P.M. We've gotta be at the airport in an hour. I got Billy's grandma to come stay at the house, so I didn't have to drive him all the way out to her place."

"Were the deputies there?"

"Had been, left a card stuck in the door with a number to call. I did. They wanted to know if I'd seen you. Said no, didn't plan to, didn't want to. When I asked what it was about, they said they had some papers to serve. I promised if I heard from you, I'd give 'em a call."

He loaded his bag into the Sable.

"Follow me," he said. "I'm gonna get rid of my car."

"Why not just leave it here?"

"Too close to your neighborhood. What did you tell your mother-in-law and Billy?"

"As little as possible. Told her there was trouble in the family, my favorite cousin up in Tallahassee. Said I was drivin' up there. Said I'd 'splain it all later. Promised Billy we'd go to Disney World when I git back."

"Good. Didn't know you had a cousin in Tallahassee."

"I don't."

"You're good."

"Yeah, I think I'm gettin' the hang a this. Startin' to like it. We'da made great fugitives."

She followed him to South Beach where skateboarders and in-line skaters flashed through the neon glitz of early twilight. The streets were jammed, the curbs lined with cars awaiting valet parking at eight dollars a pop. He pulled into a tow-away zone, stepped out and locked the car.

"You can't leave it there!" Rory said, when he opened her car door. "They'll tow it in twenty minutes. You know how they are here. There's a tow truck around every corner."

"Right. If it's impounded, I know where it is." He slid in beside her. He had heard the horror stories from people whose cars had been towed after joyriders stole, then abandoned them. They had not been notified for weeks, even months, until storage charges had mounted to astronomical heights.

"If by some quirk of fate the system works and Kathleen is notified that they've got the car, so what? It leads them to South Beach, not the airport, or your neighborhood. I want them to think I'm still here. One more stop," he said, "and we're on our way."

Parked at a meter, outside the big art deco post office on Washington Avenue, he scrawled a quick note on a piece of letterhead stationery from the office.

> *Shandi, darling. I know this will be painful, it always is when someone you care for is a disappointment and not all you expect him to be. I wish I knew how to make this easier. But in time you will learn, as I did, that the human heart is a tough and resilient organ. I will always love you. Dad.*

He folded the note around the Bowden tape, sealed it into a stamped eight-by-ten manila envelope addressed to Shandi, marked it "Personal" and dropped it into a box at the curb.

Instead of the airport, where a persistent investigator could cruise the garages and spot Rory's car, they left the Sable in a nearby park-and-lock lot and rode the shuttle bus into the terminal.

Rory helped him recomb his hair, the way Daniel wore it in his driver's license picture.

The man who checked their bags and ID at the curb barely glanced at the picture.

"Concourse D, Gate Five." He pocketed the ten-dollar tip. "Have a nice flight, Mister Alexander. You too, ma'am."

"Thank you," Frank replied. One hand on Rory's arm, his briefcase in the other, he had become Daniel Alexander.

CHAPTER
NINETEEN

The roar of the jet engines matched the roar inside him as they streaked through the night to the great Northwest.

They half watched the movie, snacked, and she dozed, her head on his shoulder. Rory called him Daniel in front of the flight attendants as he had instructed. Both still wore their wedding bands. They shared the same last name. No one would have guessed that they were married, but not to each other.

He tried to put Miami behind him, but wondered what Kathleen and his daughters were doing and thinking. This was the first night since they met that Kathleen did not know exactly where he was. Could she imagine that he would be two thousand miles away, sharing a strange bed with another woman? He could not have imagined it himself a few short weeks ago.

Arrival time was just after eleven P.M., but their bodies were still on Miami time, and Rory was exhausted. He felt energized, alert, already scanning faces, searching the crowd.

The weather was cool, but not as cold as he had expected. He bought a sweatshirt, lined windbreaker and a woolen scarf in an airport shop. Rory wore a leather jacket she had brought with her.

The cab ride into the city was long, the highway dark. He would use Daniel Alexander's credit card to rent a car in the morning after studying maps and forming a plan.

The hotel suggested by the airport shopkeeper was exquisite. Four-star, turn-of-the-century, tucked away downtown, its bar a former bookstore, volumes still lining the shelves, a wood-burning fireplace in the lobby. The bellman brought complimentary glasses of evening sherry to their door.

The colors and fabrics were rich and textured, the furniture polished cherry wood. The ambiance, the room and the double bed were warm. She called him Daniel. It seemed natural even to him now.

His thoughts were only of what lay ahead, but when she touched him and opened her arms, soft and sweet, to him in their bed, it, too, seemed natural. Unlike the first time, their wordless lovemaking was oddly enhanced by their feelings of isolation, as though each had come to the other without a past, together at the end of the world.

"We belong together," she whispered in a moment of passion.

"Yes," he murmured. "Yes."

But afterward, spent, heart pounding retroactively, he wondered about the distant coast left behind them, the southern end of that flat peninsula. Miami. Whatever chaos reigned at this home, his stately home on Rivo Alto island, must have quieted for the night. They all would be in bed by now. Were they dreaming of him? What had they told Casey?

Despite her exhaustion, Rory also seemed restless.

"What are you thinking?" The unfamiliar darkness echoed around them.

" 'Bout Billy. Wonderin' if he's all right." She sighed, turned to him, and stroked his hair. He rested his hand on the curve of her hip, stared into the darkness and knew there was no way to put Miami behind them.

He had dressed and ordered room service by the time Rory yawned awake, hair tumbled down all around the soft curves of her shoulders, beautiful au naturel, sans clothes, sans cosmetics, without artifice. Or was she? She had done nothing to arouse his suspicions, he believed in her, but his heart was wary.

"Cover up," he told her, "room service is on the way. Didn't think you'd want bacon or sausage . . ."

She wrinkled her nose.

". . . so I ordered you fruit and yogurt."

"How do you always know exactly what I want? Come over here," she invited, throwing back the sheet, smiling and patting the bed beside her.

A sound at the door spoiled the moment. Breakfast had arrived.

"Look." She stood at the window. "What a beautiful day! The paper says the high will be sixty. Who said it always rains here? I wanna see the Seattle Aquarium and the Space Needle. The SuperSonics are playin' tonight." She'd been shuffling through the newspaper and the brochures on the coffee table.

"We're not on vacation."

She frowned. "I wish we were." She sat cross-legged on the bed and gazed up at him, resigned. "Okay, where is Denise staying at out here?"

"I have no idea. I don't even know that she's here, or if she was, how long she stayed."

Rory's mouth opened in dismay.

"This is a perfect jumping-off place for Canada, Alaska, the Orient," Frank said. "But if somebody wanted to put as many miles as possible between them and Miami, yet still stay in mainland U.S.A., this is the place."

"But this is a big city, must be more than a million people. How do we ever find her?"

"Hopefully she's a creature of habit. Her old neighbors said she worked out, did aerobics every day. She had her hair done and had fancy manicures, decorated nails."

"Nail salons and hairdressers. That's only a majority of the female population. What else?"

He shrugged.

"Shouldn't we check with the local police departments, see if she got a job?"

"Doubt if she did, but it makes sense to go with the obvious."

"What about the chamber of commerce? They might keep a listing of new residents. You know, like a welcome-wagon kinda thing."

By early afternoon, after hours on the telephone, they knew that Denise Watson had not applied to any law enforcement agency, security agency or employment agency in the Seattle area.

"What did Daniel like to do? Where would he take someone in a town like this?"

"Daniel isn't here," she said quietly.

"You've trusted me this far, Rory. Indulge me."

She sighed. "Daniel liked to dine in good restaurants, drink in intimate bars with good music. Liked jazz, good steak houses, Italian food. Liked a good piano player. Always requested 'My Funny Valentine.' "

Frank got maps of the city and directions from the concierge and they walked to a photo mart to have the pictures of Daniel and Denise blown up to eight-by-ten size, two sets.

The weather was cool and crisp under blue sky. They were here somewhere, he knew it. Frank felt their presence like an electrical charge in the air. He watched faces on the street, in passing traffic. Rory, her long red hair loose, in jeans, boots and her leather jacket, turned heads.

"We have to stop and buy you some scarves."

"Why? I never wear them, it's not that cold."

"They don't know me. But they both know you. With that hair, they could spot you a block away. We don't want them to see us first."

She looked exasperated, but bought a cheap scarf in a five-and-dime and covered her hair.

The city felt strange, yet familiar to Frank. Miami and Seattle share musical three-syllable names and a distance from Middle America that is more than geographic. Both are cities on the edge, gateways to exotic capitals, watery outposts at far reaches of the map, natural destinations for wanderers, the restless and people on the run from the law, each other and the personal demons no one can ever escape.

But there was something else about Seattle, the older of the two. Though Frank saw as many young people with pierced noses and eyebrows and punk purple hair as on the streets of South Beach, there was a difference. The city exuded a discernible character, a stability and sense of history foreign to Miami's wild, raw and ever-evolving atmosphere where life lurches from crisis to crisis and nothing is ever remembered beyond next hurricane season.

They began the rounds that evening, starting with upscale steak houses and Italian restaurants. They would order a drink, small-talk the bartender or the maître d', and show the photos, saying they were in search of long-lost family members. Frank didn't know if they bought the story, but all looked, then shook their heads.

When they were hungry enough, they ordered dinner. Rory seemed to be enjoying herself. Frank remained as alert as a cat, expecting one of the faces he sought to step unaware at any moment from around a corner, to emerge from a rest room, or ride in on a gust of wind off the street.

More bars, more nightspots, after dinner, ordering drinks, leaving them virtually untouched. He ordered Perrier, she white wine. They returned to the hotel, he frustrated, she tipsy and laughing.

The sky was gray, with a drizzling rain, when they awoke on the second day. He took his medication at seven A.M. and seven P.M. now, to stay on his Miami schedule. They tore out the Yellow Pages listing Beauty Salons and Services and began those rounds, salons by day, saloons at night. He would frequently pause, scan the street and turn to check behind them. Increasingly anxious, he feared that somehow they were just missing them.

"You're making me jittery," Rory said more than once. The routine and the rain continued for five days.

At a jazz concert in Pioneer Square, she listened to the music and held his hand. He insisted she wear her scarf and never stopped searching the crowd.

Then they hit the bars again, this night the watering holes at the poshest hotels, the Vintage Park, the Claremont and Cavanaugh's.

At what would be their last stop that evening, Frank leaned over to better scrutinize a well-dressed man passing through the lobby. His height and build were correct, but he was not Daniel.

"He killed himself," Rory said too loudly. "He committed suicide." Tonight the wine did not make her laugh.

"He didn't," Frank said quietly.

The bartender lounged nearby reading a newspaper. He glanced up. "I'm with the lady," he said. "Suicide."

They stared.

He motioned to the front page of his newspaper. "Definitely suicide. Kurt Cobain killed himself. Totally messed up on drugs and couldn't handle success. All these stories now, murder theories, speculation that it was this, that it was that, that it was something else." He shook his head. "Some people want to make everything into a conspiracy. Some people just don't wanna accept the simple truth."

"Thank you very much. That's exactly what I've been saying." Rory sounded emotional, near tears. "You are absolutely right."

"She was a big fan," Frank explained, then caught her arm and got her out of there.

"Hope you find your cousin," the barkeep called after them as they departed into the drizzle.

"Why did you insist on coming, if you're not committed?" he asked bitterly as they walked through the rain.

"Maybe the search isn't what I'm committed to."

A man and a woman brushed by laughing, huddled together beneath an umbrella, illuminated for only an instant in the lamplight.

"You see." He was annoyed. "I missed getting a good look at them. You're distracting me. They could walk right by us. And you're not wearing your scarf."

She yanked the scarf from her neck and threw it down in the street. He stooped to retrieve it, sopping wet from a puddle.

Perhaps she was deliberately trying to sabotage the search, he thought bitterly.

They neither spoke nor touched for the rest of the night. She watched, quiet in the morning, as he mapped their itinerary for the day. He feared that she might announce plans to return to Miami alone. Perhaps, he thought, it would be better if she did.

No one recognized Denise's photo in a swanky salon full of women in pale pink smocks. When he turned, Rory was seated in a chair in front of a slim, dark young man who wore five earrings in one ear. Frank thought of Shandi and his heart ached. She had seen the tape by now.

"This color is real." The young man spoke in awe, trailing a wisp of Rory's long hair between his fingers. "I know people who would kill for color like this."

"Daniel," she said, "you go on and come back for me in a couple of hours. I'm staying, Raymond can take me right now."

He felt freer alone on the street, invisible and more powerful. Neither of those for whom he searched even knew that he existed and was hunting them. If their paths crossed now, he held the advantage, the element of surprise. He toured a large health club, telling the manager he might want to surprise his wife with a membership for her birthday. He scrutinized the participants in three aerobics classes in progress, beginners, advanced and a step class. He watched the men and women working out on the machines in the cardiovascular room and even stopped to peruse the candid snapshots of members posted on a bulletin board. He showed the pictures of Denise and Daniel to two employees at the front desk as he left. They shook their heads.

He visited two nail salons, then checked the time and returned for Rory. She wasn't there.

The redhead with the dramatic long curly mane was gone. A brunette with bangs and a boyish haircut was wearing her clothes.

"No more scarves," she announced. She jerked her head at the colorist, who looked nervous. "Tip the man."

A young woman was sweeping mounds of red hair from the floor. "I couldn't believe she wanted it brown," the young man said, pocketing the twenty.

"It's great," Frank said, and handed him another twenty.

"What a difference," he said, as they walked out onto the street. "You didn't have to cut it all off."

She shrugged. "You believe I'm committed now?"

"If we could just find enough putty to fill in the dimples, but there probably isn't enough in this city."

She punched his shoulder, her expression ferocious. "All I kept thinking in that chair, while he had at me with those scissors, was that if you came back and said you'd just found Denise, that it was all over and we could go home now, I was gonna snatch those scissors and cut your heart out."

She took his arm. "Two more stops." They bought a pair of dime-store glasses, wire frames. She knocked out the lenses and put them on. At Sears she bought a shapeless gray raincoat.

"Satisfied?" Posing in front of the mirror, she looked drab, like an old-maid schoolteacher.

"We've got a problem," he said.

"What now?"

"How am I going to explain to the hotel clerk this strange woman I'm bringing back to our room?"

"Thank you," he whispered later, in their rumpled, sweat-soaked bed. Their lovemaking had become all-consuming, the only time he was free of the other woman and the constant pressure to find them.

"What more could I do to prove I love you?" she said.

Neither had mentioned love before.

"I love you too," he said solemnly, wondering if this was fantasy or real life.

He saw her from time to time, regarding her reflection in the mirror, trying without success to fluff up the cropped hair.

She caught him watching and gamely shrugged. "It'll grow out. If it don't, you're a dead man."

On day ten they studied the maps spread out on the coffee table. "You know," he said, "there are all these islands, like the Florida Keys, off Seattle between here and British Columbia. Accessible only by ferry boat. Visitors can tour a few of them by bicycle."

"I saw a brochure that says some have whale sightings," she said. "Wouldn't it be wonderful to see a pod of whales in the wild?" She looked up at him. "I know, I know, we're not on vacation. But you owe me one after this, big time, April in Paris, the Orient Express, or cruising the Nile. Actually . . ." She leaned back in the room's one comfortable armchair, her voice dreamy. "What I really want is to go to upstate Florida, to Saint Marks in the Panhandle, when the monarchs are migrating."

"Butterflies?"

She nodded. "Millions and millions of them, on their way to Mexico. I've heard that their wings make a wonderful sound, like soft rain, and turn the woods and the trees into an orange flame."

"When this is over," he promised. He meant it. Until now, neither had mentioned anything beyond the immediate future. Miami seemed farther away than ever.

"Look at these, the San Juan Islands." He pointed them out on the map. She leaned forward and frowned. "Hundreds of them," he said, "some pristine and uninhabited, some inhabited by only one person, others with little villages."

"We can't check out every one."

"I want to show the pictures to the crews who operate the ferries."

They split up, to move faster. With her new look, he was less concerned about her being seen. If he could not trust her now, he could trust no one, and her own mother would not recognize her. She hit salons that day, using taxi cabs. He drove the car to health clubs and aerobics studios. The ever-present drizzle had stopped, but the sky stayed gray and the day damp and chilly.

He had parked in the wrong place, mistaking the address. Rather than move the car, he huffed and puffed up a steep inclining sidewalk. Miamians are unaccustomed to hills. Next to the health club at the top stood a small strip shopping center, brand-new with construction under way in two of the still vacant storefronts. GRAND OPENING banners streamed from a French bakery, a custom bike shop, a gourmet market with blue awnings and outdoor produce bins, and Nails by Nila. Too new to be in the phone book. He would kill two birds with one stone. He reached into his jacket, fingers closing around the envelope containing the pictures. He almost didn't notice the woman until she had walked by. It was Denise.

He spun around. She must have sensed it because she glanced back over her shoulder. He was staring. It was definitely her. Startled for a moment, she flashed a small, almost flirtatious smile and moved on, briskly. Her hair, swept back from her face, was longer than in her official police ID picture, but it was her. He would know her anywhere. She wore tight black corduroy pants, high-heeled leather boots and a white leather anorak with white fur trim on the collar and cuffs. Her nails glittered, long and decorated.

A loaf of crisp French bread protruded from the top of the cloth shopping bag she carried, along with green stalks from the produce bins at the gourmet market.

He panicked. He couldn't let her get away, but she had already seen him. He dashed up to the news racks in front of the bakery and, hands shaking, fumbled to insert the right change. He slid out a newspaper, then walked quickly downhill after her, pretending to scan the front page. He felt staggered by the emotional impact of seeing her face. He had nearly called out her name.

She walked into a shop close to where he had parked. He slipped into the rental and watched. She emerged with an armload of dry cleaning. Did it include men's clothes? He couldn't see. She deposited it and the shopping bag into a shiny black Range Rover parked two cars in front of his.

Then she set out on foot again. He jotted down the Washington tag number on the Range Rover, unsure whether to follow her or remain with her car. She crossed the street to a small travel agency, her walk confident, purposeful, a woman who knew who she was and where she was going. She came out after ten minutes, carrying a manila envelope, then back across the street to a liquor store. Minutes later she appeared carrying a brown sack containing several bottles. Before she climbed into the Range Rover, she stood for a moment, surveying the street, alert, a slightly troubled look on her face, almost as though she felt his eyes, sensed his excitement.

He wanted to call Rory. They were to meet at the hotel to eat lunch and compare notes, but she wouldn't be there for at least another hour. The Range Rover eased away from the curb. He hesitated, started the rental, let one car go between them, then cautiously followed.

She seemed to be using the phone in the Rover as she drove downtown. She parked on the street and disappeared into a corner boutique. He pulled into a "no parking" zone down the block, hoping no cop would come along. For long minutes he kept his eyes riveted to the door she had entered. Then somebody rapped on his window, startling him. A delivery truck driver, complaining that Frank blocked the loading zone. He started the engine, then saw to his horror that the Range Rover was not in its space. Gone. She must have left through another door around the corner and driven off without him seeing. Cursing, panicky, he pulled out into the flow of traffic, frantically scanning the cars up ahead, searching down side streets. She was gone. She might have picked up tickets at the travel agency. She could leave the country tonight. He searched the rearview mirror, speeded up, slowed down, uncertain what to do. Which way? Which way?

He pounded the steering wheel. He had come so close. Find her. Find her. He made a U-turn. Perhaps he could persuade the travel agent to tell him what name she was using, where she was going.

Then there she was.

Driving right by in the opposite direction. He didn't know if she saw him or not. A red light ahead. Afraid he would lose her if he circled the block, he saw a break in traffic and swerved into another quick U-turn, tires squealing. He could not risk being stopped by a cop. But he could not risk losing Denise again either. A taxi driver leaned on his horn and Frank cursed, hoping she wasn't watching in her rearview mirror.

There were four cars between them now.

He followed her through traffic for fifteen minutes, to the

docks. He parked a half block away. She stepped out of the Rover and checked her watch. Then he saw the white ferry-boat, a hefty double-decker named *The Island Queen*. He had been on the right track that morning. The Rover was among half a dozen cars lined up to board. He waited until there were two more, then joined the line. The sign said there were stops at San Juan, Orcas, Lopez and a number of smaller islands.

He bought a round-trip ticket to the end of the line and back, then drove onto the ferry, stomach taut, teeth on edge. He couldn't let her spot him. It was not crowded, this was the off season. The passengers, mostly residents, were headed home. The crew raised the ramp, cast off and they departed, motoring across the mirror-bright waters of Puget Sound. He felt a moment of panic, wondering how he could avoid her.

He tried to change his appearance. Shed his jacket and peeled off the sweater he had bought at Sears. He pulled on a hooded navy blue sweatshirt he had in the car and put on his sunglasses.

She walked the decks, upper and lower. She drew him like a magnet. He found it difficult to think of anything else, to take his eyes off her. Each time she passed, he hunched over the rail as though intent on the rocky points, sheltered coves, beaches and shorelines along a string of evergreen jewels. They made two, then three stops. One seemed to be a busy fishing village with gulls swarming the skies overlooking the harbor. The birds were leaner and more angular than South Florida seagulls. Denise made no move to disembark. He watched her with a sense of longing, on the top deck now, one booted foot up on a low railing, her hair streaming like a banner in the wind.

Was she going all the way to British Columbia?

Then he saw her on the move, headed for the Range

Rover. He climbed into the rental and hid behind the newspaper. The next stop was a small island with a narrow road and rocky shore, a tiny grocery at the landing the only sign of inhabitants.

He waited until after she drove down the ramp, then suddenly signaled that he was disembarking as well. "Sorry, I must have dozed," he apologized to an annoyed crew member. The Range Rover had already disappeared down the road. It should be no trouble to find in a place this size, Frank thought. The ferry back to Seattle would be in an hour, he was told, but would only stop if he hoisted the signal flag at the dock.

He took the rutted road slowly, eyes sweeping the brown-green landscape. He thought he saw a bald eagle, but didn't even turn his head. He was after a rarer sighting. There seemed to be only three or four rustic houses on the island. Summer places, he supposed. Smoke spiraled from the chimney of only one. The Range Rover was parked out front. He drove on about a half mile, then left the car at the side of the road and made his way back on foot. The ground was wet and slippery and he was glad he had worn athletic shoes and warm socks. The house was surrounded by madrona trees. He knew that the truth he sought was inside.

Trembling in the chill, he wondered how long he would have to wait. He did not dare approach the house in daylight. He heard voices and crouched. The front door had opened. A woman called out, her words friendly but questioning. He could not quite make them out. A man stepped onto the porch and glanced about. He wore jeans and a flannel shirt. He picked up an armload of firewood from a stack near the door, then carried it inside. He wore his hair longer and had grown a beard, but there was no doubt. It was Daniel Alexander.

CHAPTER
TWENTY

e dashed back to the car wanting to shout to the world that he was right, had been right all along. "We did it!" he muttered. "We did it!" He had to get the police, call the Miami detectives, prove to Kathleen and the girls that he was not crazy. He was right!

The island seemed deserted. He rushed to the small grocery to use the phone. The door was locked; the sign in the window said it was only open two mornings a week until spring.

He hoisted the flag at the landing and waited impatiently until he saw the ferry's slow approach in the distance. Once aboard, he nearly wept out of sheer relief. It was over. There would be answers now to all the questions. He tried to organize his thoughts, planning how to clearly explain everything to the local police. He had to tell Rory first; she had to go to the police with him.

First off the ferry, he fought the impulse to find a phone. This had to be face-to-face. Then he could tell the world, but first he had to be sure that it would listen.

He practically sprinted through the hotel lobby. Thank God she was waiting, pacing their room.

"Where were you?" She sounded annoyed. "I thought we were supposed to meet . . . Ohmigod." She saw his face. "You found her!"

He stood mute, unable to speak for a moment, scarcely able to breathe. "Both of them. Daniel is with her. Daniel is alive."

She reacted as though he had slapped her. Then she stared, shaking her head. "You know that can't be true. Why are you saying it? It's not true. It can't be."

He told her about Denise, the ferry, the island, the man on the porch.

"It's not true!"

"Rory, I'm sorry. They almost pulled it off. Thank God we came."

She kept staring, apparently in shock. "Get your coat," he said. "We're going to the police. They have to be picked up before they can get away."

"I have to see him," she said softly. "I have to see him with my own eyes."

"This is bigger than us, Rory. This is something for the police. They're murderers."

"You never set eyes on Daniel. How can you be so sure it's him, or even Denise?" Her voice grew louder. "It could be people who look like them. You never saw either one."

"I've stared at their pictures enough, but even if I hadn't"—he touched his heart—"I know."

She refused to go to the police without first seeing for herself.

"They may have spotted me," he argued fiercely. "It's too risky. What if they see us? They could take off before we get back with the police. We can't go out there ourselves."

"His brains were on my carpet," she insisted. "His blood was on my hands. Now you say you've seen my dead husband? Show me!"

She was raising her voice. He wanted the police, but not in response to a disturbance call.

He punched his fist into his palm, exasperated. He needed her help to convince the cops. He had seen them work, encountered their suspicion and bureaucracy. Cops are skeptical by nature. They do not like wild-goose chases or looking foolish. He knew what would happen if he went to them alone. First they would call Miami to check out his credibility. Rory was his credibility. "Okay," he said, "let's go. But we have to hurry."

She was stone-faced and silent. They walked the deck on the ferry and he bought her a hot chocolate. The late afternoon had grown cooler, but he was hot, seething with anger at all Daniel and Denise had done. A voice inside him rasped, "Kill them. Kill them."

The wind had picked up, but they stood in the punishing blasts on the blustery deck as the island slowly came into view. "There it is," he said.

"You know what that makes the father of my child if this is true?" Rory said. "You know what that makes my marriage? My entire life?" She looked numb.

He tried to comfort her, put his arms around her, but she was resolute, as though he had deliberately visited this pain upon her, as though he were at fault.

The next ferry would be in an hour, the last at eight-thirty P.M., he was told. They needed to hoist the flag.

"If we don't get back in a hurry, the police will have to use their own boats," he fretted to Rory. "Or wait until morning." He hoisted the flag before they left the landing.

He pulled off the road before the house was in sight, on the far side of a curve. "We should not be doing this," he warned sensibly. "What happens if they're out jogging and we come face-to-face?"

She fished her lensless spectacles from a pocket, opened the wire frames and put them on. "Daniel would never be in a place like this," she said accusingly. "You've dragged me all the way out here on some fool's errand."

The falling sun caught in the tangled branches of denuded trees as they left the car and walked, skirting the narrow road. Closer to the house, he led her off the road into the cover of woods. The cold seemed to rise from the damp leaves, rocky soil and brambles beneath their feet. Misty fog rolled in off the water. Except for seabirds and the wind, the silence was deafening. The Range Rover had not been moved. He held her hand as they crouched to watch.

"A perfect hideout," he whispered.

Rory didn't answer, her eyes fixed on the house.

"We have to get closer," she said after a long time, "so I can see."

"No," he whispered. Her hand felt like ice. "Maybe we can draw them out somehow."

No need. He heard her sharp intake of breath. A man moved quickly down the front steps and opened the door to the Range Rover. Frank panicked for a moment. If Alexander drove toward the landing, he would see their car.

A strangled sound came from Rory; he held her as her knees buckled.

"Daniel," she breathed, eyes wide. "Daniel!"

He put his hand over her mouth and forced her to the ground. "Shhhh! Shhhh!" he warned urgently.

The man appeared to remove something from the glove compartment, swung the door closed and trotted back up into the house where a fire glowed and lights shone warm in the gloom.

Fearing she would scream, Frank half dragged her back through the woods to the car, stumbling, snapping branches as they forced their way through the brush.

She panted puffs of frozen breath. "He's alive! How could he do this to us? That son of a bitch!" she screamed, red in the face, pounding her fists on the hood as he unlocked the car.

"Get in," he said sharply. "We've got to get out of here and call the cops. We're lucky he didn't hear us."

He maneuvered into a U-turn and they careened back down the narrow road in the growing dark. "It must be pitch black out here at night," he said, reluctant to use the headlights. "I just hope the damn ferry—"

"He's alive," she said. "Then who . . ." Her look was total bewilderment.

They bounced around a curve, he hit the brakes and the car skidded sideways. Across the road, blocking the way, was the Range Rover. "How'd he . . . ?"

Alexander had obviously taken another route, through the woods or along the stony beach. The Rover looked empty.

The woods on either side were dark, the fog more dense, light nearly gone.

"Where are they?" Rory said fearfully.

"Keep quiet," he said. "They don't know me."

He got out, eyes straining into the misty shadows. He strode up to the Range Rover, glanced inside. No keys.

Then, from behind his rental, on the right, a husky figure approached through the murky haze.

"Hey, there," Frank called. "This your car? We were trying to get by."

"That's him." Denise approached from the left rear. "The one who's been following me all day." Rory was still huddled in the front seat, in the dark.

Alexander came closer, boots crunching on the gravelly road. He held a gun in his right hand.

"You've been following my lady. Let's see some ID, buddy. Now." He gestured with the weapon.

"We've got one white female in here." Denise spoke crisply. "Don't move," she told Rory. She held a gun as well, and stood pointing it in a police officer's stance at the passenger-side window.

Frank fumbled, pretending to look for his wallet.

Alexander stepped up and studied his face curiously. He reached roughly inside Frank's jacket and jerked out his billfold.

He opened it and held it up to the sky's last light. His eyes widened. "What the hell! This is my driver's license! Denise, this guy's carrying my driver's license!" He looked genuinely bewildered. "Who are you! Where the hell are you from?"

Denise had Rory out of the car and was frisking her. "Who is she?" Alexander demanded, still pointing his gun at Frank and clutching the wallet.

"You son of a bitch!" Rory broke away from Denise and rushed at Alexander. "You son of a bitch!"

"Rory? Rory? Son of a . . . What are you doing here?" He and Denise looked stunned.

Swinging wildly, Rory lunged to pound his chest with her

fists. He slipped the billfold into his pocket and caught her wrist with one hand, still holding the gun in the other.

"Rory, don't," Frank said. She stopped swinging, taking shuddering breaths, panting, staring at her husband as though he were a ghost.

"We'll take them to the house," Alexander said sharply. "Denise, pull their car off the road. We can come back for it later."

Frank and Rory sat in the back of the Rover. Alexander drove. Denise was beside him, swiveled around in her seat, training her gun on them. "I'll use it," she warned.

"I know," Frank said. Even now her voice thrilled him with a familiar longing.

"That's right," Alexander said. "Don't hesitate to put 'em away if you have to, babe."

"Why did you do this, Daniel? How could you do this to Billy and me?"

"Shut up," Denise said, disgusted.

"Who was the dead man? Who was he?" Rory demanded.

Alexander and Denise exchanged glances as they pulled up at the house. They marched Rory and Frank inside at gunpoint.

The interior was a scene of cozy domesticity, warm colors, a blazing fire, enticing aromas from the kitchen. Frank saw a pair of binoculars on a wooden table near the front window and realized they were probably being watched while they spied on the cabin. Both were ordered to sit on a sofa in the center of the room.

"Jesus Christ, Rory!" Alexander squinted at his wife in the better light. "What the hell happened to your hair? You look like shit."

She removed the glasses and touched her hair se**
consciously. "It's only temporary."

Alexander, a look of disbelief on his face, again studie**
the driver's license he thought he had discarded with his pa*
thousands of miles away.

"You a cop?"

Frank shook his head.

"Well, who the hell are you?" he shouted, patience gon**
"What are you doing with my ID, and my wife? How th**
hell did you get here? How the hell did you find us?"

"Which one of you killed Harrington? You were about **
leave. Where were you going?" Frank asked. He stared cu**
ously at the two people whose crimes had saved his life.

Alexander cursed, his face beet red. He lunged forwa**
and jammed the gun in Frank's face. Rory gasped.

"I have your heart," Frank said calmly, "the heart th**
thought was yours."

Alexander's mouth dropped open. "You're the guy!" **
stepped back, his eyes probing. "You'd never know it. Let n**
see." He pointed the gun at Frank's chest. "Let's see."

Frank pulled up his sweatshirt and the shirt beneath**
revealing his scar. For a moment he thought it might not **
there. He was healthy. Daniel Alexander was alive. Ever**
thing else had to be a dream.

"Damn! Denise, take a look at this. What do you kno**
Ron said that Rory donated *my* organs." He laughed. "Lo**
where Nick wound up. Up to this minute, pal, you were t**
best walking, talking testament that I was dead."

"Who is Nick?" Rory pleaded. "Who was that at yo**
desk, with your gun, wearing your wedding ring?"

Alexander and Denise exchanged an intimate glance.

"Well," he said, almost good-naturedly, "I guess you f**

ured out that it wasn't me. I'd sure as hell like to know how. I never thought you'da caught on in a million years.''

"It wasn't me," Rory's whispered. "I never would have guessed."

Frank's alarm watch beeped, seven P.M.

"What the hell is that?" Alexander demanded, edgy, eyes darting around the room.

"I need my medication, pills, They're in the car."

Alexander sighed. "Denise, go get their car. Take out anything personal, this guy's pills, the rental papers, any ID, and get rid of them. We can take the plates off and run the car up in the woods later. We'll be long gone by the time somebody finds it in the spring.

"No, wait!" He looked thrilled. "I've a great idea! They can be us! I love it!" He turned to Denise. "Am I a genius, or what? We leave the Rover, take their rental, turn it back in and take off. The nice young couple who rented this cabin is found after it burns to the ground. Perfect! Doubles our cover. I'm dead again!" His face lit up.

Denise grinned and nodded.

"Go get rid of their stuff," he said, "bring their car, and make sure the flag isn't up for the ferry. We don't need anybody stopping by."

Frank's eyes followed Denise until she closed the door behind her.

"Don't you want to ask about Billy?" Rory said quietly.

"How is he?" Daniel sounded almost casual, slouched into a chair across from them, still pointing the gun their way.

"Heartbroken about his daddy."

"Damn stupid bitch! Look what Mommy has done to him now!" Alexander's temper flared, launching him to his feet. "You coulda just cashed the insurance check and lived happily ever after, but oh, no, not you. I left you that money,

Rory. I coulda cashed in that damn policy like everything else, but no, I leave it for you and Billy and whaddaya do? Shit! Now the kid's an orphan. Just couldn't let well enough alone, could you?"

"So you never cared. It was all phony? That last night . . ."

"Hell, Rory, that's not the point." He shook his head exasperated, his eyes flicking toward the door Denise had exited. "You were swell, the best, great in the sack, the kid was swell, but Ron and me fell behind in paying the state and county withholding taxes, the figures kept mounting and I realized there is more to life than suburbia and working your ass off for the next twenty-five years. Denise understands that. She's like me."

"That was her boyfriend you left in your place, wasn't it?" Frank said.

"Correctimundo." Alexander glanced out the window watching for Denise. "Lucky for me she always goes for the same type. First time she saw me she said I reminded her of somebody."

"But the fingerprints," Frank persisted. "They said he had your fingerprints."

"Brilliant, huh?" Alexander looked pleased. "That just happened to be Denise's job. We do it when she's on duty. She takes the call, fingerprints the corpse at the morgue and switches fingerprint cards. Foolproof.

"But then dumb bitch here"—he waved the gun at Rory—"comes home early and decides to donate my organs. Did they take 'em all baby, everything?" He raised an eyebrow suggestively.

"It would have worked, if it hadn't been for that," Frank said.

"It *is* working, with one unexpected glitch that's being eliminated."

"We both have children to raise," Frank said.

"Did I ask you here?" Alexander paced, exuding nervous energy, glaring at them, waving the gun. "You were not invited, so don't complain about the reception. First you freak Denise out on the street, in traffic, on the ferry. Then you start snooping around through the woods. You think we're stupid?"

"You are, if you expect to get away with this. Too many people know we're here."

Alexander looked thoughtful. "I don't think so. If you were leading the cavalry, there'd be bugles by now."

The man who saved his life was going to kill him now, Frank thought calmly. He remembered his father, dead at the same early age. Some families inherit deadly diseases; had he inherited a gene that left him at risk for homicide? Was it a congenital defect?

Headlights swept up outside.

"You were right," Denise said, as she entered. "The flag was up. I took it down."

Frank's heart sank along with any hope of rescue. Rory sat quietly beside him, tears in her eyes. Why had he brought her here? He never should have allowed her to come to Seattle with him.

"Is their stuff gone?" Daniel asked.

"Hope all his pills don't hurt the sea life. He had a regular pharmaceutical fruit salad. I hate being ecologically incorrect, but"—she shrugged—"I dumped them in the drink." She looked sweetly at Frank, whose ears roared when their eyes connected.

"That's my girl. Let's all go into the kitchen," Alexander said.

"Dinner is ruined." Denise waved her gun, pouting like an irate housewife.

Why the kitchen? Frank wondered, until he saw the heavy trapdoor in the floor. Alexander strained to lift it, grunting as it creaked open.

"Don't throw your back out, hon."

Rory took offense. "You knew he was a married man with a child when you first—"

"Shut up," Denise said.

"Downstairs," Alexander ordered. He smiled again. "Farewell, Rory," he said softly.

The low-ceilinged steps descended into a darkness that smelled dank and earthy, like an open grave. This is where we disappear, Frank thought. Everybody back in Miami will believe that we abandoned our families and ran away together. They will never know the truth. Kathleen will never know.

"I won't go down there," Rory said stubbornly.

"Yes, you will." Alexander wrenched her arm, forcing her toward the door as she resisted.

Frank saw Rory's terrified eyes and lunged for Denise. She cried out as he gripped her wrist, trying to twist the gun from her hand. Surprisingly strong and quick, she clipped him sharply with her shoulder and tried to trip him, knocking him off balance. The gun flew away from them both, slid across the wooden floor and was swallowed by the dark opening, bouncing off the steps below. Distracted, Alexander released Rory, who staggered back and yanked an iron skillet off the stove. The heavy lid clattered away. She swung the skillet at Alexander, chicken parts flying.

"Get away! Get away from him, Denise!" Waving Denise aside with his left hand, Alexander leveled the gun with his right. The muzzle less than two feet from Frank's chest, he squeezed the trigger. Frank braced for the bullet, then sprang forward.

"Kill him, kill him!" Denise screamed.

Alexander tried. The gun had jammed.

The men grappled. The freezer door sprang open as they crashed heavily into the refrigerator. Denise rushed to the cellar, frantic to find her gun, as Rory tried to stop her.

Frank reached a groping arm into the freezer, jerked out an ice tray, swung it by its metal handle and bashed Alexander square in the face. Blood spurted from his nose, and he dropped to his knees.

"Get out, get out! Run!" Frank shoved Rory toward a back door.

Alexander was struggling to his feet, one hand to his nose. Frank slammed the cellar door, leaving Denise in the darkness below, as they scrambled out the back door. The first breath of cold night air seared his lungs as they dashed toward the shadowy woods.

Lucca had been right about the most reliable choice of a weapon. Frank wondered how long it would take Alexander to clear the chamber of his jammed automatic, and for Denise to find hers. Two pistol shots were his answer, cracking in the night as they crashed through the trees.

"Run!"

"Where?"

There was no place; they were trapped and alone on this fog shrouded island.

Voices, shouts back at the house.

"Should we go to the landing?"

His heart thudded. "That's probably where they'll look first. There are a few other houses on the island, they seem deserted, but maybe we can find somebody, a caretaker, or

maybe we can break into one and find a phone or a weapon."
He felt her shudder.

"I'm sorry," she said, "I didn't believe you."

She reached out to him.

"We better keep moving," he told her.

He tried to remember the direction of the houses but had lost his bearings. No moon, no stars, only dense fog. Rory cried out as they stumbled, half falling down a steep incline into the icy water of a small running stream.

Something ripped as branches jabbed at his skin and snagged his clothes. Some small furry creature brushed his legs, then careened into the dark. They tried to skirt the stream.

Headlights bloomed behind them. Two sets, one on each flank, the Range Rover and their rental. The fog lights of the Rover tunneled through the mist. Frank and Rory tried to pick up their pace. The darkness around them was like a black well, visibility so poor that they nearly ran headlong into the wall of a shed behind a house. He groped for the door. Bolted, padlocked. The house shuttered, locked. The lights and straining engines hurtled toward them, terrifying small night creatures that fled in their path. Frank groped for something, anything. A box of firewood on the front porch. He fumbled for a piece to wield as a club and grasped something else, an axe. He gripped the worn wooden handle close to the razor-sharp metal head. No time to use it for breaking into the house. Headlights closed in. They ran for their lives.

They had to be close to the far end of the island, he thought. His heart had caught up with the action and was pounding. He glanced back and saw that the headlights were fixed, no longer moving. Their pursuers were on foot now, flashlight beams stabbing the swirling mist, closer than he realized. His rib cage tightened like a vise around his heart, each breath a painful spasm. He found it difficult to breathe. What was happening to him? Had the cold and the exertion damaged his borrowed heart? "They're almost here," he gasped. "If I don't make it, try to double back to the rental. I think there's an extra key in the glove box."

She tugged at his arm. "Don't leave me. We have to stay together."

"Careful," he breathed, shocked to realize they were back at the drop-off over the stream. They had been circling blindly through the mist. The sounds and the beams of light closed in.

"Go, go," he croaked, his strength spent. "I'll stay here."

"No."

"Go!" His chest about to explode, he pushed her away and into the darkness.

A figure loomed, blocking the Rover's fog lights. From the size it had to be Alexander.

Frank tried but failed to catch his breath, the pain in his chest worse. Desperately he marshaled whatever strength he had left as the footfalls came closer. Tightening his grip on the axe handle, he crouched, heart pounding.

Alexander still did not see him, his flashlight nearly useless in the fog. Frank lurched toward him, swung the axe at his knees, and connected. Alexander cried out and stumbled forward. The two wrestled to the ground, Alexander rolling atop him. Together they slid down the incline; their bodies crashed into logs, branches and stones, then splashed into frigid water. The shock felt like a thousand needles piercing his skin.

The axe lay somewhere in the brush halfway up the slope. Where was the gun? The world spun as he struggled to sit up. Roaring with anger and pain, Alexander slammed him back into the icy water, onto the rocks, fists hammering his chest. His heart in spasms, Frank felt light-headed and queasy, as helpless as before his surgery. His new heart, some-one else's heart, could no longer endure the stress, the cold and the physical combat. The water was only about three or four feet deep, but he remained submerged, at rest on the rocky bottom. He no longer felt the cold, he felt the warmth of Biscayne Bay, saw blazing sun and silver Miami skyline against a blue backdrop. The bay and the pastel towers of Miami Beach shimmered behind him. Beyond that, the blue-green Atlantic stretched east to Africa. He was earth, sea and sky, part of it all. He caught the stare of a prehistoric bird with ancient eyes and saw Rory's hair flashing bright in the water. Endless streams of brilliant orange butterflies fluttered across his vision, their wings like wind chimes gently rippling. He took a deep breath and relaxed.

Something inside him errupted, forcing him up and out of the water. He surfaced raging and murderous, gagging and cursing as though possessed. He caught Alexander by his jacket, dragged him down and rolled him over into the stream, hands gripping his throat, his own strength frighten-ing. As they thrashed in the shallows, Frank's fingers closed around a jagged stone the size of his fist. He smashed it into Alexander's forehead again and again until the man stopped struggling.

Frank crawled onto the bank breathing heavily. A woman was calling. He didn't know if it was Denise or Rory. Denise slid halfway down the bank sideways, a gun in her hand.

He gazed up at her as he struggled slowly to his feet, wet clothes leaden. "You killed me once," he heard himself say. "Are you going to kill me again?"

She gasped, motionless in the dark. He tried but could not see her eyes.

"Don't you move, Denise! I'll shoot the hell outa you if

you do. I've got the gun!" Rory was above them, her voice bold, a flashlight trained on Denise.

Dazed and blinking in the light, he slogged forward to take Denise's gun.

"You killed him," she cried, peering over his shoulder to the figure lying motionless in the water.

Daniel was not dead. He regained consciousness and was helped, moaning, out of the water by Denise. As she did so, Frank staggered up the slope to Rory and stumbled upon Daniel's gun in the dried grass.

"You lied!" he whispered in shock. "You didn't have the gun!"

"What else was I gonna say? 'Pretty please don't shoot or I'll scream'?"

"You know I never meant to hurt you, Rory," Daniel pleaded, bloodied and hobbling. "Just listen to me, we can work something out."

"Forget it, Daniel. I'm grown accustomed to bein' a widow, I'd just as soon be one again, so shut your damn mouth."

They managed to get them both back to the house and into the cellar. "Don't leave me down here," Denise begged, before Frank could close the door. "Please?"

He hesitated; after everything, she still moved him. "My medication," he asked. "Where is it? Is it really gone?"

"No." Her lips twitched in a small, quick smile. "I can show you, I threw it in the woods at the edge of the road. We can find it."

He closed the door, bolted it and turned to Rory.

"She was lying," he said simply, "it's gone."

"Are you sure?"

"I know when she's lying."

Frank changed into dry clothes from Alexander's suitcase, which was already packed. Tucked inside the bag was the gold pocket watch engraved with the words *Gratitude Is Greater Than Gold* and presented in 1897 to a hero named Daniel Alexander. Frank gave it to Rory to take home for Billy, then broke into the grocery at the landing, found a phone that worked and summoned help.

CHAPTER
TWENTY-ONE

The first rescue boat arrived as the fog lifted at dawn. The paramedics brought his backup medication from their hotel room as Frank had requested, but because he had been registered under Alexander's name, police ordered it withheld. The pills were finally released to him at noon, after medics who saw his bracelet and his scar, confirmed with the national registry and insisted. He had been deprived of his life-sustaining antirejection medication for nearly thirty hours.

The local cops were confounded, but by early evening, with the help of computer-generated fingerprints and long-distance conference calls, Alexander's identity and his "death" in Miami had been confirmed.

He and Denise had planned to leave for the Orient. Instead, they were charged with kidnaping, assault and attempted murder, pending more serious warrants from Miami.

Alexander had suffered head injuries, a broken nose and a shattered right kneecap. Hospitalized in a prison ward, he stonewalled, the police said. Not Denise. "She's talking her brains out," a detective said, adding that she appeared eager to make a deal with prosecutors.

Their flirtation caught fire soon after the burglary at the Alexander house, she told them. They were bored with their jobs, and dissatisfied with their personal lives. Tax troubles would have eventually led to the Tree Taverns being padlocked by the state. A divorce would have divided Daniel's assets and multiplied his problems. When the lovers hatched their plot to seize it all and more, Nick Bolton was a natural for the role of body double. A loner, a Gulf War veteran from Galveston, Bolton had no one to report him missing. All he had was Denise, whom he loved. He stayed, despite their rocky romance. She repaid his devotion by using her professional expertise to choreograph his death. She wore a red wig at the house that day, in case she was seen. Later, in her official capacity, she fingerprinted the corpse of her former lover, then switched the dead man's fingerprint card with a prepared card bearing Alexander's prints.

Cold, Frank thought. How incredibly cold.

Denise now claimed that she, too, was a victim. Her only crime, she insisted, was loving a man who coerced, influenced and intimidated her into joining his deadly scheme. She blamed him for everything, including both murders. An unlikely defense for a woman who wore a badge and a gun but probably the only one that might win sympathy from a jury.

Ron Harrington, also an accomplice, had agreed to split the million-dollar life insurance he had collected on his former partner. Daniel had returned to Miami for his share, according to Denise, and killed Harrington to keep him quiet.

The long day at police headquarters stretched into night before Frank and Rory were free to return to the hotel.

"Want me to stay?" asked the deputy who had whisked them away from headquarters.

"Why?"

"To run interference," he said.

Frank shook his head, perplexed by the offer. He and Rory walked into the lobby hand in hand, bruised, exhausted beyond belief and totally unprepared. They were surrounded, overwhelmed by reporters, cameras, lights and microphones.

Local newspapers were in hot pursuit of the story; versions had already moved on the wires. Crews from all the TV tabloids had arrived or were on the way. They said as little as possible and retreated to their room.

Rory offered him the phone after a long and tearful conversation with Billy and his grandmother. "Do you want to call home?"

He shook his head. "Not yet."

They slept exhausted, in each other's arm.

Heart Transplant Patient Tracks 'Donor' to Seattle, read the morning paper's front-page headline. The subhead said, *Murder Plot Suspected as 'Widow' Joins Search*. Frank and Rory looked haggard and disheveled in the accompanying photos. There was also a picture of Denise wearing a number under her chin.

Rory stayed with Frank during hours of tests at Seattle Medical Center. He showed no symptoms of rejection and an echocardiogram indicted his heart was still functioning normally. During a phone consult with the Miami team, doctors determined that preliminary results were good and a heart biopsy could wait until his return to South Florida.

317

They made arrangements to fly back to Miami the next day.

There were still reporters in the lobby when they returned to the hotel that evening. Clearly impressed, the desk clerk told them they had been on the *NBC Nightly News, Hard Copy* and *Inside Edition*. There were messages from Geraldo Rivera and Larry King.

They asked that all calls be held and ordered dinner in their room. They soaked in a hot tub, nursed each other's cuts and bruises and relaxed in silence, lying on the big bed, holding hands, the lights out and the drapes open to the sparkling skyline of the city.

They arose early, ordered coffee and a light breakfast, then packed to go home. The hotel limo would shuttle them to the airport at noon.

The unspoken question hung between them.

"What are we going to do?" he finally said. He sat on the small sofa, she in a chair. He took her hand.

"Me?" she said brightly. "I'm gonna hire a lawyer and file for divorce. Nobody 'ud deny I have grounds. Never dreamed I'd go from widow to divorcée without a weddin' in between."

"I mean us. What do we do?"

The pause was painful. "I think you know."

He did, he saw it in her eyes.

"We both have enough scar tissue around our hearts to know that hurting other people don't make you happy."

"Oh my God, Rory." His voice sounded weary.

"I know," she said. "I know."

"I don't know where I am in my marriage. What about you, will you be okay?"

"Yes." She paused and looked surprised. "I will, I really will, me and Billy. 'Member when I didn't think I could make it, and I thought I heard Daniel sayin', 'You can do it, you can do it'? I was such a fool. That obviously wasn't Daniel, it was somethin' tough inside me. What doesn't kill you makes you stronger." Her eyes locked on his. "We can't spend life looking in rearview mirrors. I can raise my child and be strong enough not to intrude on you and yours."

He held her hand. "If you remember, I'm the one who intruded in your life. Look, you have a mess ahead of you. The insurance company will want the money back. We'll have to find Daniel's assets and fight him for them."

"Isn't that how all this started? Me, not we. I can do that, without draggin' you into it, without messin' up your life."

"You saved my life, twice."

"You gave me mine back."

He wanted to return to Twin Palms to say good-bye to Billy, but during the flight they decided against it. No reason to confuse the boy further.

The plane stopped in Denver. Saying he had to stretch his legs, he hurried into an airport shop and bought a tiny gold heart on a chain. He slipped it into her bag while she dozed over the Midwest.

The sight of soft pink and gray mists rising over the great swamp as they swept in over the Everglades brought tears to his eyes. Home at last.

He did not realize he would never have the chance to kiss her good-bye, hadn't counted on yet another gauntlet of reporters, cameras and microphones. He put Rory and her bags in a cab. Their eyes caught as he closed the door. He watched it glide into airport traffic.

He stood for a while, alone in the crowd, then found a pay phone, fumbled for a quarter and punched in the familiar number.

"Where are you?" Kathleen gasped. "Oh, Frank, I'm s‹ sorry. I've been so worried."

"I'm coming home."

They were waiting in the driveway as the cab made th‹ turn beneath the overhanging branches of the huge poincian tree. Shandi's hair was all one color again. Apparently sh‹ had kept the ship on course while he was gone. She and Case‹ hugged him hard. Kathleen was thinner, her eyes swollen. The‹ talked for hours, first the four of them, then the two of them They might never be the all-American magazine-cover famil‹ of his fantasies. But they resolved to try. History and th‹ future were on their side. Together, they decided, they coul‹ make it.

Frank slept well that night for the first time since hi‹ surgery. In his own bed, beside his wife, he dreamed of run‹ ning. He was not alone, the other runner matched him, strid‹ for stride, then in a burst of speed forged ahead, into th‹ blinding sun. When Frank looked again, the runner had van‹ ished, leaving only sky and water and a pelican that spirale‹ lazily over the shimmering bay.

ACKNOWLEDGMENTS

I am grateful to Charles Delmonico, the man with heart, and to all the other heroes: Sandra Gerity, R.N., coordinator of the Heart and Lung Transplant Program at the University of Miami, Jackson Memorial Hospital; Lynn Cravero, assistant director, and Linda McBeath, aftercare coordinator, of the University of Miami Organ Procurement Agency; and to the incomparable Dr. Joseph H. Davis. My thanks, respect and admiration go to Darlene and Harry Kelton of the Pelican Harbor Seabird Station for all their noble deeds. Miami Beach Fire Fighter John Carlisle, Hungarian Honorary Consul Alexander S. Tar, Robert Feldman, Mike Sahr, Paul Steinberg and private investigator William Venturi all generously shared their expertise, as did Joel Hirschhorn, Steve Waldman, photojournalist Bill Cook and Miami Police Lt. Gerald Green—again. The usual suspects: Renee Turolla, Arnold Markowitz, Cynnie Cagney, Marilyn Lane, Ed Gadinsky, Peggy Thornburgh, David M. Thornburgh, and the Rev. Garth Thompson kept me on course, along with Michael Congdon, my agent, co-conspirator and chief accomplice.

Thanks to all of the above from the bottom of my heart.

Nationally Bestselling Author
of the Peter Decker and Rina Lazarus Novels
Faye Kellerman
"Faye Kellerman is a master of mystery."
Cleveland Plain Dealer

JUSTICE
72498-7/$6.99 US/$8.99 Can
L.A.P.D. Homicide Detective Peter Decker and his wife
and confidante Rina Lazarus have a daughter of their
own. So the savage murder of a popular high school
girl on prom night strikes home . . . very hard.

SANCTUARY
72497-9/$6.99 US/$8.99 Can

PRAYERS FOR THE DEAD
72624-6/$6.99 US/$8.99 Can
"First-rate. . . fascinating. . .
an unusually well-written detective story."
Los Angeles Times Book Review

SERPENT'S TOOTH
72625-4/$7.50 US/$10.50 Can

And Coming Soon
MOON MUSIC

Fall Victim to Pulse-Pounding Thrillers
by *The New York Times*
Bestselling Author

JOY FIELDING

SEE JANE RUN   71152-4/$6.99 US

Her world suddenly shrouded by amnesia, Jane Whittaker
wanders dazedly through Boston, her clothes blood-
soaked and her pocket stuffed with $10,000. Where did
she get it? And can she trust the charming man claiming
to be her husband to help her untangle this murderous
mystery?

TELL ME NO SECRETS   72122-8/$5.99 US

Following the puzzling disappearance of a brutalized rape
victim, prosecutor Jess Koster is lined up as the next
target of an unknown stalker with murder on his mind.

DON'T CRY NOW   71153-2/$6.99 US

Happily married Bonnie Wheeler is living the ideal life—
until her husband's ex-wife turns up horribly murdered.
And it looks to Bonnie as if she—and her innocent,
beautiful daughter—may be next on the killer's list.